THE STUDENT BODY

Also by John McNally

Troublemakers (short stories), 2000

High Infidelity: 24 Great Short Stories about Adultery by Some of Our Best Contemporary Authors (anthology), 1997

THE STUDENT BODY
Short Stories about College Students and Professors

Edited by
John McNally

THE UNIVERSITY OF WISCONSIN PRESS

The University of Wisconsin Press
1930 Monroe Street
Madison, Wisconsin 53711

www.wisc.edu/wisconsinpress/

3 Henrietta Street
London WC2E 8LU, England

5   4   3   2   1

Printed in the United States of America

Library of Congress Cataloging-in-Publication Data
The student body: short stories about college students and professors /
edited by John McNally.
     pp.   cm.
     ISBN 0-299-17404-2 (cloth: alk. paper)
     1. College stories, American. 2. College students—Fiction. 3. College teachers—
Fiction. I. McNally, John, 1965–
PS648.C64 S78   2001
813'.0108352375—dc21   2001001947

"A Different Kind of Imperfection" by Thomas Beller. From *Seduction Theory* by Thomas Beller. Copyright ©
1995 Thomas Beller. Reprinted by permission of W. W. Norton & Company. "Strip Battleship" by Amy Knox
Brown. Copyright © by Amy Knox Brown. Reprinted by permission of the author. "Hartwell" by Ron Carlson.
"Hartwell" originally appeared in *Playboy* and also appeared in *Plan B for the* Middle Class by Ron Carlson.
Copyright © 1990, 1992 by Ron Carlson. Reprinted by permission of W. W. Norton & Company. "Fraternity" by
Dan Chaon. From *Fitting Ends* and Other Stories by Dan Chaon. Copyright © 1995 by Dan Chaon. Reprinted by
permission of Northwestern University Press. "What My Boss Is Thinking" by Art Grillo. "What My Boss Is
Thinking" first appeared in *Masque: A Journal of Queer Expression* (January 1999). Copyright © by Art Grillo.
Reprinted by permission of the author. "In Loco Parentis" by Gillian Kendall. "In Loco Parentis" originally
appeared, in slightly different form, in *The Sun*. Copyright © by Gillian Kendall. Reprinted by permission of
the author. "Strawberry Spring" by Stephen King. Copyright © 1976 by Stephen King. Reprinted by permission
of the author. "The Banks of the Vistula" by Rebecca Lee. "The Banks of the Vistula" first appeared in the
Atlantic Monthly. Copyright © by Rebecca Lee. Reprinted by permission of the author. "Fundamentals of
Communication" by Thisbe Nissen. Reprinted from *Out of the Girls' Room and Into the Night* by Thisbe Nissen by
permission of the University of Iowa Press. Copyright © 1999 by Thisbe Nissen. "Free Writing" by Sondra Spatt
Olsen. Reprinted from *Traps* by Sondra Spatt Olsen by permission of the University of Iowa Press. Copyright ©
1991 by Sondra Spatt Olsen. "The Wife of the Indian" by Lucia Perillo. Copyright © by Lucia Perillo. Reprinted by
permission of the author. "The Whore's Child" by Richard Russo. "The Whore's Child" first appeared in *Harper's*
(February 1998). Copyright © by Richard Russo. Reprinted by permission of the author. "Mr. Eggplant Goes
Home" by Alex Shishin. Reprinted from *Prairie Schooner* by permission of the University of Nebraska Press.
Copyright © 1996 by the University of Nebraska Press. "Like Whiskey for Christmas" by Joe Schraufnagel.
Copyright © by Joe Schraufnagel. Reprinted by permission of the author. "The Rhythm of Disintegration" by
Marly Swick. Reprinted from *A Hole in The Language* by Marly Swick by permission of the University of Iowa
Press. Copyright © 1990 by Marly Swick. "Q: Questing" by Gordon Weaver. Copyright © by Gordon Weaver.
Reprinted by permission of the author. "Professors" by Tom Whalen. Copyright © 1986 *Florida Review*. Reprinted
by permission of the author.

This book is dedicated to my undergraduate creative writing teachers, Rodney Jones, Jim Solheim, and Rick Russo, for their early encouragement.

Contents

Acknowledgments

Editing an anthology is a group effort, and the following people provided help, suggestions, and advice at various stages of this project: Ron Wallace, Jesse Lee Kercheval, Kelly Cherry, Jim Harris, Gerald Shapiro, Gregg Palmer, Andrew Snee, Bob Marrs, Carol Houck Smith, Frances M. Kuffel, and the fine folks at the University of Iowa Press. Many thanks to Scott Mackay Smith for his computer expertise. Special thanks to Raphael Kadushin, Sheila McMahon, and everyone at the University of Wisconsin Press. Also, thanks to Carl Djerassi for a generous fellowship, without which I would not have been in Madison, Wisconsin, in the first place. I corresponded with most of the authors in this book, and without their help and understanding, this anthology would not exist. I couldn't ask for stronger support than that given by my father, Bob McNally, so once again, *thank you*. Most of all, I'd like to thank my wife, Amy, for her tireless help and support.

The Student Body

Introduction
John McnaIly

University campuses, small and large, are treasure-troves of material for fiction writers, so it's no surprise that some of the more respected contemporary novelists have zeroed in on the academy for a book or two. In the past two decades readers have been treated to a wide variety of excellent college novels, including Richard Russo's *Straight Man*, Donna Tartt's *The Secret History*, Jane Smiley's *Moo*, Michael Chabon's *Wonder Boys*, Tim O'Brien's *Tomcat in Love*, Philip Roth's *The Human Stain*, Francine Prose's *Blue Angel*, Don Delillo's *White Noise*, Jon Hassler's *Rookery Blues* and *The Dean's List*, J. M. Coetzee's *Disgrace*, Denis Johnson's *The Name of the World*, Richard Powers's *The Gold Bug Variations*, Jonathan Lethem's *As She Climbed Across the Table*, and Saul Bellow's *Ravelstein*—in short, novels by some of today's most important writers.

Despite this the campus novel is still often viewed as lower-rung literature—frequently dismissed by critics, written with trepidation, or read as a guilty pleasure. Why the stigma? Even Richard Russo, who wrote the enormously successful *Straight Man*, a novel about the lunacies of an English department, confides that he was "dead set against ever writing an academic novel" (Hogan). Dead set, perhaps, but write it he did, and *Straight Man* was universally praised by critics and academics alike as the funniest college novel to come down the literary pike in years. But it's what Russo says in explanation for his desire *not* to write such a novel that gets to the root of the problem with the genre's stigma: "It's always been my view that there are already enough academic novels and most of them aren't any good."

Russo's right. John O. Lyons acknowledges in his 1962 study of the genre, *The College Novel in America,* that most campus novels are bad and that "[m]any of the worst are interesting by reason of the particular axe the author has to grind, or simply because of their abysmal ineptness" (xiii). Based on Lyons's analysis, that would leave two rather narrow groups of readers: those who enjoy playing parlor games, trying to match a novel's character with his or her real-life counterpart, and those who like to torture themselves with bad prose.

For years the campus novel, even in the most capable hands, has been scorned by critics, the argument going something like this: a novel of academic life, by virtue of its subject, smacks of elitism; therefore, the subject matter is too insular, too trite. For these critics blue-collar life—the life of the common laborer—is a more worthy subject for literature. Literature, that is, with a capital *L.*

It's not that these critics don't have a point. The concerns of academicians *are* often trivial, and one would be hard pressed to find anything more mind-numbing than reading a realistic portrayal of a department meeting where colleagues, using the often tiresome jargon of their own particular discipline, play games of petty one-upmanship. Readers are more likely to feel sympathy for the Joads in *The Grapes of Wrath* than for the tenured professor who's having a fling with a student. But critics who are so blinded by their aversion to the subject matter that they dismiss the entire genre risk wandering onto the shaky ground of logical fallacy. Just because the subject matter is inherently insular doesn't mean that a novel that examines the subject can't achieve some universality.

A good writer transcends his or her subject matter, whatever that subject happens to be, and both the campus novel and campus short story have certainly had their share of good writers: Nathaniel Hawthorne (whose *Fanshawe,* published in 1828, is cited as the first

American college novel), Wallace Stegner, James Thurber, Mary Mc-Carthy, Willa Cather, Sinclair Lewis, E. B. White, F. Scott Fitzgerald, Robert Penn Warren, Bernard Malamud, Kingsley Amis, Saul Bellow, Vladimir Nabokov, John Gardner, Joyce Carol Oates, John Barth, Raymond Carver, John Irving, A. S. Byatt, and Tobias Wolff, to name but a few. And by the looks of it, more writers than ever are turning toward the academy for material.

John E. Kramer, Jr.'s, *The American College Novel: An Annotated Bibliography,* published in 1981, documents nongenre campus novels (genre here meaning sci-fi, crime, or sex novels), and his study reveals that the output of campus novels has been increasing at a nearly exponential rate. He counts twenty-six American college novels published for the seventy-one-year period between 1828 and 1899. He then breaks his book down into spans of nineteen years each. Between 1900 and 1919, thirty-seven were published. Between 1920 and 1939, ninety-three. Between 1940 and 1959, 106 college novels. And finally, between 1960 and 1979, a whopping 163 college novels. While I don't have any recent statistics, I imagine that the pattern has continued and that the output between 1980 and 1999 is far greater than the output of the preceding nineteen years. Even as I write this barnesandnoble.com has published an essay by Mark Winegardner titled "The University Connection," listing several recent college novels and citing their growing appeal to readers. Winegardner's theory?

> [T]he audience for literary fiction is overwhelmingly made up of
> people with some kind of university connection: professors,
> would-be professors, or people who've spent a lot more than four
> years in college. It's like the audience for war fiction, composed of
> morbidly fascinated outsiders and insiders who delight in seeing if
> an author's invented absurdities can compare with the reader's
> own war stories.

As for the ever-increasing output of novels and stories set in universities, one can't ignore the staggering increase of graduate programs in creative writing across this country in the past twenty years. It's not uncommon for a writer to earn a B.A. with a concentration in creative writing, move on to an M.A. program in creative writing, followed by the requisite M.F.A., and if the poor writer is still standing, a Ph.D. with a creative dissertation. The dismal college teaching job market has encouraged writers-in-training to remain in school well beyond what writers thirty years ago were doing. It only stands to reason that sooner or later a number of these writers will turn to the material that they know best—academia.

The campus short story is the offspring of—or, perhaps, the lesser-known cousin to—the campus novel. In the past ten years the campus short story has crept up on us, appearing in authors' collections, sandwiched between noncampus stories, or in literary journals. Where the campus novel seems to lend itself to satire and humor, the range of the campus short story tends to be broader, more varied. *The Student Body* is an attempt to capture some of that variety, while showcasing the work of both well-known and up-and-coming writers.

It's fitting for Richard Russo to lead the pack with his National Magazine Award–winning story, "The Whore's Child," which couldn't be more different than *Straight Man,* despite its common denominator of an English department. Here, a nun signs up for a creative writing course, and through a series of submitted chapters for workshop, the professor and her fellow students begin to piece together the darker secrets of the nun's life.

Greek life is under scrutiny in stories by Amy Knox Brown and Dan Chaon. In Brown's "Strip Battleship," loyalty, in its many forms, becomes the central question to a fraternity brother who's been purposely left behind during the house president's bachelor party. In Dan Chaon's "Fraternity," one of the frat's brothers must come to terms with a car accident, in which he was the driver, that seriously injured the fraternity's president.

Genre novels, particularly mysteries, that use college as a setting far outnumber literary or mainstream novels doing the same, so it stands to reason to include a story by the master of many genres, Stephen King. College graduate, former college teacher, and writer King employs the old saw *write what you know* by returning from time to time to college settings and characters who are either teachers or writers—or both. His short story "Strawberry Spring," from his first collection *Night Shift,* is one of his very first campus stories, a reminiscence about a time in the narrator's life when a serial killer roamed the university town where he lived.

Though the novel as a form may lend itself more readily to academic comedy than academic drama, there is certainly no shortage of humorous short stories on the subject. Joe Schraufnagel, in his debut short story, "Like Whiskey for Christmas," intersperses, à la Laura Esquivel, ingredients for junk food, song lists, and recipes for cocktails, in this over-the-top tale of a graduate student infatuated with his married professor. In Lucia Perillo's "The Wife of the Indian," a scholar fakes an American Indian identity in order to get a teaching job, then gets found out. Sondra Spatt Olsen's protagonist reveals her intense dislike of her boss, the director of composition, while free writing along with her students in the aptly named "Free Writing." Gordon Weaver's politically incorrect "Q: Questing" is the story of a desperate adjunct professor who commutes between four schools while carrying on four affairs with four very different women.

For balance, Marly Swick offers a more melancholy story in "The Rhythm of Disintegration," where a professor of history, under the delusion that he can conjure up old times, meets with his ex-wife at the university's student union. Ron Carlson's beautifully rendered "Hartwell" lets readers peek into the life of a lonely professor who denies, over and again, that he is not like his poor, sad-sack colleague Hartwell. A new female student meets a series of unsavory profs in Tom Whalen's short-short, "Professors." Gillian Kendall's "In Loco Parentis"—the story of a lesbian professor in the deep South whose favorite student dies in an alcohol-related accident—grips the reader like a literary page-turner in its first few sentences and never lets up.

Along with well-established writers like Stephen King, Thomas Beller, and Marly Swick, readers will discover in *The Student Body* a host of new and exciting faces, such as Thisbe Nissen, Art Grillo, Rebecca Lee, and Alex Shishin—writers, I'm sure, you're bound to hear more from soon.

Inside each of these stories you'll hear a distinct voice. It's the voice you hear while walking across campus, the voice that makes you hesitate to hear what comes next. Listen.

WORKS CITED

Hogan, Ron. "Richard Russo." *Beatrice Interview.* 1997. <http://www.beatrice.com/interviews/russo/>.

Kramer, John E., Jr. *The American College Novel: An Annotated Bibliography.* New York and London: Garland Press, 1981.

Lyons, John O. *The College Novel in America.* Carbondale and Edwardsville: Southern Illinois University Press, 1962.

Winegardner, Mark. "The University Connection." Barnes and Noble.com. 28 August 2000. <http://www.bn.com/>.

PART ONE
The Students

The Whore's Child
Richard Russo

Sister Ursula belonged to an all but extinct order of Belgian nuns who conducted what little spiritual business remained to them in a decrepit old house purchased by the diocese seemingly because it was unlikely to outlast them. I'd seen Sister Ursula many times before the night she turned up in class, though we had never spoken. She drove an old, rusted-out station wagon with bald tires that was always crowded with elderly nuns who needed assistance getting in and out. St. Francis Church was only a few blocks away, but too far to walk for any of the nuns but Sister Ursula herself, whose gait, at seventy, was awkward but relentless. "You should go over there and introduce yourself someday," my wife had suggested more than once. "Those old women have been left all alone." Her suspicion was later confirmed by Sister Ursula herself. "They are waiting for us to die," Sister Ursula confessed to me, in reference to the diocese that had housed them on Forest Avenue, a block from our house. "Impatient of how we clutch to our miserable existences."

"I'm sure you don't mean that," I told her, an observation that was to serve as my mantra with Sister Ursula, who seemed to enjoy hearing me say it.

She appeared in class that first night and took up residence at the center of the seminar table as if she had every right to be there, despite the fact that her name did not appear on my computer print-out. Fiction-writing classes are popular and invariably oversubscribed at most universities, and never more so than when the teacher has recently published a book, especially one that had received as much press attention as mine had in the spring. It was my first in over a decade, and initially I'd thought my fleeting celebrity might have been responsible for Sister Ursula's presence in my classroom the first chilly evening of the fall semester, though she gave no indication of this, or that she recognized me as her neighbor.

No, Sister Ursula seemed innocent not only of me but of all department and university protocol. When informed that students petition to take the advanced fiction-writing class by means of a manuscript submission the previous semester, and that prerequisite to the advanced seminar were beginning and intermediate courses, Sister Ursula disputed neither the existence nor the wisdom of these procedures. Nor did she gather her things and go, which left me in an odd position. Normally it was my policy not to allow unregistered students to sit through even one class, because doing so encourages their mistaken belief that they will be able to wheedle or cajole or flatter their way in. In the past I'd shown even football players the door without the slightest courtesy or ceremony, but this was a different challenge entirely. Sister Ursula was herself nearly as big as a linebacker, but more persuasive than her size was her body language, which suggested that once settled, she was not used to moving. And she was settled. I let her stay.

After class I explained why it would be highly unprofessional of me to allow her to remain in the advanced fiction workshop. After all, she freely admitted she'd never attempted to write a story before, which, I explained, put her at an extreme disadvantage. My mistake was in not leaving the matter there. Instead I went on. "This is a storytelling class, Sister. We're all liars here. The whole purpose of our enterprise is to become skilled in making things up, of substituting our own truth for THE truth. In this class we actually prefer a well-told lie," I explained, certain that this would dissuade her.

She patted my hand, as you might the hand of a child. "Never you mind," she assured me, after adjusting her wimple for the journey home. "My whole life has been a lie."

"I'm sure you don't mean that," I told her.

~

"In the convent," Sister Ursula's first submission began, "I was known as the whore's child."

"Nice opening," I wrote in the margin, as if to imply my belief that her choice had been a purely artistic one. It wasn't, of course. She was simply starting with what was for her the beginning of her torment. She was writing—and would continue to write—a memoir. By mid-semester I would give up asking her to invent things.

The first installment weighed in at a robust twenty-five pages. In it she detailed the suffering of a young girl taken to live in a Belgian convent school where the treatment of the children was determined by the social and financial status of the parents who abandoned them there. As a charity case and the daughter of a prostitute, young Sister Ursula (there could be no doubt that the child in the first-person narrative *was* Sister Ursula) found herself at the very bottom of the ecclesiastical food chain. What little wealth she possessed—some pens and paper her father had purchased for her the day before they left the city, along with a pretty new dress— was taken from her, and she was informed that henceforth she would have no use for her few pitiful possessions. Her needs—food, a uniform, and a single pair of shoes—would be provided for her, though she would doubtless prove unworthy to receive them. The shoes she was given were two sizes too small, an accident, Sister Ursula at first imagined, until she asked if she might exchange them for the shoes of a younger girl that were two sizes too large and was scorned for the suggestion. As a result of the shoes that did not fit, Sister Ursula developed the tortured gait of a cripple, which was much imitated by the other children, who immediately perceived in their new playmate a suitable object for their cruelest derision.

The mockery of her classmates was something Sister Ursula quickly accommodated by shunning their companionship. In time she grew accustomed to being referred to as the whore's child, and she hoped that the children would eventually tire of calling her this if she could manage not to show how deeply it wounded her. During periods of recreation in the convent courtyard she perfected the art of becoming invisible, avoiding all games and contests, during which, she knew, even those on her team would turn on her. What she was not prepared for was the cruelty she suffered at the hands of the nuns, who seemed to derive nearly as much satisfaction from tormenting her as the children did. When she'd asked if she might exchange the shoes, she had not merely been told that this was not permitted. She had been told why. The chafing caused by the too-small shoes had caused Sister Ursula's heels to bleed into her coarse white socks and then into the shoes themselves. Only a wicked child, Sister Veronique had explained, would foul with her own blood the shoes she'd been given, then beg to exchange them for the shoes of an innocent child. Did she think it fair, the old nun had wondered out loud, that another child, one who had not only a virtuous mother but also a father, be asked to wear the polluted shoes of a whore's child?

Worse than the sting of the old nun's suggestion that anything Sister Ursula touched was thereafter contaminated was the inference that trailed in the wake of the remark about the other girl's parents. The innocent girl had not only a virtuous mother—Sister Ursula knew what this meant—but *also a father*, which seemed to imply that Sister Ursula herself did not have one. Of course she knew that she did have a father, a tall, handsome father who had promised to rescue her from this place as soon as he could find work. Indeed, it was her father who had brought her to the convent, who had assured Mother Superior that she was a good girl and not at all wicked. How then had Sister Veronique concluded that she had no father? The young girl tried to reason it through but became confused. She knew from experience that evil, by its very nature, counted for more in the world than good. And she understood that her mother's wickedness diminished her father's value, but did it negate his very existence? How could such a thing be? She dared not ask, and so the old nun's remark burrowed even deeper, intensifying her misery, which already bordered on despair.

Sister Ursula's first installment ended here, and the other students, whose job it was to criticize it constructively, approached the narration the way you would an alien spacecraft. Several had gone to Catholic schools where they'd been tutored by nuns, and they weren't sure, despite my encouragement, that they were allowed to be critical of this one. The material itself was foreign to them. They'd never encountered anything like it in the workshop. On the plus side, Sister Ursula's story had a character in it, and the character was placed in a dire situation, and those were good things for stories to do. On the other hand, the old nun's idiom was imperfect, her style stiff and old-fashioned, and the story seemed to be moving forward without exactly getting anywhere. It reminded them of stories they'd heard other elderly people tell, tales the tellers eventually managed to forget the point of, narratives that would gradually peter out with the weak insistence that all these things really did happen. "It's a victim story," one student recognized. "The character is being acted upon by outside forces, but she has no choices, which means there can be no consequence to anything she does. If she doesn't participate in her own destiny, where's the story?"

Not having taken the beginning and intermediate courses, Sister Ursula was much enlightened by these critiques, and she took feverish notes on everything that was said. "I liked it though," added the student who'd identified it as a victim story. "It's different." By which he seemed to mean that Sister Ursula herself was different.

The old nun stopped by my office the next day, and it was

clear that she was still mulling things over. "To be so much . . . a victim," she said, searching for the right words, "it is not good?"

"No," I said, smiling. Not in stories. Not in life, I was about to add, until I remembered that Sister Ursula still wasn't making this distinction and my doing so would probably confuse her further. "But maybe in the next installment?" I suggested.

She looked at me hopefully.

"Maybe your character will have some choices of her own as your story continues?"

Sister Ursula considered this possibility for a long time, and I could tell by looking at her that the past wasn't nearly as flexible as she might have wished.

She was about to leave when she noticed the photograph of my daughter that I keep on my desk. "Your little girl," she said, "is a great beauty?"

"Yes," I said, indicating that it was okay to pick up the photo if she wanted to.

"Sometimes I see her when I am driving by," she explained. When I didn't say anything to that, she added, "Sometimes I don't see her anymore?"

"She and her mother are gone now," I explained, the sentence feeling syntactically strange, as if English were also my second language. "They're living in another state."

Sister Ursula nodded as though she was not certain what I meant by the term.

"She will return to this state?"

I nodded. "I hope so, Sister."

~

"And so I became a Catholic," began the second lengthy installment of Sister Ursula's story, and again I scribbled "nice beginning" in the left margin before hunkering down. I'd had students like Sister Ursula before; they'd inspired the strictly enforced twenty-five-page limit in all my workshops. I noted that for this second submission Sister Ursula had narrowed her margins, fiddled with her font, wedging the letters closer together, and it looked like the spacing was not quite double, maybe 1.7. Venial sins.

Having had no religious training prior to entering the convent, Sister Ursula was for some time unable to recite prayers with the other children, further evidence, were any needed, of her moral depravity. She discovered that it was not an easy task to learn prayers to the cadence of public ridicule, but learn them Sister Ursula eventually did, and although in the beginning the ritual words tormented her, they eventually became a comfort. Most of the prayers she fought to memorize were adamant as to the existence of a God who, at least in the person of the crucified Christ, was infinitely more loving and understanding and forgiving than the women He led to His altar as His brides.

To be loved and understood and forgiven seemed to Sister Ursula the ultimate indulgence, and so she became a denizen of the convent chapel, retreating there at every opportunity from the taunts and jeers of the other children, the constant moral reprimand of the crowlike nuns. She liked the way the chapel smelled— damp and cool and clean—at least when she had the place to herself. Often she would hide there for an hour or more before she was missed, until finally one of the side doors would creak open, momentarily flooding the chapel with bright light. Then the long, dark shadow of a nun would fall across Sister Ursula where she knelt in prayer at the foot of the cross, and she would have no choice but to rise and be led back to her torment, often by a twisted ear.

In addition to the authorized prayers she'd memorized, Sister Ursula learned to compose others of her own. She prayed that Sister Veronique, who had suggested that she had no father and who worked in the convent stable, might be kicked in the head by a horse and paralyzed. She prayed that Sister Joseph, who worked in the kitchen and who took seriously her duty to ensure that the charity children received the poorest food in the smallest quantities, might one day slip and fall into one of her boiling vats. Required to stay at the convent most holidays, Sister Ursula prayed that the children who were allowed to go home might perish in railway accidents. Sometimes, in an economical mood, she just prayed that the convent would burn to the ground, that the air would be full of black ash. She saw nothing wrong with praying such prayers, especially since none of them, no matter how urgently offered, were ever answered. She felt a gentle trust in the Jesus on the cross who hung above the main altar of the convent chapel. He seemed to know everything that was in her heart and to understand that nothing dwelt there that wasn't absolutely necessary to her survival. He would not begrudge her.

In truth, Jesus on the cross reminded Sister Ursula of her beloved father, who, she knew, had never wanted her packed off to the convent, who had not forgotten her, and who missed her every day, as she missed him. Like Jesus on the cross, her father was slender and handsome and sad, and, like Jesus, he was stuck where he was, unable to find work and married to a woman who was his shame. And yet if the prayers she had struggled to memorize were true, there was hope. Had not Jesus shed his crown of thorns, stepped down from the cross to become the light and salvation of the world, raising up with Him the lowly and the true of heart? When she wasn't praying that Sister Veronique would be kicked in the head by a horse, Sister Ursula fervently prayed that her father might one day be free as well. The first thing he would do, she felt certain, was come for her, and so every time the side door to the chapel opened, she turned toward the harsh light with a mixture of hope and fear, and although it was always a dark nun whose shadow filled the doorway, she held tenaciously to the belief that one day it would be her father standing there.

One Christmas season—was it her third year in the convent

school?—Sister Ursula was summoned to the chamber of Mother Superior, who told her to ready herself for a journey. It was a full week before any of the other students would be permitted to leave for the Christmas holiday, and Sister Ursula was instructed to tell no one of her impending departure. Indeed, Mother Superior seemed flustered, and this gave Sister Ursula heart. During her years of secret vengeful prayer she'd indulged many fantasies of dramatic liberation from the convent. Sometimes she'd imagined her father's arrival on horseback, his angry pounding on the door at the main gate, his purposeful stride through the courtyard and entrance through the side door of the chapel. Perhaps Mother Superior's anxiety stemmed from the fact that her father was on his way to effect just such a rescue.

At the hour appointed for her departure, Sister Ursula stood, as instructed, in the courtyard by the main gate, beyond which no men save priests were permitted entry, and awaited her father's arrival. She hoped he would come by coach or carriage, that she and he might be conveyed to the village train station in this fashion, but she was more than happy to make the long journey on foot if necessary, so long as she and her father were together. She had better shoes now, though she still hobbled like a cripple. And so when a carriage came into view in the dusty road beyond the iron gate, her heart leapt, until she recognized the carriage as the one that belonged to the convent. Inside sat not her father but Sister Veronique, who had not been kicked in the head by a horse despite three years' worth of Sister Ursula's dogged prayers. When the carriage drew to a halt, Sister Ursula knew her imagination had been led astray by her need. She was to be banished from the convent, not rescued from it. She did not fear a worse existence than her present one, because a worse existence was not within her powers of imagination. Rather, what frightened her was the possibility that if she was taken from the convent school, her father would not know where to find her when the time came. This terrible fear she kept to herself. She and Sister Veronique did not speak a word on the long journey to the city.

They arrived at a hospital and were taken to the charity ward late that evening only to learn there that Sister Ursula's mother the prostitute had expired that morning at about the time their journey had begun, too late to notify them. A nun dressed all in white informed Sister Veronique that it would be far better for the child not to see the deceased, and a look passed between them. All that was left by way of keepsake was a brittle, curling, scalloped-edged photograph, which the white nun gave to Sister Ursula, who had offered no reaction to the news that her mother was dead. "Where is my father?" was all she'd wanted to know. The white nun and Sister Veronique exchanged another glance, and in that glance Sister Ursula understood that the white nun shared Sister Veronique's belief that she had no father, and she saw too that it would be useless for her, a child, to try to convince the white nun otherwise. Sister Ursula's fury supported her most of the way home, first the long journey by train, then the shorter carriage ride. But when they came within sight of the convent Sister Ursula broke down and began to sob. To her surprise if not comfort, Sister Veronique placed a rough, calloused hand on her shoulder and said softly, "Never mind, child. You will become one of us now." In response Sister Ursula slid as far away from the old nun as she could and sobbed even harder, knowing it must be true.

"Are we ever going to meet the father?" one student wanted to know. "I mean, she yearns for him, and he gets compared to Christ, but we never see him directly. We're, like, told how to feel about him. If he doesn't show up, I'm going to feel cheated."

Sister Ursula dutifully made a note of this criticism, but you had only to look at the old woman to know that the father was not going to show up. Anybody who felt cheated by this could join the club.

The day after Sister Ursula's second workshop the doorbell rang at seven-thirty in the morning. I struggled out of bed, put on a robe, and went to the door. Sister Ursula stood on the porch, clearly in a state of agitation. The rusted-out station wagon idled at the curb with its full cargo of curious, myopic nuns, returning, I suspected, from morning Mass. The yard was strewn with dry, unraked November leaves, several of which had attached themselves to the bottom of Sister Ursula's flowing habit. "He must be in the story? He must return?" Sister Ursula wanted to know.

"He's already *in* the story," I pointed out, cinching my robe tightly at the waist.

"But I never saw him after she died. That is what my story is about."

"How about a flashback?" I suggested. "You mentioned there was one Christmas holiday . . ."

But she was no longer listening. Her eyes, slate gray, had gone hard. "She died of syphilis."

I nodded, feeling something harden in me too. Behind me I heard the bathroom door open and close, and I thought I saw Sister Ursula's gaze flicker for an instant. She may have caught a glimpse of Jane, the woman I was involved with, and I found myself hoping she had.

"My father's heart was broken."

"How do you know that, if you never saw him again?"

"He loved her," she explained. "She was his ruin."

～

"It was my hatred that drew me deeper into the Church," Sister Ursula's third twenty-five-page installment (the font even smaller, more squeezed) began, eliciting my now standard comment in the margin. As a writer of opening sentences, Sister Ursula was without peer among my students.

In the months that followed her mother's death, an explanation occurred to Sister Ursula. Her father had booked passage to

America to search for work. Such journeys, she knew, were fraught with unimaginable peril. Perhaps he now lay at the bottom of the ocean. Gradually Sister Ursula came to accept the inevitability of Sister Veronique's cruel prophecy. She would become one of them she detested. Ironically, that prophecy was hastened by the prophet's own untimely death when she was kicked by a horse, not in the head as Sister Ursula had prayed, but in the chest, causing severe internal hemorrhaging and creating an opening in the convent stable. During her long sojourn at the convent school Sister Ursula had learned to prefer the company of animals to that of humans, and so at the age of sixteen, already a large, full woman like her mother, she became herself a Bride of Christ.

Sister Ursula's chronicle of the years following her vows, largely a description of her duties in the convent stable, was interspersed with several brief recollections of the single week she'd spent at home in the city during the Christmas holiday of that first year she entered the convent school. During that week she'd seen very little of her mother, and this was a relief to Sister Ursula, who dreaded the heat of her mother's embrace, the cloying stench of her whore's perfume. Rather, her beloved father took her with him on his rounds, placing her on a convenient bench outside the dark buildings he entered, telling her how long he would be, how high a number she would have to count to before he would return. Only a few times did she have to count higher. "Did you find work, Father?" she asked each time he reappeared. It seemed to Sister Ursula that in buildings as large and dark as the ones he entered, with so many other men entering and exiting, there should have been work in one of them, but there was none. Still, that they were together was enough for Sister Ursula. Her father took her to the wharf to see the boats, to a small carnival where a man her father knew let her ride a pony for free, and finally on a bitter cold picnic in the country where they ate warm bread and cheese. At the end of each of these excursions her father promised again that she would not have to remain much longer in the convent school, that another Christmas would find them together.

The installment ended with Sister Ursula taking her final vows in the same chapel that for years had provided her with refuge from the taunts of the other children, for whom she would always be the whore's child. There at the very altar of God, Sister Ursula, like a reluctant bride at an arranged marriage, continued to indulge her fantasy of rescue right up to the last moment, and when she was asked to state in words her irrevocable devotion to God and Church, she paused a long moment and turned toward the side door of the chapel, the one where she'd always imagined her father would appear, and she willed it to open, willed her father's silhouette to appear there, a man prepared to scatter these useless women and hateful children before him.

But the door remained shut, the chapel dark except for the flickering light of a hundred candles, and so Sister Ursula became a bride.

"There's a lot of misogyny in the story?" observed a male student who I happened to know was taking a course with the English department's sole radical feminist and was therefore alert to all of misogyny's insidious manifestations. I took his stating this opinion in the form of a question to indicate that maybe the observed distrust, even hatred, of women evinced in Sister Ursula's writing might be okay in this instance because the author was, sort of, a woman.

The young man was right to be cautious. What would you expect? a chorus of his female classmates sang out. The whole thing takes place in a girls' school. There were only two men in the story and one was Jesus, so the statistical sample was bound to be skewed. Besides, the whole structure of the society that was responsible for all the cruelties suffered by the girl in the story existed within the context of male domination. The worst that could be said of such a microcosm was that these women had been conditioned to imitate the behavior of men. No, read correctly, Sister Ursula was clearly a feminist.

"I *would* like to see more of the mother though," one young woman conceded. "It was a major cop-out for her to die before they could get to the hospital."

"You wanted a deathbed scene?" said the student who'd been worried about the story's misogyny. "Wouldn't that be sort of melodramatic?"

A pause in the discussion. Melodrama was a bad thing, almost as bad as misogyny.

"Why was the daughter sent for?" wondered another student. "If the mother didn't love her, why send for her?"

"Maybe the father sent for her?"

"Then why wasn't he there himself?"

"I know I was the one who wanted to see more of the father after the last submission," said the student who'd made this request, "but now I think I was wrong. All the stuff with her father over the Christmas holiday? It was like we kept learning what we already knew. And then he's not there at the hospital when the mother dies. I'm confused." He turned and appealed to me directly. "Aren't you?"

"Maybe somebody in the hospital contacted the convent," another student suggested, letting me off the hook.

"For a dying prostitute in a charity ward? How would they even know where the daughter was if the mother didn't tell them?"

Everyone now turned to Sister Ursula, who seemed to have slipped into a trance as a result of the barrage of questions.

"I don't care. I really like this story," said another student. "It feels real."

~

The fourth and final installment of Sister Ursula's story was only six and a half pages with regular margins, normal fonts, and standard double spacing.

"My life as a nun has been one of terrible hatred and bitterness," it began. I thought about writing, "You don't mean that," in the margin, but refrained. Sister Ursula always meant what she said. It was now late November, and she hadn't veered a centimeter from literal truth since Labor Day. The last perfunctory pages of her story summarized her remaining years in the convent until the school was partially destroyed by fire. It was then that Sister Ursula came to America. She was still a relatively young woman, but by then she had no thoughts of leaving the order she had always despised. She had become, as Sister Veronique predicted, one of them, and one of them she would remain.

Once, in her late forties, she had returned to Belgium to search for her father, but she had little money, and no trace of the man could be found. It was as if, as Sister Veronique had always maintained, he had never existed. When her money was exhausted, Sister Ursula gave up and returned to America to live out what remained of her life among the other orphans of her order. This was her first college course, she explained, and she wanted everyone to know that she had enjoyed meeting the other students and reading their stories, and she thanked them for helping her to write hers. All of this was contained in the final paragraph of the story, an unconscious postmodern gesture.

"This last part sort of fizzled out," one student admitted. It clearly pained him to say this after its author had thanked her readers for all their help. "But it's one of the best stories we've read all semester."

"I liked it, too," said another, whose voice didn't fall quite right.

Everyone seemed to understand that there was more to say, but no one knew what it was. Sister Ursula stopped taking notes and silence descended on the room. For some time I'd been watching a young woman who'd said next to nothing all term but who wrote long, detailed end comments on the stories of her fellow students. She'd caught my attention now because her eyes appeared to be full of tears. I sent her an urgent telepathic plea. No. Don't. "But the girl in the story never got it," she protested.

The other students, including the author, all turned toward her then. "Got what?"

I confess it. My own heart was in my throat.

"About the father," she explained. "He was the mother's pimp, right? Is there another explanation?"

~

"So," Sister Ursula said sadly. "I was writing what you call a fictional story after all."

It was now mid-December, my grades were due, and I was puzzling over what to do about Sister Ursula's. She had not turned in a final portfolio of revised work to be evaluated, nor had she returned to class after her final workshop, and no matter how hard I tried I couldn't erase from my memory the image of the old nun that had haunted me for weeks, of her face coming apart in terrible recognition of the willful lie she'd told herself over a lifetime.

And so I'd decided to pay her a visit at the old, run-down house where she and five other elderly nuns had been quartered now for nearly a decade. I had brought a Christmas tree ornament, only to discover that they had no tree, unless you counted the nine-inch plastic one in the center of the mantle in the living room. Talk about failures of imagination: in a house inhabited by infirm, elderly nuns, who did I think would have put up and decorated a tree?

Sister Ursula seemed surprised to see me standing there on her sloping porch, but she led me into a small parlor room off the main hallway. "We must be very still," she explained. "Sister Patrice has fallen ill. I am her nurse, you see. I am nurse to all of them."

In the little parlor we took seats opposite each other across a small gateleg table. I must have looked uncomfortable, because Sister Ursula said, "You have always been nervous of me, and you should not. What harm was in me has wasted away with my flesh."

"It's just that I was bitten by a nun as a child," I explained.

Sister Ursula, who had said so many horrible things about nuns, looked momentarily shocked by this revelation, until it dawned on her. "Oh, I understand that you made a joke," she said. "I thought that you might be . . . what was that word the boy in our class used to describe those like me?"

I had to think a minute. "Oh, a misogynist?"

"Yes, that. Would you tell me the truth if I asked you do you like women?"

"Yes, I do. Very much."

"And I men, so we are the same. We each like the opposite from us."

Which made me smile. And perhaps because she had confided so much about herself, I felt a sudden, irrational urge to confide something in return. Something terrible perhaps. Something I believed to be true. That my wife had left because she had discovered my involvement with a woman I did not love, who I had taken up with, I now realized, because I felt cheated when the book I'd published in the spring had not done well, cheated because my publisher had been irresponsibly optimistic, claiming the book would make me rich and famous, and I'd been irresponsibly willing to believe it, so that when the book provided neither fame nor fortune, I began to look around for a consolation prize and found her. I am not a good man, I might tell Sister Ursula. I have not only failed but also betrayed those I love. If I said such things to Sister Ursula, maybe she would find some inconsistency in my tale, some flaw. Maybe she'd conclude that I was judging myself too harshly and say, "You don't mean that."

But I kept my truths to myself, because she was right. I was "nervous of her."

After an awkward moment of silence, she said, "I would like to show you something, if you would like to see it?"

Sister Ursula struggled heavily to her feet and left the room, returning almost immediately. The old photograph was pretty much as described—brown and curled at its scalloped edges, the womanly image at its center faded nearly into white. But still beautiful. It might have been the photo of a young Sister Ursula, but of course it wasn't. Since there was nothing to say, I said nothing. Sister Ursula left it on the small table when I set it there.

"You? You had loving parents?"

I nodded. "Yes."

"You are kind. This visit is to make sure that I am all right, I understand. But I am wondering for a long time. You also knew the meaning of my story?"

I nodded.

"From the beginning?"

"No. Not from the beginning?"

"But the young woman was correct? Based on the things that I wrote, there could be no other . . . interpretation?"

"Not that I could see."

"And yet I could not see."

There was a sound then, a small, dull thud from directly overhead. "Sister Patrice," Sister Ursula informed me, and we got to our feet. "I am needed. Even a hateful nun is sometimes needed."

At the front door, I decided to ask. "One thing," I said. "The fire . . . that destroyed the convent school?"

Sister Ursula smiled and took my hand. "No," she assured me. "All I did was pray."

She looked off across the years though, remembering. "Ah, but the flames," she recalled, her old eyes full of a young woman's fire. "They reached almost to heaven."

Strip Battleship
Amy Knox Brown

The air this early March afternoon is like a gift: warm and dimmed by clouds, a sudden surprise after an unusually cold Nebraska winter. Snow that has lingered for months along the curbs melts within hours, and Michael walks, alone, along O Street, listening to water rush through the grates above storm sewers, the murmur of a season dissolving. The time and temperature sign outside the defunct Security Savings and Loan flashes 75 degrees, 3:15.

He's done with classes for the day. The fraternity, when he stops there, seems oddly empty and quiet. Only Peter and Wallace, the two chemistry majors no one particularly likes, are sitting in the front room, smoking. The warm air pulls him back outside, and he wanders toward downtown, past the law firm where he's a runner, past the tile and carpet stores, past Walgreens. Outside Ali Baba Gyros, he inhales the tantalizing smell of cooked meat and grease. A couple strolling ahead of him wear shorts, their pasty legs a sign of hope that this warm spell will continue.

In front of Miller and Paine, he stops to examine the display windows. Mannequins in bathing suits stand, hips cocked, the seams of their wrists visible like scars; a male figure in Bermuda shorts crouches on a square of astroturf, gazing at a golf ball; crystal vases and china gleam, a big white sign reads "Register now for your summer wedding!"

The word *wedding* reminds him that he needs to buy a gift for the upcoming wedding of his pledge father, Tom. Michael presses through the revolving doors into the store, brightly lit and populated with women his mother's age who stand against counters and stroke scarves or lean forward, allowing salesclerks to dab cosmetics against their faces. He knows Tom's fiancée, Ann, works in Miller's china department, but Friday is one of her days off, so he'll let one of the old, anonymous clerks help him pick out something "nice." All around him, the low sound of women speaking. The air smells of powder and perfume. He rides the escalators to the fifth floor, and there, in the china department, he sees Ann, standing behind a cash register. She's wrapping a box in silver paper and nodding enthusiastically at the customer facing her.

He approaches the counter. The customer takes the wrapped box and heads for the escalator. Ann glances up, and when she sees Michael she pantomimes surprise: her eyebrows raise, her mouth opens. She has long dark hair, brown eyes, a too-loud laugh Michael finds oddly compelling.

"I didn't know you were working today," he tells her. How can he buy a gift from the person it's *for*?

"One of the regular clerks was sick. It was a last-minute thing." She shrugs. "So how come you guys haven't left yet? Tom said he wanted to get started this morning."

"Started for where?"

Her brows come together and her hand rises off the counter. The light in the department is dim and casts dark shadows under her eyes. The china surrounding them seems poised, waiting to break. "Well, the stag party—the stag party in Kansas City—" Her fingers touch her lips and he can see she feels as bad as he feels, comprehending: Tom's stag party, an all-weekend bash held out of town, a *big deal* . . . And Michael, standing here in Miller and Paine, hasn't heard a word about it until now.

He swallows, understanding the reason for the almost-vacant fraternity; thirty or forty of his brothers must be on their way south to celebrate the upcoming nuptials of the Sigma Chi president. How hard had it been for them to keep the planning a secret from him? *Why* wasn't he invited? The enormity of the slight—and it's worse than a *slight,* isn't it, the feeling in his chest an actual weight, heavy as plutonium?—makes him look down at the counter.

"Michael?"

He forces himself to meet Ann's eyes and grin. "Oh, there's this project I have to work on for the law firm, I had to bow out at the last minute." Did Tom leave him behind because of last week, when Michael and Ann stopped at Cliff's Bar after their Wednesday night American Authors class? Around eleven, Tom had stormed in, looking around angrily. When he saw Ann and Michael together, he frowned. "I've been trying to call you for *hours,*" he hissed at Ann. Chastised, she stood, waved goodbye to Michael, and left. Is that the reason?

Ann nods. "A project?" she prompts.

"Well." He runs his fingers along the smooth counter. He does, indeed, have an assignment from the senior partner, but it doesn't need to be finished for a couple weeks. And it's the kind of project he could discuss with the brothers, but explaining it to a girl is, well, embarrassing.

"What kind of project?"

"Well . . ." She stares at him, waiting. He sighs. "You know that case against the Video Box? For renting obscene materials?"

"Yeah?"

"The firm I work at is defending the Video Box on the grounds that the videos aren't actually obscene. For something to be obscene, you know, it has to be judged that way considering the community's standards." Ann blinks rapidly, listening. "So I have to watch a few of those movies, the ones that are supposed to be ob-scene—the other runners do, too, and the attorneys—to see if we feel offended. As members of the community, if we feel offended. If we don't, the movies aren't obscene and Video Box isn't breaking the law."

Ann laughs—too loudly, of course. A couple of women on the far side of the department glance over. "That's wild. Do you get paid?"

He nods.

"Wow." Another customer approaches the register and Michael steps away to examine a pyramid of goblets. Behind him, Ann says, "No, I'm sorry, that pattern's been discontinued, but here's the manufacturer's direct number. Sometimes they have old stock available."

"Thank you, dearie," the customer says. Her thick heels tap against the linoleum as she walks away.

"Hey, Michael."

He turns from the goblets. Ann is leaning on the counter.

"I'm done here at nine—do you want to meet at Cliff's for a couple drinks? Or do you have too many pornos to watch?"

For the first time since he realized he'd been left behind, *purposely left behind,* he feels the muscles in his jaw relax. "I have time for Cliff's," he says.

～

The clientele of Cliff's consisted, for years, of businessmen, but lately students have infiltrated the dim bar, which is furnished with dark veneered tables and black padded chairs. Tonight, older men in suits compete with frat rats for the attention of college girls. Michael sits at the long table by the pay phone so he can see Ann when she comes in, and she does, a few minutes after nine.

"Hey," she says, sitting, smiling at him. He notices that one of her front teeth slightly overlaps the one next to it. How many years has he known her—three? And he's observed this tiny flaw only now. "I can't believe how nice it is outside."

"I know."

The waitress brings two bottles of Moosehead. "I went ahead and ordered," Michael says. "Is that okay?"

"Sure." Ann lifts the bottle to her lips and drinks. "So, you get any of your pornos watched? I bet that's what they're doing in Kansas City." She looks at him, speculatively. "Or maybe worse. Do you know?"

He doesn't know, not having been included in the planning (why wasn't he included in the planning?), but he can guess. There'll be a stripper or two, possibly some local girls picked up at the bar, Tom locking himself into a bathroom with a couple of them, coming out later with his hair tousled, his shirt wrinkled and buttoned wrong, a smug expression: *Two of them, one of me.* "Probably a lot of drinking, you know, they sent me out to buy a case of tequila—"

"Mm."

Or the stripper standing on the bed, a young stripper with firm silicone breasts and shaved pubic hair, waiting for Tom to pull out his wallet and hand over money before she kneels between his legs and lets everyone watch what she does to make him come. Michael coughs and continues, "And everybody loves telling stories, Hell Week and all those myths about what guys did in the old days."

"Yeah." She peels the label off the Moosehead bottle and presses it flat against the table. "Tom hates it when I do that."

"Do what?"

"Peel the labels off."

"Why?"

"I don't know."

"Do you want another one? Or a Kamikazee?"

"Kamikazee."

The waitress brings two tall glasses filled with ice, lime juice, and vodka. They drink in silence. Why is the air between them a little tense, as if one is keeping a secret from the other? Usually conversation comes easily. At the Sigma Chi Halloween party, he and Ann stood in one corner of the basement for hours, talking. She was dressed as a flapper, and Michael wore a complicated costume that consisted of a shirt and trousers he'd spray-painted orange, an orange toolbox, and a welder's mask. "What ARE you?" people kept asking. "A monster? A convict?"

"Agent Orange," Michael said. Ann had laughed–each time he'd said it, in fact–but everyone else frowned at him, puzzled. "You're WHAT?"

At the party, Tom stood in the middle of a group of the brothers. Their voices rose over the music of the B-52's. Tom punched at the air–he must have been describing a fight he'd been in–and Ann and Michael watched. Tom was the sort of guy who commanded attention. He was tall, his big white teeth flashed when he grinned, his voice could move from a high-pitched imitation of a grocery store clerk to the deep notes of his own sincere self telling the brothers how much the fraternity, how much all of them, meant to him.

"Hm," Ann had said after Tom finished the story and everyone around him appeared paralyzed with laughter. *Hm:* at the time, Michael assumed the sound was one of admiration, satisfaction.

"How're the wedding plans going?" Michael asks. "Only two months 'til the big day, right?"

She looks at him. "Two and a half. I think." Her lips stretch into a straight line. "I'm sure Tom's been telling everyone at Sigma Chi about it."

"About what?"

"About wanting to postpone the wedding?"

"What?"

"Well, I guess he didn't actually say the word *postpone*. He just wants to wait to send the invitations out."

"Wait? Why?"

"You tell me. They're all addressed and ready to go, but he said he wants to hold onto them for a couple of weeks." Her shoulders raise and lower, a theatrical shrug. "I figured this stag party was a good sign, you know, why would he have a big stag party if he *didn't* want to get married?"

"Right." Michael rattles the ice in his Kamikazee. The only problem with the stag party is its timing. All the other stag parties he's gone to have been the week of the wedding itself, sometimes even the night before. Why is Tom holding his stag so far in advance?

"Right," he says again and lifts the glass to his mouth.

Was Tom the reason Michael had pledged Sigma Chi? With his toothy grin, too-firm handshake, Tom had welcomed Michael into the big brick house on Vine Street. Ann stood next to him, smiling. Inside, light glowed warmly and pretty girls clustered in the room, holding cups of beer. Michael stepped into the soothing smell of cigarette smoke and perfume. He liked the idea that he was welcome here, that he belonged.

Hell Week, early December, Michael and his fellow pledges were forbidden from showering or brushing their teeth. They carved spoons from small planks of wood the actives supplied, and they ate all their meals with these primitive tools. Each time you lifted the filled spoon from your plate, you had to say, "Square meal, square deal," before you put the food in your mouth. The pledges were forced to sleep in shower stalls, and every night at 3 A.M., a group of actives charged into the bathroom, shouting. In the same dirty clothes he'd worn all week, a cap over his greasy hair, a wad of gum in his mouth, Michael sat in the back of his classes, trying to stay awake.

Friday was Hell Night. All week the pledges had been whispering rumors among themselves: there'd be beatings, there'd be hookers. Someone said, *I heard they brand you.* Blindfolded, the pledges were led into the Sigma Chi basement. Michael could smell the damp walls as they moved, slowly, down the stairs. Around them the voices of actives were pitched too low for him to identify words. Sweat sprang out under his arms and on his palms. He smelled heat, sensed a flickering brightness around the edges of his blindfold. Torches?

On the basement floor, the pledges kneeled. Their shirts were removed, their hands tied together in front of them. The pledge next to Michael breathed too fast, the sound of a dog panting. "Now, little brothers," Tom intoned. "You have reached the last step in your journey to brotherhood. With this last step, you will be marked, permanently, as a member of the sacred tribe of Sigma Chi."

Marked, Michael thought. Did he mean *branded?* His throat felt swollen. Beads of sweat seeped into his blindfold. An active barked, "Brother Peter, stand up!" There was a shuffling at the end of the line of pledges. Metal clanged against the floor. "Careful," Tom said. "Don't want to damage the equipment." The actives laughed. Michael tried to swallow. He heard a hissing noise, like water poured on fire. Then his blindfold slipped down over his left eye, and the bright room became visible.

Two of the actives held Peter's shoulders. Peter's mouth was stiff with fear. The muscles in his arms quivered. Tom grasped a pair of tongs in one hand and brought them, slowly, toward Peter's chest. Smoke curled off the tongs. *They're going to brand us!* Michael thought for that one horrible moment before he saw the open ice chest behind Tom emitting the same wisps of smoke. *Dry ice,* Michael realized; a joke, a perfectly calibrated joke that only the actives would understand. "Brother Peter," Tom said and pressed the ice into Peter's chest. Peter screamed and the line of pledges convulsed. Before he shut his eye, his exposed eye, Michael saw Tom's shoulders shaking, his hand over his mouth, his face gleaming with mirth.

In Cliff's, Michael studies Ann's face. The waitress brings another round of Kamikazees. Should he tell her about the Hell Night scene, what he had witnessed—Tom's capacity for cruelty? His first loyalty, he knows, should lie with Tom, his *brother.* The secrets of the fraternity are secrets forever.

The bartender props open the front door, and warm air pours

in the room to dissipate the smoke. At the bar, the lawyers and bankers have loosened their ties. They shout over each other's heads, drape their arms around the shoulders of pretty girls, order shots. Michael looks out the open door. The black sky appears softer than the sky of winter, less brittle and flat.

"You know," he says. "If you and Tom didn't end up getting married, it might not be the worst thing that could happen." Her eyes widen, and he adds, "I'm not saying he doesn't want to get married, I don't know, he hasn't said anything to me. Not mailing the invitations might just be cold feet or something, everybody gets that, don't they?"

Ann nods.

"Are you okay?"

"Yeah." She smiles, unconvincingly.

They finish their drinks in silence and walk outside. Overhead, the low cover of clouds parts momentarily to reveal a sliver of moon. "I can give you a ride home," Ann offers.

"Okay."

They cross the street to a small, decrepit parking lot. Michael climbs in the passenger seat of Ann's Citation. "Are you okay to drive?"

She nods, shifts the car, too carefully, and turns on the radio. Halos of light hover around the streetlamps. Michael rolls down his window and holds his arm out in the night air. It flows around his skin like water around a rock. He wonders if he said the wrong thing or the right thing. He wonders if he should have said anything at all. But even silence can get you into trouble, can't it? Even momentary silence, like the episode at this year's Hell Night. Maybe the reason Tom didn't invite him to the stag had happened months ago.

After the activities—the blindfolding, the false branding—the pledges were sent to shower, then everyone gathered in the fraternity's living room. Logs burned and popped in the fireplace. In the dim light, you couldn't see the cigarette burns on the sofa cushions or the scratches that scarred the top of the old baby grand piano no one ever played.

Tom, as president, opened bottles of Irish whiskey, and Michael, his dutiful pledge son, helped pour drinks. Outside the window, snow drifted down, soundlessly. Tom and Ann were already engaged. In two weeks it would be Christmas.

Tom raised his glass. "To our new brothers in the bond." All around the room, the brothers tapped their plastic cups together and drank. "You know," Tom began, "we're more of a family than most regular families because we've all *chosen* Sigma Chi. And Sigma Chi has chosen us. If you look around you, these are the guys that will be here for you whenever you need them." He raised his glass. "To the pledge class of 1987, on the most important day of your life." He cleared his throat and looked around the room. "People say, you know, that it's the day you graduate from college or the day you get married, but to me, I know the most important day of my life was four years ago when I got through Hell Night and stood here listening to Newby say the same things I'm saying to you." Tom's voice cracked a little, and he gave them a sheepish smile.

In the firelight, Michael could see that his pledge father's face was damp. Sweat? Tears? Surely Tom wasn't *serious* about this being the most important day of anyone's life. Tom raised his glass again. "To all my brothers." Everyone drank, then Tom turned to Michael—who was, after all, the person closest to him, physically and fraternally—and hugged him. "My son," Tom said. Crushed against Tom's shoulder, Michael was surrounded by the scent of cologne and smoke. Tom's damp cheek pressed against his. All around them, pledge fathers embraced pledge sons; the pledges turned to embrace one another. Some of them sniffed and wiped their eyes. "My son," Tom said again and patted Michael's back. In his voice, Michael heard a certain tone, as if the statement *my son* had been a question and Tom was waiting for an answer. But what should Michael say? *Dad? Brother?* What, really, did Tom mean to him?

And so there had been this space of silence between them, Tom's arms growing stiff against Michael's back. Finally, Michael said, "Tom, man, you're it." Weak words, the voice of a traitor.

Ann slows now in front of Michael's apartment building. The car bumps against the curb when she tries to park. "Oops. So it's back to work for you, huh?"

"Yeah." Michael rolls up the window. "Have you ever seen one?"

"A porno? No." She frowns. "I'd remember if I'd seen one, wouldn't I?"

"Oh yeah."

"Then no."

"Well, you're welcome to check one out, let me know your opinion as a member of the community—"

Ann laughs, then squints at him, considering. "You've seen one before. I mean, before this project."

"Yeah."

"Where?"

"Newby's stag party."

"Why not, then." She turns off the car. The sudden capitulation startles Michael—but if he didn't want her to say yes, why did he ask? He clears his throat and climbs out of the car.

Ann follows Michael across the lawn to his apartment. His key moves effortlessly into the lock and he pushes open the door. The apartment looks the way it always looks: mismatched furniture, a little barren. "Do you want something to drink?"

"Beer's fine." Ann stands next to the television, where Michael has piled the pornos. "*One Lay at a Time*," she reads. "*Sexual Freak Show*." Michael hands her a can of Budweiser. "Thanks." She sits on the couch.

"*One Lay at a Time* is probably a takeoff on *One Day at a Time*."

"Ah." Ann nods. "I get it."

"They like to do that, make a pun on a title of a TV show or something."

"You're quite the expert."

"Not really. You'd notice it yourself if you looked at a bunch of them all at once." He turns on the television and picks up one of the videos: *Bimbo Bowlers from Buffalo*. The mechanics of opening the box, sliding the tape into the VCR, adjusting knobs, makes him feel as if everything he's doing is calculated. Here is Michael, inviting his pledge father's fiancée to watch a porno. What is he thinking? He sets the movie back on the stack but leaves the television on. "You know, I don't think we should do this."

"No? Are they that disgusting?"

"Well, sort of."

Ann sets her beer on the coffee table and leans back against the couch, stretching. "All right. Do you have any games? Trivial Pursuit or something?"

"I've got Monopoly." Michael goes to the closet where he keeps his winter clothes, boots, textbooks he should sell back to the bookstore. On the top shelf, he sees the Monopoly box underneath another game. "Battleship, too."

"Battleship!" Ann hoots. "Perfect."

Michael pulls the box off the shelf. "More beer?"

"Sure." He takes two more cans from the refrigerator and brings them, along with the Battleship box, into the living room.

Ann has one leg draped over the arm of the couch. She leans her head against the cushions and stares up at the ceiling. "You know what my high school boyfriend and I used to do?"

"What?"

"We used to play Strip Battleship, you know, like Strip Poker. If one of your ships got sunk, you had to take off a piece of clothes. I haven't thought about that in years."

"Sounds like fun," Michael says. He permits himself to imagine a younger version of Ann: She's sitting on the floor in a basement, parents' footsteps creaking above her and the boyfriend who looks on, dumbly, as she reaches behind her to unclasp her bra.

"Yeah, it was all right. I won most of the time."

Michael opens the Battleship box. Inside, the two rectangular cases nestle together, pins and ships scattered around them.

"So, you want to play?" Ann asks.

He looks up. Her eyes are a little glassy, she's grinning, and her crooked front tooth seems charming to him, not a flaw at all. How much have they had to drink? Michael weighs his obligations, carefully. At the same time he's counting her clothes: a white blouse, patterned scarf tied over her shoulders, black slacks, white socks, black shoes. Underneath, there'd be a bra and panties. Seven.

"I won't tell," she says.

His spine tingles, the hair on his arms raises. And on his own self: A denim shirt over a T-shirt, briefs, jeans, shoes and socks. His watch. Seven. "Are you sure?"

He means, are you sure you want to do this? But Ann says, "Who would I tell?"

"Right."

"But you can't tell, either."

"I won't."

"And earrings count." Now she has an advantage, eight items to his seven.

"But not your ring."

"Oh, no, not that."

Ann stays on the couch; Michael sits facing her, on the floor. They open the cases and arrange their ships on the bottom grid. "Ready?" he asks.

"Yes." She leans forward to take her beer off the table. "You can go first."

"B-7," he says, looks up, and sees her eyes widen with dismay. "Hit!"

He presses a pin into the grid to mark the spot.

"A-17," she says.

"Miss."

"B-8."

"Hit." She shakes her head. "Damn. You're good at this."

When he sinks Ann's first ship, she takes off her earrings, presses the backs against the posts, and sets them on the table. The blank blue screen of the television glows, the tall floor lamp in one corner stands in a pool of light. Shadows shade Ann's face. When she sinks his tugboat, he pulls off his shoes, wriggling his freed toes inside his socks.

How long will it be before one of them sobers up enough to say, "We've got to stop"? If he thinks too hard about what they're doing, Michael is aghast at his own behavior, playing a game designed for seduction with his pledge father's fiancée. But if he doesn't think too hard, if he concentrates instead on the grid in front of him, trying to figure out where Ann's put her ships, getting up to open new beers for both of them, waiting and *not peeking* at her board when she goes down the hall to the bathroom, grinning at her when she returns, he realizes he's only having fun. Given what Tom is likely doing in Kansas City, what Tom said to Ann about postponing the wedding, does what they're doing here in Lincoln make any difference?

His socks and denim shirt come off, then Ann's shoes and socks, then her scarf. She rests her bare feet on the edge of the coffee table. Her big toes lean in slightly toward her second toes. The nails are polished red.

When Michael sinks Ann's battleship, he watches her frown, debating: blouse or slacks? She unbuttons the blouse, then shrugs her arms out of the sleeves. Underneath, a white lacy bra covers her breasts. Michael swallows.

"Now we have to start over, you know, to finish the game, since all my ships are gone."

"All right." He nods, forces himself to look down at the grid, re-arrange his ships in a new pattern, fiddle with the little pegs used to mark hits and misses.

"Ready?"

"Ready."

A few weeks after Christmas Break, Newby—former house president, now married and employed—returned for a visit. He stood in the Sigma Chi foyer, rubbing his hands together and yelling for Tom. "Where the hell is he? Isn't he ready yet?" Newby and Tom had some of the same mannerisms, the too-firm handshake, the toothy grin, but Newby was taller than Tom, his voice even louder. He slapped the new actives on the back and cuffed Michael under the chin. "How's my little brother?"

Michael pitched his voice low, like Tom's voice on Hell Night when he talked about the most important day of their lives, and said, "Fine, brother." He and Newby embraced each other, playfully. "My brother," Michael said. He aimed to make his voice crack sincerely between the two syllables, the way Tom's did. "Oh, bro-ther." Some of the new actives looking on laughed.

"Jesus, man, you're good," Newby said. "You sound just like him."

Michael tried another line. "Newby, man, you mean so much to me." He opened his arms. A draft blew across his back when someone opened the door behind him.

"Okay, man, I get it," Newby said.

Michael turned to the others. "All you bro-thers, you're the most important thing in the world."

Then, suddenly, Tom was clattering down the stairs. Had he heard? Surely Tom would know that it was only a joke, no harm meant. Michael's arms fell to his sides.

"You ready?" Tom said to Newby.

"Right-o," Newby said. He gave them a little salute, but Tom walked across the foyer and out the door without looking at anyone.

∼

Michael loses his jeans. Ann loses her slacks. He notices that freckles spot her knees. The thin bones of her shins press against the skin. She wears lacy white panties.

They've stopped speaking. The air feels charged around them, the great looming presence of the unknown making Michael conscious of the steady thud of his heart.

Michael loses his T-shirt. Ann loses her bra. Should he look away when she sets the Battleship board on the coffee table, reaches behind her to undo the hooks? He watches her slide the straps off her shoulders. For a moment he sees her pale breasts, the dark nipples, then she picks up the Battleship case and holds it in front of her so his view is cut off. He exhales, slowly. Now they're even: only underwear is left. Ann says a letter and number that coincide with the position of his barge. Without thinking, he says, "Miss." Then he clears his throat and studies the board. "J-14."

"Hit," she says. He's going to win. In a moment, she'll be sitting completely naked on his couch. And then—?

She says, "J-14."

"Sorry," Michael says. "J-13."

"Hit," she says again. "H-7."

He says, "Miss," even though it's one of the two spots where his tugboat sits. "J-12."

"Hit." It must be her battleship. He reads off two more numbers, and she says, "Hit and sink."

"Well." He waits. She doesn't move. They stare at each other over the top of her Battleship board. He imagines their breathing

Amy Knox Brown

has become synchronized. The muscles in her neck quiver when she swallows. Is she thinking of Tom?

On his knees, wearing only his briefs, hard behind the white cotton, Michael moves toward her. The Battleship board trembles in her hand. Her knees and the slopes of her shoulders shine in the television's dim light. He's at the couch. He reaches toward the lacy waistband of her underwear and her hand stops him. His fingers close around her fingers. The setting of her engagement ring presses against his skin.

"You have to," he whispers.

"I *can't.*"

He knows she can't. He twists the ring against her finger. It's loose. He pulls. The band sticks momentarily at her knuckle, then it slides off, the reverse of what must have happened when Tom proposed, on his knees like Michael is now, slipping the ring onto Ann's finger as he said, *Will you be my wife?*

And did the words make her eyes fill with tears? She blinks at Michael and swallows again. Clutching the ring, Michael leans toward her. The scratchy carpet scours his knees, like the basement floor of Sigma Chi on Hell Night—torches flickering around him, Michael hauled out of line for the branding, a symbol of brotherhood he understood even then to be an illusion. The diamond digs into his palm. His lips touch Ann's. He closes his eyes, waiting for her fingers to descend upon his skin.

The Banks of the Vistula
Rebecca Lee

It was dusk; the campus had turned to velvet. I walked the brick
path to Humanities, which loomed there and seemed to incline
toward me, as God does toward the sinner in the Book of Psalms.
It was late on a Friday afternoon, when the air is fertile, about to
split and reveal its warm fruit—that gold nucleus of time, the
weekend.

Inside, up the stairs, the door to Stasselova's office was open,
and the professor lifted his head. "Oh," he said. "Yes." He coughed,
deep in his lungs, and motioned me in. He had requested this visit
earlier in the day, following class. His course was titled Speaking in
Tongues: Introductory Linguistics. Stasselova was about sixty-five
and a big man, his torso an almost perfect square. Behind his balding head the blond architecture of St. Gustav College rose into the
cobalt sky. It looked like a rendition of thought itself, rising out of
the head in intricate, heartbreaking cornices that became more abstract and complicated as they rose.

I was in my third week of college. I loved every moment of it,
every footfall. The students resembled the students I'd known in
high school, Scandinavian Midwesterners like myself, whose fathers
were all pastors or some declension thereof—but the professors
thrilled me. Most had come from the East Coast, and seemed fragile
and miserable in the Midwest. Occasionally during class you could
see hope for us rising in them, and then they would look like great
birds flying over an uncertain landscape, asking mysterious questions, trying to lead us somewhere we could not yet go.

I wanted to be noticed by them, to distinguish myself from the ordinary mass of students, and to this end I had plagiarized my first paper for Stasselova's class. This was why, I presumed, he had called me to his office.

The paper, titled "The Common Harvest," was on the desk between us. I had found it in the Kierkegaard Library. It was a chapter in an old green-cloth book that was so small I could palm it. The book had been written in 1945, by a man named Delores Tretsky, and it hadn't been signed out since 1956. I began to leaf through it, and then crouched down to read. I read for a full hour; I thought it beautiful. I had not once in all my life stopped for even a moment to consider grammar, to wonder how it rose out of history like a wing unfurling.

I had intended to write my own paper, to synthesize, as Stasselova had suggested, my own ideas with the author's, but I simply had nothing to contribute. It seemed even rude to combine this work with my own pale, unemotional ideas. So I lifted a chapter, only occasionally dimming some passages that were too fine, too blinding.

"This is an extraordinary paper," he said. He was holding his coffee cup over it, and I saw that coffee had already spilled on the page to form a small, murky pond.

"Thank you," I said.

"It seems quite sophisticated. You must not have come here straight out of high school."

"I did," I said.

"Oh. Well, good for you."

"Thanks."

"You seem fully immersed in a study of oppression. Any reason for this?"

"Well, I do live in the world."

"Yes, that's right. And you say here—a shocking line—that a language must sometimes be repressed, and replaced, for the larger good. You believe this?"

"Yes."

"You think that the Eastern-bloc countries should be forced to speak, as you say here, the mother tongue?"

Some parts of the paper I had just copied down verbatim, without really understanding, and now I was stuck with them. Now they were my opinions. "Yes," I said.

"You know I am from that region."

"Is that right?"

"From Poland."

"Whereabouts in Poland?" I asked conversationally.

"I was born on the edge of it, in the dark forest land along its northeastern border, before the Soviet Union took it over completely, burning our towns. As children we were forced to speak Russian, even in our homes, even when we said good-night to our mothers as we fell asleep."

This was turning into a little piece of bad luck.

"When did you write this?" he asked.

"Last week."

"It reads like it was written fifty years ago. It reads like Soviet propaganda."

"Oh," I said. "I didn't mean it that way."

"Did somebody help you?"

"Actually, yes. Certainly that's all right?"

"Of course, if done properly. Who was it that helped you, a book or a person?"

"My roommate helped me," I said.

"Your roommate. What is her name?"

"Solveig."

"Solveig what?'

"Solveig Juliusson."

"Is she a linguistics scholar?"

"No, just very bright."

"Maybe I can talk to Solveig myself?"

"Unfortunately, you can't."

"Why not?"

"It's complicated."

"In what way?"

"Well, she's stopped eating. She's very thin. Her parents were worried, so they took her home."

"Where does she live?"

"I don't know."

We both sat silent. Luckily, I had experience lying in my ado-lescence, and knew it was possible to win even though both parties were aware of the lie. The exercise was not a search for truth but rather a test of exterior reserve.

"I'm sure she'll be returning soon," I said. "I'll have her call you."

Stasselova smiled. "Tell her to eat up," he said, his sarcasm curled inside his concern.

"Okay," I said. I got up and hoisted my bag over my shoulder. As I stood, I could see the upper edge of the sun falling down off the hill on which St. Gustav was built. I'd never seen the sun from this angle before, from above as it fell, as it so obviously lit up an-other part of the world, perhaps even flaming up the sights of Stas-selova's precious, oppressed Poland, its dark contested forests and burning cities, its dreamy and violent borders.

~

My roommate Solveig was permanently tan. She went twice a week to a tanning salon and bleached her hair frequently, so that it looked like radioactive foliage growing out of dark, moody sands. Despite all this she was very beautiful, and sensible.

"Margaret," she said when I came in that evening. "The library telephoned to recall a book. They said it was urgent."

I had thought he might check the library. "Okay," I said. As I rifled through the clothes on my closet floor, I decided it would have to be burned. I would finish the book and then I would burn it. But first there was tonight, and I had that rare thing, a date.

My date was from Stasselova's class. His name was Hans; he was a junior, and his father was a diplomat. He had almost auburn hair that fell to his neckline. He wore, always, long white shirts whose sleeves were just slightly, almost imperceptibly, puffed at the shoulders, like an elegant little joke, and very long, so they hung over his hands. I thought he was articulate, kind. I had in a moment of astonishment asked him out.

The night was soft and warm. We walked through the tiny town, wandered its thin river. We ate burgers. He spoke of Moscow, where he had lived that summer. I had spent my childhood with a vision of Russia in the distance, an anti-America, a sort of fairy-tale intellectual prison. But this was 1987, the beginning of *perestroika*, of *glasnost,* and views of Russia were changing. Television showed a country of rain and difficulty and great humility, and Gorbachev was always bowing to sign something or other, his head bearing a mysterious stain shaped like a continent one could almost but not quite identify. I said to Hans that I wanted to go there myself, though I had never thought of the idea before that moment. He said, "You can if you want." We were in his small, iridescent apartment by now. "Or perhaps to Poland," I said, thinking of Stasselova.

"Poland," Hans said. "Yes. What is left of it, after men like Stasselova."

"What do you mean, men like Stasselova?"

"Soviet puppets."

"Yet he is clearly anti-Soviet," I said.

"*Now,* yes. Everybody is anti-Soviet now." The sign for the one Japanese restaurant in town cast a worldly orange light into the room, carving Hans's body into geometric shapes. He took my hand, and at that moment the whole world seemed to have entered his apartment. I found him intelligent, deliberate, large-hearted. "Now," he said, "is the time to be anti-Soviet."

~~~

On Monday afternoon, in class, Hans sat across from me. We were all sitting around a conference table, waiting for Stasselova. Hans smiled. I gave him the peace sign across the table. When I looked back at him, moments later, Hans's hands were casually laid out on the table, palms down. I saw then, for the first time, that his left hand tapered into only three fingers, which were fused together at the top knuckle. The hand looked delicate, surprising. I had not noticed this on our date, and now I wondered if he had purposely kept me from seeing it, or if I had somehow just missed it. For a brief, confused moment, I even wondered if the transformation had occurred between then and now. Hans looked me squarely in the eye. I smiled back.

Stasselova then entered the room. In light of my date with Hans, I had almost forgotten my visit with him the previous Friday. I'd meant to burn the book over the weekend in the darkness at the ravine, though I dreaded this. My mother was a librarian, and I knew that the vision of her daughter burning a book would have been like a sledgehammer to the heart.

Throughout the class Stasselova seemed to be speaking directly to me, still chastising me. His eyes kept resting on me disapprovingly. "The reason for the sentence is to express the verb—a change, a *desire*. But the verb cannot stand alone; it needs to be supported, to be realized by a body, and thus the noun—just as the soul in its trajectory through life needs to be comforted by the body."

The sun's rays slanted in on Stasselova as he veered into very interesting territory. "All things in revolution," he said, "this way, need protection. For instance, when my country, Poland, was annexed by the Soviet Union, we had the choice of joining what was called Berling's army, the Polish wing of the Russian army, or the independent Home Army. Many considered it anti-Polish to join the Russian army, but I believed, as did my comrades, that more could be done through the system, within the support of the system, than without."

He looked at me. I nodded. I was one of those students who nod a lot. His eyes were like brown velvet under glass. "This is the power of the sentence," he said. "It acts out this drama of control and subversion. The noun always stands for what is, the status quo, and the verb for what might be, the ideal."

Across the table Hans's damaged hand, spindly and nervy, drummed impatiently on the tabletop. I could tell he wanted to speak up. Stasselova turned to him. "That was the decision I made," he said. "Years ago. Right or wrong, I thought it best at the time. I thought we could do more work for the Polish cause from within the Red Army than from outside it."

Hans's face was impassive. He suddenly looked years older— austere, cold, priestly. Stasselova turned then to look at me. This was obviously an issue for him, I thought, and I nodded as he continued to speak. I really did feel supportive. Whatever army he thought was best at the time, that was fine with me.

⁓

In the evening I went to the ravine in the elm forest, which lay curled around the hill on which the campus was built. This forest seemed deeply peaceful to me, almost conscious. I didn't know the reason for this at the time—that many elms in a forest can spring from a single tree. In this case a single elm had divided herself into a forest, an individual with a continuous DNA in whose midst one could stand and be held.

The ravine cut through like an old emotional wound. I

crouched on its bank and glanced at the book one last time. I flicked open my lighter. The book caught fire instantly. As the flame approached my hand, I arced the book into the murky water. It looked spectacular, a high wing of flame rising from it. Inside, in one of its luminous chapters, I had read that the ability to use language and the ability to tame fire arose from the same warm, shimmering pool of genes, since in nature they did not appear one without the other.

As I made my way out of the woods and into the long silver ditch that lined the highway, I heard about a thousand birds cry, and I craned my neck to see them lighting out from the tips of the elms. They looked like ideas would if released suddenly from the page and given bodies—shocked at how blood actually felt as it ran through the veins, as it sent them wheeling into the west, wings raking, straining against the requirements of such a physical world.

⌒

I returned and found Solveig turning in the lamplight. Her hair was piled on her head, so unnaturally blonde it looked ablaze, and her face was bronze. She looked a thousand years old. "Some guy called," she said. "Stasselova or something."

He called again that night, at nearly midnight. I thought this unseemly.

"So," he said. "Solveig's back."

"Yes," I said, glancing at her. She was at her mirror, performing some ablution on her face. "She's much better."

"Perhaps the three of us can now meet."

"Oh," I said, "it's too early."

"Too early in what?"

"In her recovery." Solveig wheeled her head around to look at me. I smiled, shrugged.

"I think she'll be okay."

"I'm not so sure."

"Listen," he said. "I'll give you a choice: you can either rewrite the paper in my office, bringing in whatever materials you need, or the three of us can meet and clear this up."

"Fine, we'll meet you."

"You know my hours."

"I do." I hung up and explained to Solveig what had happened—Stasselova's obsession with language and oppression, my plagiarism, the invocation of her name. Solveig nodded and said of course, whatever she could do she would.

~

When we arrived that Wednesday, the light had almost gone from his office but was still lingering outside the windows, like the light in fairy tales, rich and creepy.

Solveig was brilliant. Just her posture, as she sat in the narrow chair, was enough initially to chasten Stasselova. In her presence men were driven to politeness, to sincerity, to a kind of deep, internal apology. He thanked her, bowing a little at his desk. "Your work has interested me," he said.

"It is not my work, sir. It's Margaret's. We just discussed together some of the ideas."

"Such as?"

"Well, the necessity of a collective language, a mutual tongue."

"And why is that necessary?" Stasselova leaned back and folded his hands across his vast torso.

"To maintain order," she said. And then the sun fell completely, blowing one last blast of light across the Americas before it settled into the Soviet Union, and some of that light, a glittery, barely perceptible dust, settled around Solveig's head. She looked like a dominatrix, an intellectual dominatrix, delivering this brutal news.

"And your history in psycholinguistics?" he said.

"I have only my personal history," she said. "The things that have happened to me." I would not have been surprised if at that declaration the whole university had imploded, turned to liquid, and flowed away. "Besides," she said, "all the research and work was Margaret's. I saw her working on it, night after night."

"Then, Margaret," he turned his gaze on me, "I see you are intimately connected with evolutionary history as well as Soviet ideology. As well, it appears, you've been steeped in a lifetime's study of linguistic psychosocial theory."

"Is it because she's female," Solveig asked, "that she's made to account for every scrap of knowledge?"

"Look," he said after a long, cruel silence, "I simply want to know from what cesspool these ideas arose. If you got them from a book, I will be relieved, but if these ideas are still floating around in your bloodlines, in your wretched little towns, I want to know."

I was about to cave in. Better a plagiarist than a fascist from a tainted bloodline.

"I don't really think you should be talking about our bloodlines," Solveig said. "It's probably not appropriate." She enunciated the word "appropriate" in such a way that Stasselova flinched, just slightly. Both he and I stared at her. She really was extraordinarily thin. In a certain light she could look shockingly beautiful, but in another, such as the dim one in Stasselova's office, she could look rather threatening. Her contact lenses were the color of a night sky split by lightning. Her genetic information was almost entirely hidden—the color of her hair and eyes and skin, the shape of her body—and this gave her a psychological advantage of sorts.

⁓

Stasselova's lecture on Thursday afternoon was another strange little affair, given as long autumn rays of sun, embroidered by leaves, covered his face and body. He was onto his main obsession again, the verb—specifically, the work of the verb in the sentence, and how it relates to the work of a man in the world.

"The revolution takes place from a position of stability, always. The true revolutionary will find his place within the status quo."

"And this is why you joined the Russian army in attacking your own country?" This was Hans, startling us all.

"I did not attack my own country," Stasselova said. "Never."

"But you watched as the Nazis attacked it in August of 1944, yes? And used that attack for your own purposes?"

"This night I was there, it's true," he said, "on the banks of the Vistula, and I saw Warsaw burn. And I was wearing the fur hat of Russia, yes. But when I attempted to cross the Vistula, in order to help those of my countrymen who were escaping, I was brought down—clubbed with a rifle to the back of the head by my commanding officer, a Russian."

"That's interesting, because in accounts of the time you are referred to as an officer yourself—Officer Stasselova, of course."

"Yes. I was a Polish officer though. Certainly you can infer the hierarchy involved?"

"What I can infer . . ." Hans's voice rose, and then Stasselova's joined in, contrapuntally, "What you can infer . . . ," and for a moment the exchange reminded me of those rounds we sang at summer camp. "What you can infer," Stasselova said, drowning out Hans, "is that this was an ambiguous time for those of us who were Polish. You can't judge after the fact. Perhaps you think that I should be dead on those banks, making the willows to grow." Stasselova's eyes were shot with the dying light; he squinted at us and looked out the window momentarily. "You will stand there and think maybe certain men in certain times should not choose their own lives, should not want to live." And then he turned away from Hans. I myself scowled at Hans. So rude!

"And so I did live," Stasselova said finally. "Mostly because I was wearing my Russian hat, made of the fur of ten foxes. It was always Russia that dealt us blows, and it was always Russia that saved us. You see?"

~

The next day I was with Hans in the woods. We were on our stomachs in a clearing, looking to the east, from where the rain was stalking us through the trees.

"What I want to know," Hans was saying, "is why is he always asking for you to see him?"

"Oh," I said, "he thinks I plagiarized that first paper."

"Did you?"

"Not really."

"Why does he think so?"

"Says it smacks of Soviet propaganda."

"Really? Well, he should know."

"I agree with him—that you're judging him from an irrelevant stance."

"He was found guilty of treason by his own people, not me—by the Committee for Political Responsibility. Why else would he be here, teaching at some Lutheran college in Minnesota? This is a guy who brought martial law down on his own people, and now we sit here in the afternoon and watch him march around in front of us, relating everything he speaks of—*comma splices,* for Christ's sake—to his own innocence."

"Yet all sorts of people were found guilty of all sorts of meaningless things by that committee."

"I bet he thinks you're a real dream—this woman willing to absolve the old exterminator of his sins."

"That's insulting," I said. But I realized how fond I'd grown of this professor in his little office, drinking his bitter coffee, night descending into the musky heart of Humanities.

And then the rain was upon us. We could hear it on the tiny

ledges of leaves above us more than feel it. "Let's go," Hans said, grabbing my hand with his left, damaged hand. The way his hand held mine was alluring; his hand had the nimbus of an idea about it, as if the gene that had sprung this hand had a different world in mind, a better world, where hands had more torque when they grasped each other, and people held things differently, like hooks—a world where all objects were shaped something like lanterns, and were passed on and on.

~

Monday was gray, with long silver streaks of rain. I dragged myself out of the warmth of my bed and put on my rain slicker. At 9:45 I headed toward Stasselova's office.

"Hello," I said, knocking on the open door. "I'm sorry to disturb you outside your office hours." I was shivering; I felt pathetic.

"Margaret," he said. "Hello. Come in." As I sat down, he said, "You've brought with you the smell of rain."

He poured me coffee in a Styrofoam cup. During our last class I had been so moved by his description of that night on the Vistula that I'd decided to confess. But now I was hesitating. "Could I have some of this cream?" I asked, pointing to a little tin cup of it on his windowsill.

"There it is again," he said, as he reached for the cream.

"There is what again?"

"That little verbal tic of yours."

"I didn't know I had one," I said.

"I noticed it first in class," he said. "You say 'this' instead of 'that'; 'this cream,' not 'that cream.' The line people draw between the things they consider *this* and the things they consider *that* is the perimeter of their sphere of intimacy. You see? Everything inside is *this*; everything inside is close, is intimate. Since you pointed at the cream and it is farther from you than I am, 'this' suggests that I am among the things you consider close to you. I'm flattered," he said, and handed me the creamer, which was, like him, sweating. What an idea—that with a few words you could catch another person in a little grammatical clutch, arrange the objects of the world such that they bordered the two of you.

"At any rate," he said, "I'm glad you showed up."

"You are?"

"Yes. I've wanted to ask you something."

"Yes?"

"This spring the college will hold its annual symposium on language and politics. I thought you might present your paper. Usually one of the upperclassmen does this, but I thought your paper might be more appropriate."

"I thought you hated my paper."

"I do."

"Oh."

"So you'll do it?"

"I'll think about it," I said.

He nodded and smiled, as if the matter were settled. The rain was suddenly coming down very hard. It was loud, and we were silent for a few moments, listening. I stared beyond his head out the window, which was blurry with water, so that the turrets of the campus looked like a hallucination, like some shadow world looming back there in his unconscious.

"This rain," he said then, in a quiet, astonished voice, and his word *this* entered me as it was meant to—quietly, with a sharp tip, but then, like an arrowhead, widening and widening, until it included the whole landscape around us.

～

The rain turned to snow, and winter settled on our campus. The face of nature turned away—beautiful and distracted. After Christmas at home (where I received my report card, a tiny slip of paper that seemed to have flown across the snows to deliver me my A in Stasselova's class) I hunkered down in my dorm for the month of January, and barely emerged. The dorm in which most of us freshman girls lived was the elaborate, dark Agnes Mellby Hall, named after the stern, formidable virgin whose picture hung over the fireplace in our lounge.

As winter crept over us, we retired to Mellby earlier and earlier. Every night that winter, in which most of us were nineteen, was a slumber party in the main sitting room among its ornate furnishings, all of which had the paws of beasts where they touched the floor. There, nightly, we ate heavily, like Romans, but childish foods, popcorn and pizza and ice cream, most of us spiraling downstairs now and then to throw up in the one private bathroom.

On one of those nights I was reading a book in the sitting room when I received a phone call from Solveig, who was down at a house party in town and wanted me to come help her home. She wasn't completely drunk, but calculated that she would be in about forty-five minutes. Her body was like a tract of nature that she understood perfectly—a constellation whose movement across the night sky she could predict, or a gathering storm, or maybe, more accurately, a sparkling stream of elements into which she introduced alcohol with such careful calibration that her blood flowed exactly as she desired, uphill and down, intersecting precisely, chemically, with time and fertility. Solveig did not stay at the dorm with us much, but rather ran with an older pack of girls, feminists mostly, who that winter happened to be involved in a series of protests, romantic insurrections, against the president of the college, who was clearly terrified of them.

About ten minutes before I was to leave, Stasselova appeared in the doorway of the sitting room. I had not seen him in more than a month, since the last day of class, but he had called a few times. I had not returned his calls, in the hopes that he would forget about

Rebecca Lee

my participation in the symposium. But here he was, wearing a long gray coat over his bulkiness. His head looked huge, the bones widely spaced, like the architecture of a grand civic building.

The look in his eyes caused me to gaze out across the room and try to see what he was seeing: perhaps some debauched canvas of absolute female repose, girls lying everywhere in various modes of pajamas and sweats, surrounded by vast quantities of food and books. Some girls—and even I found this a bit creepy—had stuffed animals that they carried with them to the sitting room at night. I happened to be poised above the fray, straddling a piano bench, with a book spread in front of me, but almost all the rest were lying on their backs with their extremities cast about, feet propped on the couch or stretched up in the air at weird, hyperextended angles. We were Lutherans, after all, and unlike the more experienced, secular girls across the river, at the state college, we were losing our inno- cence right here, among ourselves. It was being taken from us physi- cally, and we were just relaxing until it fell away completely.

Stasselova, in spite of all he'd seen in his life, which I'd gleaned from what he said in class (the corpulent Goering marching though the forest, marking off Nazi territory, and later Stalin's horses breaking through the same woods, heralding the swath that would now be Soviet), still managed to look a little scared as he peered into our sitting room, eventually lifting a hand to wave at me.

I got up and approached him. "Hey," I said.

"Hello. How are you, Margaret?"

"It's good to see you. Thanks for the A."

"You deserved it. Listen. I have something for you," he said, mildly gesturing for us to leave the doorway, because everybody was looking at us.

"Great," I said. "But you know, right now I need to walk down- town to pick up Solveig at a house party."

"Fine," he said. "I'll walk you."

"Oh. Okay."

I got my jacket, and the two of us stepped into the night. The snow had arranged itself in curling waves on the Mellby lawn, and stuck in it were hundreds of silver forks, which, in a flood of early-evening testosterone, the freshman boys had placed in the earth, a gesture appropriate to their sexual frustration and also to their faith in the future. Stasselova and I stepped between them. They looked spooky and lovely, like tiny silver grave sites in the snow. As we walked across campus, Stasselova produced a golden brochure from his pocket and handed it to me. On the front it said, in emerald-green letters, "9th Annual Symposium on Language and Politics." Inside, under "Keynote Student Speaker," was my name. "Margaret Olafson, 'The Common Harvest.'" I stopped walking. We paused at the top of the stairs that floated down off the campus and into the town. I felt extremely, inordinately proud. Some winter lightning, a couple of great wings of it, flashed in the north. Stasselova looked paternal, grand.

The air at the party was beery and wildish, and the house itself—its many random rooms and slanting floors—seemed the product of a drunken adolescent mind. At first we could not spot Solveig, so Stasselova and I waited quietly in the hallway until a guy in a baseball cap came lurching toward us, shouting in a friendly way over the music that we could buy plastic glasses for the keg for two dollars apiece. Stasselova paid him and then threaded through the crowd, gracefully for such a large man, to stand in the keg line. I watched him as he patiently stood there, the snowflakes melting on his dark shoulders.

And then Hans was on my arm. "What on earth?" he said. "Why are you here? I thought you hated these parties." He'd been dancing, apparently. He was soaked in sweat, his hair curling up at his neck.

I pointed to Stasselova.

"No kidding," Hans said.

"He showed up at my dorm as I was leaving to get Solveig."

"He came to Mellby?"

"Yes."

"God, look at him. I bet they had a nickname for him, like the Circus Man or something. All those old fascists had cheery nicknames."

Stasselova was now walking toward us. Behind him the picture window revealed a nearly black sky, with pretty crystalline stars around. He looked like a dream one might have in childhood. "He is not a fascist," I said quietly.

"Professor!" Hans raised his glass.

"Hans, yes, how are you? This is a wonderful party." Stasselova said, and it actually was. Sometimes these parties could seem deeply cozy, their wildness and noise an affirmation against the formless white midwestern winter surrounding us.

He handed me a beer. "So," he said rather formally, lifting his glass. "To youth."

"To experience," Hans said, smiling, and lifted his glass.

"To the party." Stasselova looked pleased, his eyes shining from the soft lamplight.

"The Party?" Hans raised an eyebrow.

"This party," Stasselova said forcefully, cheerfully.

"And to the committee," Hans said.

"The committee?"

"The Committee for Political Responsibility."

In one of Stasselova's lectures he had taken great pains to explain to us that language did not describe events, it handled them, as a hand handles an object, and that in this way language made the world happen under its supervision. I could see that Hans had taken this to heart and was making lurching attempts in this direction.

Mercifully, Solveig appeared. Her drunkenness and her dignity had synergized into something quite spectacular, an inner recklessness accompanied by great external restraint. Her hair looked the color of heat—bright white. She was wearing newly cut-off jeans and was absently holding the disassociated pant legs in her hand.

"The professor," she said, when she saw Stasselova. "The professor of oppression."

"Hello, Solveig."

"So you came," she said, as if this had been the plan all along.

"Yes. It's nice to see you again."

"You as well," she said. "Why are you here?"

The whole scene looked deeply romantic to me. "To take you home," he said.

"Home?" she said, as if this were the most elegant and promising word in the language. "Yours or mine?"

"Yours, of course. Yours and Margaret's."

"Where is your home again?" she asked. Her eyes were glimmering with complexity, like something that is given to human beings after evolution, as a gift.

"I live downtown," he said.

"No, your real home. Your homeland."

He paused. "I am from Poland," he said finally.

"Then there. Let's go there. I have always wanted to go to Poland."

Stasselova smiled. "Perhaps you would like it there."

"I have always wanted to see Wenceslaus Square."

"Well, that is nearby."

"Excellent. Let us go." And Solveig swung open the front door and walked into the snow in her shorts and T-shirt. I kissed Hans good-bye, and Stasselova and I followed her.

Once outside, Stasselova took off his coat and hung it around Solveig. Underneath his coat he was wearing a dark jacket and a tie. It looked sweet, and made me think that if one kept undressing him, darker and darker suits would be found underneath.

Solveig was walking before us on the narrow sidewalk. Above her, on the hill, hovered Humanities—great, intelligent, alight. She reached into the coat pocket and pulled out, to my astonishment, a fur hat. The hat! The wind lifted, and the trees shook off a little of their silver snow. Humanities leaned over us, interested in its loving but secular way. I felt as sure about everything as those archaeologists who discover a single bone and can then hypothesize the entire animal. Solveig placed the hat on her head and turned to vamp for a moment, opening and closing the coat and raising her arms above her head in an exaggerated gesture of beauty. She looked like some stirring, turning simulacrum of communist and capitalist ideas. As she was doing this, we passed by the president's house. It was an old-fashioned house, with high turrets, and had a bizarre modern wing hanging off one end of it. Solveig studied it for a moment as she walked, and then suddenly shouted into the cold night, "Motherfucker!"

Stasselova looked as if he'd been clubbed again in the back of the head, but he kept walking. He pretended that nothing had happened, didn't even turn his head to look at the house, but when I turned to him, I saw his eyes widen and his face stiffen with shock. I said "Oh" quietly, and grabbed his hand for a moment to comfort him, to let him know that everything was under control, that this was Minnesota. Look—the president's house is still as dark as death, the moon is still high, the snow sparkling everywhere.

His hand was extraordinarily big. After Hans's hand, which I'd held for the past few months, Stasselova's more ordinary hand felt strange, almost mutant, its five fingers splayed and independent.

~

The next night, in the cafeteria, over a grisly neon dish called Festival Rice, I told Hans about the hat. "I saw the hat," I said.

A freshman across the cafeteria stood just then and shouted, in what was a St. Gustav tradition, *"I want a standing ovation!"* The entire room stood and erupted into wild applause and hooting. Hans and I stood as well, and as we clapped, I leaned over to yell, "He's been telling the truth about that night overlooking Warsaw: I saw the hat he was wearing."

"What does that mean? That means nothing. I have a fur hat."

"No," I said. "It was this big Russian hat. You should have seen it. This big, beautiful Russian hat. Solveig put it on. It saved his life."

Hans didn't even try to object; he just kind of gasped, as if the great gears of logic in his brain could not pass this syllogism through. We were still standing, clapping, applauding. I couldn't help thinking of something Stasselova had said in class: that at rallies for Stalin, when he spoke to crowds over loudspeakers, one could be shot for being the first to stop clapping.

~

I avoided my paper for the next month or so, until spring crashed in huge warm waves and I finally sought it out, sunk in its darkened drawer. It was a horrible surprise. I was not any more of a scholar, of course, than I had been six months earlier, when I'd plagiarized it, but my eyes had now passed over Marx and a biography of Stalin (microphones lodged in eyeglasses, streams of censors on their way to work, bloody corpses radiating out of Moscow) and the gentle Bonhoeffer. Almost miraculously I had crossed that invisible line beyond which people turn into actual readers, when they start to hear the voice of the writer as clearly as in a conversation. "Language," Tretsky had written, "is essentially a coercive act, and in the case of Eastern Europe it must be used as a tool to garden collective hopes and aspirations."

As I read, with Solveig napping at the other end of the couch, I felt a thick dread forming. Tretsky, with his suggestions of annexations and, worse, of *solutions,* seemed to be reaching right off the page, his long, thin hand grasping me by the shirt. And I could almost hear the wild mazurka, as Stasselova had described it, fading, the cabarets closing down, the music turning into a chant, the bootheels falling, the language fortifying itself, becoming a stronghold—a fixed, unchanging system, as the paper said, a moral framework.

~

Almost immediately I was on my way to Stasselova's office, but not before my mother called. The golden brochures had gone out in the mail. "Sweetie!" she said, "What's this? Keynote speaker? Your father and I are beside ourselves. Good night!" She always exclaimed "Good night!" at times of great happiness. I could not dissuade her from coming, and as I fled the dorm, into the rare, hybrid air of early April, I was wishing for those bad, indifferent parents who had no real interest in their children's lives.

The earth under my feet as I went to him was very sticky, almost lugubrious, like the earth one sometimes encounters in dreams. Stasselova was there, as always. He seemed pleased to see me.

I sat down and said, "You know, I was thinking that maybe somebody else could take my place at the symposium. As I reread my paper, I realized it isn't really what I meant to say at all."

"Oh," he said. "Of course you can deliver it. I would not abandon you at a moment like this."

"Really, I wouldn't take it as abandonment."

"I would not leave you in the lurch," he said. "I promise." I felt myself being carried, mysteriously, into the doomed symposium, despite my resolve on the way over to back out at all costs. How could I win an argument against somebody with an early training in propaganda? I had to resort finally to the truth, that rinky-dink little boat in the great sea of persuasion. "See, I didn't really write the paper myself."

"Well, every thinker builds an idea on the backs of those before him—or her, in your case." He smiled at this. His teeth were very square, and humble, with small gaps between them. I could see that Stasselova was no longer after a confession. I was more valuable if I contained these ideas. Probably he'd been subconsciously looking for me ever since he'd lain on the muddy banks of the Vistula, Warsaw flaming across the waters. He could see within me all his failed ideals, the ugliness of his former beliefs contained in a benign vessel—a girl!—high on a religious hill in the Midwest. He had found somebody he might oppose, and in this way absolve himself. He smiled. I could feel myself as indispensable in the organization of his psyche. Behind his head, in the sunset, the sun wasn't falling, only receding farther and farther.

The days before the symposium unfurled like the days before a wedding one dreads, both endless and accelerated, the sky filling with springtime events—ravishing sun, great winds, and eccentric green storms that focused everyone's attention skyward. And then the weekend of the symposium was upon us, the Saturday of my speech rising in the east. I awoke early and went to practice my paper on the red steps of Humanities, in whose auditorium my talk was to take place. Solveig was still sleeping, hung over from the night before. I'd been with her for the first part of it, had watched her pursue a man she'd discovered—a graduate student, actually, in town for the symposium. I had thought him a bit of a bore, but I trusted Solveig's judgment. She approached men with stealth and insight, her vision driving into those truer, more isolated stretches of personality.

I had practiced the paper countless times, and revised it, attempting to excise the most offensive lines without gutting the paper entirely and thus disappointing Stasselova. That morning I

Rebecca Lee

was still debating over the line "If we could agree on a common language, a single human tongue, perhaps then a single flag might unfurl over the excellent earth, one nation of like and companion souls." Reading it now, I had a faint memory of my earlier enthusiasm for this paper, its surface promise, its murderous innocence. Remembering this, I looked out over the excellent earth, at the town below the hill. And there, as always, was a tiny Gothic graveyard looking peaceful, everything still and settled finally under the gnarled, knotty, nearly human arms of apple trees. There were no apples yet, of course: they were making their way down the bough, still liquid, or whatever they are before birth. At the sight of graves I couldn't help thinking of Tretsky, my ghost-writer, in his dark suit under the earth, delightedly preparing, thanks to me, for his one last gasp.

By noon the auditorium had filled with a crowd of about two hundred, mostly graduate students and professors from around the Midwest, along with Hans and Solveig, who sat together, and two rows behind them, my long-suffering parents, flushed with pride. I sat alone on a slight stage at the front of the room, staring out at the auditorium, which was named Luther. It had wooden walls and was extremely tall; it seemed humble and a little awkward, in that way the tall can seem. The windows stretched its full height, so that one could see the swell of earth on which Humanities was built, and then, above, all manner of weather, which this afternoon was running to rain. In front of these windows stood the reformed genius of martial law himself, the master of ceremonies, Stasselova. Behind him were maple trees, with small green leaves waving. He had always insisted in class that language as it rises in the mind looks like a tree branching, from finity to infinity. Let every voice cry out! He had once said this, kind of absently, and water had come to his eyes—not exactly tears, just a rising of the body's water into the line of sight.

After he introduced me, I stood in front of the crowd, my larynx rising quite against my will, and delivered my paper. I tried to speak each word as a discrete item, in order to persuade the audience not to synthesize the sentences into meaning. But when I lifted my head to look out at my listeners, I could see they were doing just that. When I got to the part where I said the individual did not exist—citizens were "merely shafts of light lost, redemptively, in the greater light of the state"—I saw Hans bow his head and rake his otherworldly hand through his hair.

". . . And if force is required to forge a singular and mutual grammar, then it is our sacred duty to hasten the birthpangs." Even from this distance I could hear Stasselova's breathing, and the sound of blood running through him like a quiet but rushing stream.

And then my parents. As the speech wore on—"harmony," "force," "flowering," "blood"—I could see that the very elegant parental machinery they had designed over the years, which sought always to translate my deeds into something lovely, light-bearing, full of promise, was spinning a little on its wheels. Only Solveig, that apparatchik of friendship, maintained her confidence in me. Even when she was hung over, her posture suggested a perfect alignment between heaven and earth. She kept nodding, encouraging me.

I waited the entire speech for Stasselova to leap forward and confront me, to reassert his innocence in opposition to me, but he did not, even when I reached the end. He stood and watched as everybody clapped in bewilderment, and a flushed floral insignia rose on his cheeks. I had come to love his wide, excited face, the old circus man. He smiled at me. He was my teacher, and he had wrapped himself, his elaborate historical self, into this package, and stood in front of the high windows, to teach me my little lesson, which turned out to be not about Poland or fascism or war, borderlines or passion or loyalty, but just about the sentence: the importance of, the sweetness of. And I did long for it, to say one true sentence of my own, to leap into the subject, that sturdy vessel traveling upstream through the axonal predicate into what is possible; into the object, which is all possibility; into what little we know of the future, of eternity—the light of which, incidentally, was streaming in on us just then through the high windows. Above Stasselova's head the storm clouds were dispersing, as if frightened by some impending good will, and I could see that the birds were out again, forming into that familiar pointy hieroglyph, as they're told to do from deep within.

Strawberry Spring
Stephen King

Springheel Jack . . .

I saw those two words in the paper this morning and my God,
how they take me back. All that was eight years ago, almost to the
day. Once, while it was going on, I saw myself on nationwide TV—
the Walter Cronkite Report. Just a hurrying face in the general background behind the reporter, but my folks picked me out right away.
They called long-distance. My dad wanted my analysis of the situation; he was all bluff and hearty and man-to-man. My mother just
wanted me to come home. But I didn't want to come home. I was
enchanted.

Enchanted by that dark and mist-blown strawberry spring,
and by the shadow of violent death that walked through it on those
nights eight years ago. The shadow of Springheel Jack.

In New England they call it a strawberry spring. No one knows
why; it's just a phrase the old-timers use. They say it happens once
every eight or ten years. What happened at New Sharon Teachers'
College that particular strawberry spring . . . there may be a cycle
for that, too, but if anyone has figured it out, they've never said.

At New Sharon, the strawberry spring began on March 16,
1968. The coldest winter in twenty years broke on that day. It
rained and you could smell the sea twenty miles west of the
beaches. The snow, which had been thirty-five inches deep in
places, began to melt and the campus walks ran with slush. The Winter Carnival snow sculptures, which had been kept sharp and clear-

cut for two months by the subzero temperatures, at last began to sag and slouch. The caricature of Lyndon Johnson in front of the Tep fraternity house cried melted tears. The dove in front of Prashner Hall lost its frozen feathers and its plywood skeleton showed sadly through in places.

And when night came the fog came with it, moving silent and white along the narrow college avenues and thoroughfares. The pines on the mall poked through it like counting fingers and it drifted, slow as cigarette smoke, under the little bridge down by the Civil War cannons. It made things seem out of joint, strange, magical. The unwary traveler would step out of the juke-thumping, brightly lit confusion of the Grinder, expecting the hard clear starriness of winter to clutch him . . . and instead he would suddenly find himself in a silent, muffled world of white drifting fog, the only sound his own footsteps and the soft drip of water from the ancient gutters. You half expected to see Gollum or Frodo and Sam go hurrying past, or to turn and see that the Grinder was gone, vanished, replaced by a foggy panorama of moors and yew trees and perhaps a Druid-circle or a sparkling fairy ring.

The jukebox played "Love Is Blue" that year. It played "Hey, Jude" endlessly, endlessly. It played "Scarborough Fair."

And at ten minutes after eleven on that night a junior named John Dancey on his way back to his dormitory began screaming into the fog, dropping books on and between the sprawled legs of the dead girl lying in a shadowy corner of the Animal Sciences parking lot, her throat cut from ear to ear but her eyes open and almost seeming to sparkle as if she had just successfully pulled off the funniest joke of her young life—Dancey, an education major and a speech minor, screamed and screamed and screamed.

The next day was overcast and sullen, and we went to classes with questions eager in our mouths—who? why? when do you think they'll get him? And always the final thrilled question: Did you know her? Did you know her?

Yes, I had an art class with her.

Yes, one of my roommate's friends dated her last term.

Yes, she asked me for a light once in the Grinder. She was at the next table.

Yes,

Yes, I

Yes . . . yes . . . oh yes, I

We all knew her. Her name was Gale Cerman (pronounced Kerr-man), and she was an art major. She wore granny glasses and had a good figure. She was well liked but her roommates had hated her. She had never gone out much even though she was one of the most promiscuous girls on campus. She was ugly but cute. She had been a vivacious girl who talked little and smiled seldom. She had been pregnant and she had had leukemia. She was a lesbian who had been murdered by her boyfriend. It was strawberry spring, and on the morning of March 17 we all knew Gale Cerman.

Half a dozen state police cars crawled onto the campus, most of them parked in front of Judith Franklin Hall, where the Cerman girl had lived. On my way past there to my ten o'clock class I was asked to show my student ID. I was clever. I showed him the one without the fangs.

"Do you carry a knife?" the policeman asked cunningly.

"Is it about Gale Cerman?" I asked, after I told him that the most lethal thing on my person was a rabbit's-foot key chain.

"What makes you ask?" he pounced.

I was five minutes late to class.

It was strawberry spring and no one walked by themselves through the half-academical, half-fantastical campus that night. The fog had come again, smelling of the sea, quiet and deep.

Around nine o'clock my roommate burst into our room, where I had been busting my brains on a Milton essay since seven. "They caught him," he said. "I heard it over at the Grinder."

"From who?"

"I don't know. Some guy. Her boyfriend did it. His name is Carl Amalara."

I settled back, relieved and disappointed. With a name like that it had to be true. A lethal and sordid little crime of passion.

"Okay," I said. "That's good."

He left the room to spread the news down the hall. I reread my Milton essay, couldn't figure out what I had been trying to say, tore it up and started again.

It was in the papers the next day. There was an incongruously neat picture of Amalara—probably a high-school graduation picture—and it showed a rather sad-looking boy with an olive complexion and dark eyes and pockmarks on his nose. The boy had not confessed yet, but the evidence against him was strong. He and Gale Cerman had argued a great deal in the last month or so, and had broken up the week before. Amalara's roomie said he had been "despondent." In a footlocker under his bed, police had found a seven-inch hunting knife from L. L. Bean's and a picture of the girl that had apparently been cut up with a pair of shears.

Beside Amalara's picture was one of Gale Cerman. It blurrily showed a dog, a peeling lawn flamingo, and a rather mousy blond girl wearing spectacles. An uncomfortable smile had turned her lips up and her eyes were squinted. One hand was on the dog's head. It was true then. It had to be true.

The fog came again that night, not on little cat's feet but in an improper silent sprawl. I walked that night. I had a headache and I walked for air, smelling the wet, misty smell of the spring that was slowly wiping away the reluctant snow, leaving lifeless patches of last year's grass bare and uncovered, like the head of a sighing old grandmother.

For me, that was one of the most beautiful nights I can remember. The people I passed under the haloed streetlights were murmuring shadows, and all of them seemed to be lovers, walking with hands and eyes linked. The melting snow dripped and ran, dripped and ran, and from every dark storm drain the sound of the sea drifted up, a dark winter sea now strongly ebbing.

I walked until nearly midnight, until I was thoroughly mildewed, and I passed many shadows, heard many footfalls clicking dreamily off down the winding paths. Who is to say that one of those shadows was not the man or the thing that came to be known as Springheel Jack? Not I, for I passed many shadows but in the fog I saw no faces.

The next morning the clamor in the hall woke me. I blundered out to see who had been drafted, combing my hair with both hands and running the fuzzy caterpillar that had craftily replaced my tongue across the dry roof of my mouth.

"He got another one," someone said to me, his face pallid with excitement. "They had to let him go."

"Who go?"

"Amalara!" someone else said gleefully. "He was sitting in jail when it happened."

"When what happened?" I asked patiently. Sooner or later I would get it. I was sure of that.

"The guy killed somebody else last night. And now they're hunting all over for it."

"For what?"

The pallid face wavered in front of me again. "Her head. Whoever killed her took her head with him."

New Sharon isn't a big school now, and was even smaller then —the kind of institution the public relations people chummily refer to as a "community college." And it really was like a small community, at least in those days; between you and your friends, you probably had at least a nodding acquaintance with everybody else and their friends. Gale Cerman had been the type of girl you just nodded to, thinking vaguely that you had seen her around.

We all knew Ann Bray. She had been the first runner-up in the Miss New England pageant the year before, her talent performance consisting of twirling a flaming baton to the tune of "Hey, Look Me Over." She was brainy, too; until the time of her death she had been editor of the school newspaper (a once-weekly rag with a lot of political cartoons and bombastic letters), a member of the student dramatics society, and president of the National Service Sorority, New Sharon Branch. In the hot, fierce bubblings of my freshman youth I had submitted a column idea to the paper and asked for a date—turned down on both counts.

And now she was dead . . . worse than dead.

I walked to my afternoon classes like everyone else, nodding to people I knew and saying hi with a little more force than usual, as if that would make up for the close way I studied their faces. Which was the same way they were studying mine. There was someone dark among us, as dark as the paths which twisted across the mall or wound among the hundred-year-old oaks on the quad in back of the gymnasium. As dark as the hulking Civil War cannons seen through a drifting membrane of fog. We looked into each other's faces and tried to read the darkness behind one of them.

This time the police arrested no one. The blue beetles patrolled the campus ceaselessly on the foggy spring nights of the eighteenth, nineteenth, and twentieth, and spotlights stabbed into dark nooks and crannies with erratic eagerness. The administration imposed a mandatory nine o'clock curfew. A foolhardy couple discovered necking in the landscaped bushes north of the Tate Alumni Building were taken to the New Sharon police station and grilled unmercifully for three hours.

There was a hysterical false alarm on the twentieth when a boy was found unconscious in the same parking lot where the body of Gale Cerman had been found. A gibbering campus cop loaded him into the back of his cruiser and put a map of the county over his face without bothering to hunt for a pulse and started toward the local hospital, siren wailing across the deserted campus like a seminar of banshees.

Halfway there the corpse in the back seat had risen and asked hollowly, "Where the hell am I?" The cop shrieked and ran off the road. The corpse turned out to be an undergrad named Donald Morris who had been in bed the last two days with a pretty lively case of flu—was it Asian that year? I can't remember. Anyway, he fainted in the parking lot on his way to the Grinder for a bowl of soup and some toast.

The days continued warm and overcast. People clustered in small groups that had a tendency to break up and re-form with surprising speed. Looking at the same set of faces for too long gave you funny ideas about some of them. And the speed with which rumors swept from one end of the campus to the other began to approach the speed of light; a well-liked history professor had been overheard laughing and weeping down by the small bridge; Gale Cerman had left a cryptic two-word message written in her own blood on the blacktop of the Animal Sciences parking lot; both murders were actually political crimes, ritual murders that had been performed by an offshoot of the SDS to protest the war. This was really laughable. The New Sharon SDS had seven members. One fair-sized offshoot would have bankrupted the whole organization. This fact brought an even more sinister embellishment from the campus right-wingers: outside agitators. So during those queer, warm days we all kept our eyes peeled for them.

The press, always fickle, ignored the strong resemblance our murderer bore to Jack the Ripper and dug further back—all the way to 1819. Ann Bray had been found on a soggy path of ground some

twelve feet from the nearest sidewalk, and yet there were no foot-
prints, not even her own. An enterprising New Hampshire newsman
with a passion for the arcane christened the killer Springheel Jack,
after the infamous Dr. John Hawkins of Bristol, who did five of his
wives to death with odd pharmaceutical knickknacks. And the
name, probably because of that soggy yet unmarked ground, stuck.

On the twenty-first it rained again, and the mall and quadran-
gle became quagmires. The police announced that they were salting
plainclothes detectives, men and women, about, and took half the
police cars off duty.

The campus newspaper published a strongly indignant, if
slightly incoherent, editorial protesting this. The upshot of it seemed
to be that, with all sorts of cops masquerading as students, it would
be impossible to tell a real outside agitator from a false one.

Twilight came and the fog with it, drifting up the tree-lined
avenues slowly, almost thoughtfully, blotting out the buildings one
by one. It was soft, insubstantial stuff, but somehow implacable
and frightening. Springheel Jack was a man, no one seemed to
doubt that, but the fog was his accomplice and it was female . . .
or so it seemed to me. It was as if our little school was caught between them, squeezed in some crazy lovers' embrace, part of a marriage that had been consummated in blood. I sat and smoked and
watched the lights come on in the growing darkness and wondered
if it was all over. My roommate came in and shut the door quietly
behind him.

"It's going to snow soon," he said.

I turned around and looked at him. "Does the radio say that?"

"No," he said. "Who needs a weatherman? Have you ever
heard of strawberry spring?"

"Maybe," I said. "A long time ago. Something grandmothers
talk about, isn't it?"

He stood beside me, looking out at the creeping dark.

"Strawberry spring is like Indian summer," he said, "only much

more rare. You get a good Indian summer in this part of the country once every two or three years. A spell of weather like we've been
having is supposed to come only every eight or ten. It's a false
spring, a lying spring, like Indian summer is a false summer. My
own grandmother used to say strawberry spring means the worst
norther of the winter is still on the way—and the longer this lasts,
the harder the storm."

"Folk tales," I said. "Never believe a word." I looked at him.
"But I'm nervous. Are you?"

He smiled benevolently and stole one of my cigarettes from
the open pack on the window ledge. "I suspect everyone but me
and thee," he said, and then the smile faded a little. "And sometimes
I wonder about thee. Want to go over to the Union and shoot some
eight-ball? I'll spot you ten."

"Trig prelim next week. I'm going to settle down with a magic
marker and a hot pile of notes."

For a long time after he was gone, I could only look out the
window. And even after I had opened my book and started in, part
of me was still out there, walking in the shadows where something
dark was now in charge.

That night Adelle Parkins was killed. Six police cars and seventeen collegiate-looking plainclothesmen (eight of them were
women imported all the way from Boston) patrolled the campus.
But Springheel Jack killed her just the same, going unerringly for
one of our own. The false spring, the lying spring, aided and abetted him—he killed her and left her propped behind the wheel of her
1964 Dodge to be found the next morning and they found part of
her in the back seat and part of her in the trunk. And written in
blood on the windshield—this time fact instead of rumor—were two
words: HA! HA!

The campus went slightly mad after that; all of us and none
of us had known Adelle Parkins. She was one of those nameless, harried women who worked the break-back shift in the Grinder from

six to eleven at night, facing hordes of hamburger-happy students on study break from the library across the way. She must have had it relatively easy those last three foggy nights of her life; the curfew was being rigidly observed, and after nine the Grinder's only patrons were hungry cops and happy janitors—the empty buildings had improved their habitual bad temper considerably.

There is little left to tell. The police, as prone to hysteria as any any of us and driven against the wall, arrested an innocuous homosexual sociology graduate student named Hanson Gray, who claimed he "could not remember" where he had spent several of the lethal evenings. They charged him, arraigned him, and let him go to scamper hurriedly back to his native New Hampshire town after the last unspeakable night of strawberry spring when Marsha Curran was slaughtered on the mall.

Why she had been out and alone is forever beyond knowing— she was a fat, sadly pretty thing who lived in an apartment in town with three other girls. She had slipped on campus as silently and as easily as Springheel Jack himself. What brought her? Perhaps her need was as deep and as ungovernable as her killer's, and just as far beyond understanding. Maybe a need for one desperate and passionate romance with the warm night, the warm fog, the smell of the sea, and the cold knife.

That was on the twenty-third. On the twenty-fourth the president of the college announced that spring break would be moved up a week, and we scattered, not joyfully but like frightened sheep before a storm, leaving the campus empty and haunted by the police and one dark specter.

I had my own car on campus, and I took six people downstate with me, their luggage crammed in helter-skelter. It wasn't a pleasant ride. For all any of us knew, Springheel Jack might have been in the car with us.

That night the thermometer dropped fifteen degrees, and the whole northern New England area was belted by a shrieking norther that began in sleet and ended in a foot of snow. The usual number of old duffers had heart attacks shoveling it away—and then, like magic, it was April. Clean showers and starry nights.

They called it strawberry spring, God knows why, and it's an evil, lying time that only comes once every eight or ten years. Springheel Jack left with the fog, and by early June, campus conversation had turned to a series of draft protests and a sit-in at the building where a well-known napalm manufacturer was holding job interviews. By June, the subject of Springheel Jack was almost unanimously avoided—at least aloud. I suspect there were many who turned it over and over privately, looking for the one crack in the seemless egg of madness that would make sense of it all.

That was the year I graduated, and the next year was the year I married. A good job in a local publishing house. In 1971 we had a child, and now he's almost school age. A fine and questing boy with my eyes and her mouth.

Then, today's paper.

Of course I knew it was here. I knew it yesterday morning when I got up and heard the mysterious sound of snowmelt running down the gutters, and smelled the salt tang of the ocean from our front porch, nine miles from the nearest beach. I knew strawberry spring had come again when I started home from work last night and had to turn on my headlights against the mist that was already beginning to creep out of the fields and hollows, blurring the lines of the buildings and putting fairy haloes around the streetlamps.

This morning's paper says a girl was killed on the New Sharon campus near the Civil War cannons. She was killed last night and found in a melting snowbank. She was not . . . she was not all there.

My wife is upset. She wants to know where I was last night. I can't tell her because I don't remember. I remember starting home from work, and I remember putting my headlights on to search my way through the lovely creeping fog, but that's all I remember.

I've been thinking about that foggy night when I had a headache and walked for air and passed all the lovely shadows without shape or substance. And I've been thinking about the trunk of my car—such an ugly word, *trunk*—and wondering why in the world I should be afraid to open it.

I can hear my wife as I write this, in the next room, crying. She thinks I was with another woman last night.

And oh dear God, I think so too.

Like Whiskey for Christmas
Joe Schraufnagel

CHAPTER ONE

Cheese Sandwich on Whole Wheat with Avocado Smear
2 Slices of HealthNut Whole Wheat Bread
Country Crock Easy Spread Margarine
3 Slabs of Farmer Cheese
Mayonnaise
Gulden's Mustard
Lettuce for Crunch
Very Ripe Avocado Smear

Lovingly slather creamy margarine, mayonnaise (generously, please) and mustard on HealthNut bread. Break taboo and brazenly slip a spoonful of Kraft Real mayonnaise into your mouth as if there were no German housemate watching in disbelief and horror. Lick the spoon with porcine self-satisfaction. Housemate may appear damaged. Hurry the hell up because another housemate—a wealthy Kazakhstanian wraith who apparently suffers from TB because she hawks up a lung every single morning—is waiting to use the goddamned slip of a counter that passes for a kitchen. Bitch under your breath, then conclude your performance on a low note by leaving your mess untouched. Flee and enjoy the food product in the cool solitude of your dinky little room.

⌒

Gil Poulsby.

I stared, stunned, at the card identifying him as the man I needed to see to prove competency in Spanish in order to receive my Master's Degree in Linguistics, this card that served a dual purpose because it also allowed him to check out an untranslated volume of Lorca. I passed his ID under the scanner five times unsuccessfully. I sat opposite Gil Poulsby from the business side of the checker's station, helpless and with a face-cramping grin. He had said something absurd and hilarious, but I was delirious for reasons other than good humor. His eyes were black and flashing, and I was lost completely in them. All of a sudden, I loved this man! I loved him with all my heart and soul, with every fathom of will I harbored and all the grace my god would allow. He appeared puzzled by my rapturous mien, but he didn't miss a beat.

"Do these scanner things work?" He had the boxy, sure-footed countenance of a film-noir mug, a wiseguy. He laughed. His laughter came from somewhere deep, deep inside I guessed. His spleen. His colon, perhaps.

I wanted to touch him but instead I yelled something moronic—"There's a trick to these things!"—and I whisked both his ID and Lorca along the counter and off onto the floor, as if on purpose.

He was truly baffled now, but he displayed the kind of good sportfulness that has mended hearts and raised expectations from time immemorial. He retrieved the dispatched items. "Wow! Did you catch that?" he asked the other checker. "Remember that in a pinch!"

Yael, my artfully disheveled co-checker, had missed all the hubbub and couldn't be distracted from *Cymbeline*. Oh, to be aloof and desired. I had kept a mental tally of all the married professors who had fumbled miserably in the face of her funky Upper West Side could-care-less-and-would-you-please-leave-now Teflon veneer.

Poulsby was apparently unflappable. His smile was warm and immediate. He turned back to me and said, "Good show, Harpo. *Ani-*

mal Crackers, right?" He winked. "Hey! Are you a fan of football? Did you happen to catch the Wolverines . . ."

From then on "Hey!" would take on new significance and I would try to pepper my conversations with the breathless attention-grabber but to no avail. "Hey!" just seemed drippy or sarcastic coming out of my mouth. It sounded like a come-on. Poulsby no doubt rallied his classes on to near riotous climaxes with a well-posited "Hey!"

The gap in his teeth was breathtaking. I was so easily distracted by the lush topographical charms of his face. Conversation was a little bit beyond my grasp but I plowed onward like Cortés. What was that, a scar on his lip? A trace of a harelip? Cleft palate? It's image was tattooed on my brain now for all time. The tonal nuances of his Brooklyn accent were either reminiscent of a Gershwin rhapsody or as wistful as a Joni Mitchell chord change, I couldn't decide which. He had a mild rasp that suggested a rich life and nights well spent, which sent me to the moon. I couldn't have invented a man like this; my imagination simply fell too short.

". . . safety before the half and then it was anybody's game!"

His lips were moving. His nose was doughy. His hands were long. Could he know that he was Philadelphia doo wop to my ears, Rodin's unrealized masterpiece, a hero sandwich on the best home baked bread I've never tasted, a sleek, loaded '68 Mustang? Could I tell him? Then and there? What were the rules? Doesn't this kind of thing happen between two people once in a lifetime, and don't both parties have to act on it? They have to act on it or they become catatonic, and they lay down and die in some grisly state-run institution. That's my understanding of real love, anyway.

Sadly, I had lost my place in the topic at hand. I can talk baseball and fake a basketball ramble, but football is so abysmally dull that no amount of independent research on my part could rouse the dozing hound dog of apathy. In the arena of football bullshitting, I simply cannot be present.

Anything but football. Could nothing be done? He was holding up the line with all this small talk. Why couldn't we talk about fishing? Fishing is as iconically masculine as a wad of raw ground chuck and onion on a Ritz. It's universal. Every fella fishes. How could we topic-hop and hail unsung lure strategies or piss and moan about ridiculous license violation fines? Just two normal, regular guys rapping about fishing. Wait. Didn't I have business with the man? "I love you" was the subtext to all of my nonsense which followed.

"Those Wolverines . . ." I cooed. Was I going to break into song? What could possibly follow that?

"Ah, yes." I was vamping now, buying time.

"Does Bob Schembechler still coach or . . ." I inquired, earnestly. Bob Schembechler? Any relation to Bo? Luckily for me, the man of the hour was busying himself with gloves, his longshoreman's skull cap and a Bic Round Stic cleverly cocked behind his right ear.

"Uh, Professor? I'd like to speak to you about the Spanish for Reading Knowledge exam." That's it, shaver, just start over.

"Oh yeah? Well, just drop by my office. Or call." He reached for that Bic like a man who knows what a man's ear is really for—a fleshy flap for small tools, a perch for Bics and cigarettes. Questions and directions would be heard and possibly entertained. Mindless chinning would be damned to hell. "We'll set you up." He grinned, cocked his torso, and motioned dramatically. Suddenly, it seemed as if Gil Poulsby himself were going to stop the show with his signature tune—"Mammy," perhaps, pitched to the bargain seats.

"See, the way it works is we pick out a book in Spanish that you should have at least a couple of weeks to read through so as to become familiar with it."

"Like *Ferdinand the Bull?*" What kind of dunce was I? What the hell was the matter with me? Poulsby appeared only slightly annoyed, as though he got this sort of shit from the minions daily. I was one of the minions.

"*Like Water for Chocolate* is a common choice. That one's too easy, though. Not an option anymore."

"*Mambo Kings Play Songs of Love?*" It was the only Latin-flavored book I had read to date. When was I going to shut my clot? Why not just suggest *Valley of the Dolls* or *Chicken Soup for the Soul? The Collected Prose of Rod McKuen* might be challenging. Christ, I needed an intervention. My mouth was out of control. I was beading sweat. He was doing a fine job of resisting me. So polite. What method of betrayal was next for my utterly disconnected body? Grand mal seizure? Flatulence?

"Ahhhhh." He closed his eyes at the thought. "Nestor Castillo's story is so beautiful. Heartbreaking. 'Beautiful Maria of My Soul' . . ."

Now why did he have to go and say that and look the way he did as he said it? Nestor Castillo was me. I believed *I* was Nestor and that *I* would die of heartache just as Nestor did in Hijuelos's tale of the two brothers from Cuba. The consummate romantic, Nestor Castillo. Consumed by a love supreme. My fate was sealed. I would love Gil Poulsby forever and he would never know unless my body again betrayed me and only then would I face the horrible consequence of the love that dare not speak its name. . .

". . . but, you know, Desi Arnaz was no saint. Lucy must have been some kinda woman to put up with all his garbage." He flushed when stressing a point. "Okay, then. Talk to you soon, sport." He saluted on his way through the electronic barrier.

Ten years ago I had revealed to myself that I was homosexual, and for all of those ten endless years I endured a polite, inconsequential, and asexual existence as such, untouched and undiscovered, excepting those rare occasions when I had come clean to some disinterested party or another. Their response meant nothing to me, and so the inevitable spooked-horse look or opportunistic leer could not possibly wreak havoc with my psyche. I could pass for straight whenever the occasion required heterosexuality. I had even made a few bloodless stabs at bisexuality. Some ladyfriends had been slumming; others were simply insane. The latter had run for their lives. The former, for the most part, stood by for the long haul, bemused and affectionate. The wonderful thing was that they had all been heroic drinkers, and I had had bacchanalian boozy good times with each and every one. They tried teaching me faith. They tried teaching me to care. They tried teaching me to try to do right. On all accounts, I had failed.

But Gil Poulsby would change all of that. He would make an honest man of me. We would show all the world how to love. We would build things, read a lot and grow our own food. We would be real men in real love participating in the real world, and not in some gay ghetto within some urban wasteland. I would tell him how I felt about him. It was just a matter of time.

He was gone, though, but he had left his name and office phone number on a slip of paper. I was high.

"Holy shit!"

Mary Louise, my Seventh Day Adventist supervisor, looked hurt. "Excuse me?" she said.

"Do you know him?" I asked gingerly.

"What? Why?" She was profoundly confused. My theory is that women can smell a homoerotic situation, fiction or non, from a mile away. Mary Louise looked like she had just found a copy of *ManRump* magazine under my mattress.

"That's Gil Poulsby!" I declared as if hepping her to some secret cultish pleasure.

"Take your break. You're seven minutes into it already." She was atypically snotty but I didn't care because I was in love and had twenty-three minutes to revel in it. Could I indulge and have a whiskey and water at Nick's Home of Good Food? I had gone to work lit before, a stick of Juicy Fruit my only cover, with nary a comment or sideways glance. Hell, I was drunk on Poulsby. I couldn't wait to be exposed to his Eddie Bauer threads, passionate nonsequiturs, and good fella goombah Brooklynside *Je ne sais quoi* once again. More, Professor Poulsby! More! I was a junkie for his mojo, even if it was only implied. The threat of contact, spiritual or otherwise, was enough to keep me alive for centuries, and I had waited years for this. Gil Poulsby was exactly what I deserved.

CHAPTER TWO

Sprees

> *Dextrose*
> *Sugar*
> *Maltodextrone*
> *Malic Acid*
> *Less Than 25% Magnesium Something*
> *Carnauba Wax*
> *Blue 1 Lake*
> *Blue 2 Lake*
> *Carmine Color*
> *Red 40 Lake*
> *Yellow 5 Lake*
> *Yellow 5 Lake 2*

You don't make 'em, Nestlé does, but watch out because they're a self-described kick in the mouth.

⤳

I sat in the student union, munching tangy delicious Sprees and quaffing Frangelico-flavored coffee in a Styrofoam cup. What was Gil Poulsby doing now? Was he married? Oh god, yes. He had to be in his mid-forties at least. His wife was no doubt some queenly thing with a quicksilver intellect. I loved her, too. Any woman worthy of his affections was okay in my book. Her name was probably Gemma, the fine-boned product of a long line of academics. She no doubt had knocked out all the boys on the Rutgers crew team, but only Gil had that rough and ready gypsy spirit that could dare to flame her tempest-tossed Scorpionic passion. He was Dion to her Ronnie Ronnette. Dylan to her Sad-Eyed Sarah. What the hell was I thinking? How dare I mess with something as sacred as what they

Joe Schraufnagel

90

have? Who did I think I was? Desi Arnaz? Just as Gil had said in one
of his chewy, profound proverbs: *Desi Arnaz was no saint.* He had
said it like it was no big deal.

At first I wasn't sure. Lucy Ball was no Maya Angelou, either.
Ah, but Desi was a character in *Mambo Kings* and he was rendered
a sort of untouchable "machine from the heavens" kind of character. I got it. Why didn't Gil write for *Artforum*? Obviously, he was a
cultural critic of the highest order and yet he had this street cred
that leant him all the authority in the world. A sort of Lou Reed for
the literary set. His brand of sexy made my fillings hurt. Or maybe it
was the Sprees, but I doubted it. Where did he live? I would check
the staff directory first thing at the library after break and find out.
Near East Side, I was betting. He probably hung out with Ben Si-
dran, Richard Davis, Mose Allison, and Van Morrison. That would
make sense. He seemed to fit into that naturalist, white soul-
brother mold. Tennyson, Emerson, Morrison, and Poulsby had all
walked around in fields wet with rain. So would I. Gil Poulsby had
brought about great changes in me. Already! The jukebox echoed
that sentiment, serenading me with U2's "I Still Haven't Found
What I'm Looking For." Professor Poulsby, I would run, I would
crawl, I would scale these city walls only to be with you, too, you
know. Wild horses couldn't drag me away. I would make for him a
mix tape that would move the mountain within him. I loved him
that much. Who knew it could be like this?

CHAPTER THREE

Poulsby Mix (Undelivered)

SIDE ONE

My Weakness—Alan Lomax Field Recording
So Far Away—*Sounds of Blackness*
Ou Es Tu, Mon Amour? (Where Are You, My Love?)—*Willie
Nelson*

Why Does My Heart Feel So Bad? —*Alan Lomax Field Recording*
Why Can't We Live Together? —*Timmy Thomas*
Something He Can Feel —*Aretha Franklin*
Praise You —*Fatboy Slim*
You Are My Sunshine —*Mississippi John Hurt*
A Thousand Miles Away —*Shep and the Limeliters*
Everybody Here Wants You —*Jeff Buckley*
It's Ecstasy, When You're Lying Next to Me —*Barry White*
Babalu —*Desi Arnaz*
Red Eyed and Blue —*Wilco*
You Are Too Beautiful —*Johnny Hartman and John Coltrane*
Gloomy Sunday —*Billie Holliday*
SIDE TWO
Unforgettable —*Nat 'King' Cole*
Hey Love —*Stevie Wonder*
Can't Stand the Rain —*Anne Peebles*
You Sexy Thing —*Hot Chocolate*
Magic in Your Eyes —*Rufus featuring Chaka Kahn*
Long Hot Summer Night —*Jimi Hendrix*
Love of My Life —*Santana*
I Want You —*Elvis Costello*
Needless to Say —*Loudon Wainwright III*
San Diego Serenade —*Tom Waits*
I Still Haven't Found What I'm Looking For —*U2*
Wild Horses —*Rolling Stones*
In My Mind —*Texas Tornadoes*
Le Chanson de Juin —*Enrico Caruso*
Two Grey Rooms —*Joni Mitchell*

Create this gut-wrenching tape with headphones on so as not to disturb your shrinking violet housemates. Quarantine your tender heart
from the foul, noisy fools who have never known a love, a need, of

this magnitude. Perhaps smack casualties, suicides, and Oscar Hijuelos knew, probably Gil and Gemma Poulsby and artists, or *all* of the above . . . wait a second . . . hold on . . . what in hell was that? Squirrels rutting in the walls? No. Only a scalp-tightening tap upon my door as heard above an oh-so-crucial, life-changing Joni Mitchell chord change. I responded with "*What.*"

"So sorry, Jack. Turn your music to low, please." It was the Kazakhstanian wraith. "I hear your music down the hall," she breathed through my door.

"Oh. Sorry," I replied, wanly.

Jesus H. Christ-In-All-His-Glory, what is this place, a monastic retreat? How could she possibly hear the haunting, plaintive "Two Grey Rooms" through my headphones all the way down the hall? And why on earth would she mind? What was the matter with her? Never-you-mind soldier, a forty of Schlitz Malt Liquor will heighten *el dolor* and deepen the experience of wedding your love, so unattached within, to the inarticulate speech of the heart as rendered by your friends Joni, Van, Aretha, and Mississippi John Hurt. Curse the sociopathic wretch next door, stare at your phone, and wonder what your love's tonal nuances would sound like through a few hundred miles of cable. Imagine yourself as Nipper, your head cocked as you process your master's voice. Wouldn't it be something if you actually received a call from your soul's one desire? Well, forget about it and try to get some sleep because it will never happen. Not in a hundred million years, buckaroo. Sleep a restless sleep and fight the Far Eastern wraith for bathroom rights in the morning. Dream a Technicolor downtown cityscape, a young Gil Poulsby in snug chinos executing a crafty boogaloo under a shameless Brooklyn moon to a finger-popping a cappella street choir as sweet Gemma looks on, charmed. It's a wild night. Watch yourself, naked, tear-stained, and without a word to say, as you bear witness behind an infinite chain-link fence.

CHAPTER FOUR

Hardee's Breakfast Burrito
  Tortilla
  Grease
  Refried Bean Paste
  Processed Cheese Food
  Sour Cream Substitute
  Scrambled Egg Material

Greedily clutch your breakfast burrito and slurp your acidic road coffee like the unrecovered, gifted alcoholic you believe yourself to be.
Romanticize your situation. Sometimes you believe it's all you have
left. Okay, things aren't that bad. Your parents love you on credit. Or
at least they say they do. It's November and cold as the proverbial
witch's tit. It warms your sloppy drunk heart that you're here to enjoy Professor's Poulsby's office hours. This is a happy occasion. Why
are you loitering outside in Wisconsin winter when you could be
lounging in the heated comfort of Van Hise Hall, waiting on a
bench for the man who might allow you to graduate with certified
competency in Spanish for Reading Knowledge? You could so easily
pretend that you don't care about his rooster strut or his cute neck.

    Why has the primal urge to commune, to merge profoundly,
come down to this? Why can't intellect play more of a role? Why
couldn't I be moved to testify in the wake of one of Yael's Shake-
spearean sonnet-informed bon mots? The fact that she barely whispers those theoretical knee-slappers of hers while Poulsby fairly
shouts his ripping good crowd-pleasing one-liners should weigh in
her favor. Right? But there was more to him, much more than that.
This man was, quite literally, something else altogether. Since that
fateful Sunday shift, he had diddy-bopped by the checker's desk
twice and shouted out a hardy "hey!" en route to somewhere I

wished I were, waiting there to enjoy his company. Another day, he dropped a morsel of biography which proved revealing. Did I hear him say something about a Westchester? (I was close!) Quaker upbringing? I couldn't believe he wasn't a Jew from Rockaway Beach or a Flatbush Italian Catholic! Why were my pie-eyes star-crossed and why was I given to *meshugga* for this ring a ding ding, ba-da-bing, ba-da-boom Quaker? The answer was self-evident. He was a true believer, a Friend, with salesmanship and panache and with the quavering intensity of Harvey Keitel in *Mean Streets* to boot. The Shangri-La's would crap themselves over this tuff tomcat with the soul of a poet. I was not to blame! I was absolved!

I had just met him but I knew in my heart he was different, different like Jackson Pollack. The facts told the tale. The incongruancy of it all! Yaels are a dime a dozen. Self-possessed, self-exiled, self-professed cookie-cutter bohemians are old hat. God, you run into them at every turn in every English Department at every university. They're either pumping out Beckett Society newsletters or attending ad hoc Gertrude Stein revisionist seminars or some ridiculous thing that I, Applied Linguistics drone that I am, could never understand in a million years. I might as well be peddlin' my pappy's corn squeezin's in the underfunded foothills of Appalachia. Don't ask a lit major for the time in an elevator, he/she will holler "solicitation" and campus security will expose you for the faker you were all along.

Gil was a participant in this life. Gil knew what time it was, and Gil could appreciate and even desire slabs of fried bacon alongside a plate of runny-yolked eggs. Gil didn't just read literature, move on, and chalk it up to empty experience. Gil *felt* it. He absorbed it, then bled it. Gil saw me for what I was, a man in love with words. I deserved to step into his office, my head held high. We were sure to be on equal footing. I would drop well-chosen references to Mexican artists, Cuban baseball players, Andalusian poets and soul-brothers—white, black, and otherwise. Gil would see me as raw material, a work in progress, and he would, in fact, approve. Jesus Christ, I just loved that guy. I really did!

I peered in at the throngs behind the plate-glass window of that wretched early-seventies, futuristic monument to the crapola-to-come that was Van Hise Hall, and I spied him. There he was! I hustled indoors to intercept him. He looked harried as he picked his way through the yammering student herd, as though he had stepped off a plane and into an Istanbul bazaar. I didn't want to be just another turd in his path so I reclined by the door to his office, all chill, and would ease into him. He had a class in fifteen minutes and I would make him feel relaxed. Gemma knew him best, inside and out, knew all the knots and the kinks, but at the very least I could buffer the shock of undergraduate overstimulation. The cell phones, the brain-busting inanities, the bottled waters, the inappropriate sexual charge, the vapidity of it all—I would ground him first.

"Hey! You're the guy from the library! How's things?" He appeared reasonably jazzed to see me. I extended my hand, which he took. Unexpectedly, he elaborated on what was up with him. This man was just full of surprises.

"My father-in-law just died. Man, this year has just been shit. Can you believe this weather? Winter is killing me. Just killing me."

His father-in-law died? Shouldn't he be taking a leave of absence? I was aching to give him a great big hug and tell him everything would be all right. His masculinity was intimidating. Even though I weighed in at 210 pounds, wore my beard closely trimmed, and was tattooed to an obscene degree, deep down I felt like a cheap piano bar Dusty Springfield drag queen when faced with his jivey, middle-weight physicality. He seemed to me to be the cock of the walk.

Unfortunately, I was suddenly blind-sided by images of Professor Poulsby in a torn T-shirt, sucking the meat out of crawdads, and leering wolfishly at Blanche DuBois. I stood by as sweaty, ineffectual Mitch. Jesus God, did I come off as an impotent mama's boy? It didn't help that I had actually had *momma* tattooed on my forearm, as if I were preternaturally in on the joke. Hug? Maybe I should coldcock my beloved professor. Maybe he would respect me then.

"It's going to be one hell of a drive home. Look. It's spitting out already."

Snow was spiraling down and around the campus outside. Home was a house on Snahatchee Pass. I had looked him up in the staff directory. Where the hell was that, in the Adirondacks? He was so far removed from the reality of my Madison student-ghetto life. For me, there would be no nonchalant walks by the Poulsby pad en route to the Open Pantry for a soda and AA batteries. For me, there would be no casually dropping by to discuss magic realism because I just "happened" to be jogging through the neighborhood. I would have to take a cab.

"Come on in. Grab a chair. Just let me move my crap here."

There were no telltale signs of who he was or what he liked to look at, what he liked to read. Just a cinder block replication of your average dorm room in generic, standard issue bile yellow. Somehow, this piqued my interest. Clearly, he was private and would reveal himself on his own terms. A rugged individualist, this Gilbert Alfred Poulsby. Was there no end to his complexity? He gazed at the juices left by his Poor Boy sandwich as he snatched it away from atop a carelessly arranged pile of corrected homework. He was wide-eyed and astonished at this misbegotten state of affairs which had resulted, I surmised, from what he perceived to be a capitulation to his lower nature—sloth, complacency, torpor. But I sat there taking it all in and sick with love. His humanity was spoiling me for good. I was grinning like a monkey.

"My wife has to keep after me, as you can see."

Wife. The word was as final as death. Goddamn it. My diseased heart fell to my shoes. Her name was most likely DeLinda. DeLinda would know him as I never could. DeLinda could reach over in the middle of the night and treat herself to a handful of Professor Gil Poulsby, whereas I was lucky if I could reach the bathroom for the fifth elimination of the night. Even then, I would have to wrestle the Kazakhstanian wraith for toilet privileges. She would be camped out all hours of the night, disgorging her respiratory system all over the tub, for god's sake. Why in hell wasn't she hospitalized? How could she function in life like this? How could I go on? What was to become of either of us?

Professor Poulsby leaned forward in his chair. He carried himself like a bull. No Ferdinand, he.

"I have to take a medical leave of absence. Complications. . . . I can't talk about it but it's as bad as you can imagine, pal. We'll have to work around it, but it shouldn't affect you too adversely, you know what I mean? I think we can work something out. Shit. Life can really bite you in the ass when you least expect it, don't you think?" He looked me straight in the eye.

What? What complications? I had no business asking, but I needed to know. My mind was racing, already gassed on emotions utterly foreign to its usual diet of self-interest and vanity. DeLinda must have been out of her head with worry. She was his wife. I wasn't anybody in particular and I was in near hysteria. I had to feign cool.

"Well . . . which hospital . . . where?"

He didn't hear me. On purpose, I decided later, in a moment of self-derision.

"*Like Water for Chocolate* I think would be good enough, huh, sport? What do you think? Will that be all right? I'll make an exception for you. We'll get you through this, okay?"

I choked back hiccoughy sobs and fidgeted spastically to cover my discomfort.

"Yeah. Thank you, Professor. Yes."

CHAPTER FIVE

Med Therapy for Congestive Heart Failure
  250 mcg Digoxin
  20 mg Lisinopril
  25 mg Hydrochlorothiazide
  160 mg Sotalol
  5 mg Warfarin

Every morning, fashion a pharmaceutical cocktail from these pastel party animals lurking in your very own medicine cabinet. Love them, they've been put on this earth especially for you—that's what your healer, Linda from St. Joe, Michigan, sincerely advises.

"Forget about it. Everybody has their cross to bear"—a practical homily courtesy of your Gramma Muggs. Prefer the latter hard-boiled nugget of Germanic stoicism to lovey-dovey impossibilities. Find it hard to love that which makes your man-root punk out and quite literally fall dead asleep to the point of pins and needles. Adopt a pose of crabbed cynicism and knock back a six pack every once in a while to show the world at large that you're not afraid to disrespect pharmaceuticals. That you're not afraid of death. Realize that your crimes in fact free you.

⌒)

I read *Like Water for Chocolate* breathlessly, turning pages at an alarming rate. I had not sustained a semi-erection for this long in, well, never. Something about heat and revolution and food brought out the barely latent Barry White in me. I imagined boiling pots of spiced sauces and clandestine meetings under the vast velveteen blanket of Mayan divined and timeless night skies, and I felt blessed. This was homework?! Syntax was never like this! I found myself examining condensation on water glasses and considering

Like Whiskey for Christmas

99

the erotic implications—awkward when you're practically deep-kissing a 7-Up Uncola glass in the local kosher deli. I was giving perfect strangers meaningful looks on public transportation. I was in a state. I feared my Poulsby fixation would take a turn for the worse. I was infected with the historic passion of Tita and her absolutely off-limits brother-in-law. Taboos were aching to be broken. Something was in the air all right, sniffing about for a much needed slap and tickle, an overdue pat or friendly squeeze—a little appendage friend of mine I like to call "Gordito," translated "Lil' Chubby."

~~

The day had arrived. Pam Mould, English Department high priestess, had set it up like a pimp. She coordinated dates, locations, and such, e-mailing with fingers afire. I had a date. I had a date with the rest of my life and, in an oblique way, with the light of my life, Professor Gil Poulsby. He had chosen the passage from the text that I would be translating. Three pages—a virtual menu of sensual delights that I would be treated to as handed down by one Gilbert Alfred Poulsby, a six-course meal in and of himself. I would impose my interpretation upon the lush Spanish text to extract Anglicized meaning—*so much meaning*—from the lyrical lovemaking in black and white before me. I wore Skin Bracer's spice-scented aftershave. I combed my hair and slicked it. He wouldn't be there, but he might as well have. I wore cool linens, even though Memorial Day was six months away and it was icy cold outside. I had a snort of Scotch, purchased especially for the afterglow, and raised it to him as I closed my eyes to the strains of a lugubrious rendering of "It Had to Be You" by the one and only Shirley Horn. This was voodoo. I had to live it and remember it for all time. It had at last happened. I was a complete freak. I rhumba-ed to my testing destination, in a pea coat and in a foot of snow.

It was better than I could have imagined. The passage was

damn near pornographic. Maybe not as pornographic as I had
hoped but it was provocative. Rolled Christmas pastry dough something or other in *la cucina* and a definite clandestine meeting. Or so
I thought. Something had gone awry. My Spanish was wretched. In
my fever I had forgotten to review Spanish grammar rules. My Spanish was something along the lines of Pig-Latin-derived Spanglish.
Shit. I couldn't even piece together a hot and bothered stretch of
breathy imperatives and deathless declaratives. I had anticipated a
discrete communiqué, but he might as well have tapped out "You're
a fricking moron" with a spoon on a pipe from the floor below and
it would have meant as much to me. Coitus interruptus couldn't
hold a candle to this. The stench of my own aftershave was rank,
and even though I was inadvertently awarded an extra ten minutes
by the phone dependent Ms. Mould, I gave it up and handed it in.
Okay, so Translation D-Day wasn't so great. But I signed off on my
legal pad derivation enthusiastically, an implied "hey!" in the exclamation points following "Thank you, Professor Poulsby." He could
at least feel my enthusiasm.

Chapter Six

Dewars and Water on the Rocks
   Some Ice
   A Coupla Fingers of Dewars
   Tap Water

Christmas was coming. My semester grades had been reported, and
I was looking forward to leaving town for a few days, even if it was
only to retreat to my parents' condo on a fairly rustic lake in what
my pop was prone to calling "the compound," a subdivision in a
densely wooded area which in his estimation was a holding pen for
retired folk waiting to die. I didn't think it was quite that bad, but
all of the condos did look pretty samey-same. I sat in my dinky

little room which smelled of soured tomato juice and bed, waiting for my folks to drive up in their Windstar migratory escape vehicle. They literally fled for Sun City the second they sensed that the Christmas holiday might in fact be over.

With a few minutes to kill, and with the clock approaching happy hour, I poured myself a hit of Scotch and water. I felt relieved that I was freed from the abridged version of Hell that was my first semester of graduate school. The Dewars had sat neglected upon the floor next to the foot of my bed. Finals had distracted me from my private joy—the fabled nightcap, or a little afternoon tickler, but I would right that wrong, pronto. I situated myself in front of my battered laptop, logged on to check my e-mail and there, amidst the detritus, was an e-mail from the star of our show, gapouls@facstaff.wisc.edu.

I threw back a slug of glug-a-lug and flushed from head to toe. Where had he been? How was he doing? I beamed as I double-clicked on *read*. The screen came alive with the adorable format of an unassuming archy or mehitable, the salutation lower case and single spaced.

"dear jack," it began.

"dear jack"—*jack* was such a term of endearment in contrast to the much more harsh *John* which my duff of an advisor had per-sisted in calling me as if to prove that he called the shots regarding my remaining days on earth and that he would address me any damn well way he pleased.

"dear jack, I regret to inform you that you have failed to pass the Spanish for Reading Knowledge exam. I counted 27 errors in an especially easy text. You might consider a short-term class and give it a shot once again, next semester. I don't think you will have prob-lems of a serious nature after a refresher course. Contact me or my secretary, Karyn Black, for further details. Merry Christmas! cheers, Gil P."

So Gil Poulsby was alive and well! He was out of the hospital and I was on air! I was incompetent in the untenable field of Spanish for Reading Knowledge, and yet I felt oddly renewed in the face of all this uncertainty. I couldn't read in Spanish, that much I knew, but I could feel good about Gil and Gil believed in giving it a shot. Jesus Christ, I could do that much. Couldn't I? I responded to this cyber-stocking stuffer pronto.

"dear Prof. Poulsby, my Spanish is sickly and perhaps a term in Spain would rectify this pathetic situation, but let me just state outright that I am completely enamored of you. You are everything that is real to me, everything I believe in. I believe I've found in you a kindred spirit and for that fact alone, I will love you always. You are and always will be a light in the darkness for me. Thank you and cheers, jack."

I would not look out for a response. I had fallen off the precipice. The folly of my recklessness felt fine. I could fail and fail and fail and suffer gladly. I would find him in my heart and mind again and again and again. It would be all right. Hey! Everything would be just about okay, regardless.

A Different Kind of Imperfection
Thomas Beller

And then it was Christmas vacation and he was home. "Welcome home, Alexander!" his mother said when he walked in the door, pressing her warm face against his cold one. She was the only person who used his full name. It sounded odd.

She had bought some flowers and arranged them around the house in the special way she had of making things seem nice and attended to. Having brought him up alone—his father had died when he was ten—his mother was diligent about respecting his privacy, not prying into his life. He always felt guilty about not wanting to tell her things about himself, the few times she asked. After all, he was her son, her only child, and his life would be of interest to her.

"So. Tell me about school," she said now, sitting across from him at the kitchen table. His bags were piled up behind him in the foyer and he slouched in his chair, which seemed too small for him. The whole house seemed oddly small in comparison to the high ceilings of the ancient dorm he lived in at Vassar, where he was now a sophomore.

The scene—he and his mother in the same chairs, the same look on her face—reminded him of coming home from kindergarten and having his mother and father ask him how school was, while they sat at the kitchen table. He had always shrugged and said nothing, but he sometimes wondered whether both of his parents had

spent their entire day waiting for him at the kitchen table, dis-
cussing him. All that attention seemed to demand more from him
than anything he could supply with meager details about his frac-
tions or papier-mâché cow, and so he usually said nothing. Eventually he would shrug and slouch on into his room, down the long
dark hallway. But he had always liked the idea that both his parents
had been in conference over him all day.

Now here was his mother, sitting in the same position at the
kitchen table, smiling and asking him the same questions, looking
loving and a little daunting, as usual. It was too much love to live
up to.

"There's really nothing much to say," he answered, thinking
about Sloan, his suddenly ex-girlfriend. She lived in Baltimore. He
had never thought about that city, but now that Sloan lived there,
was in fact there that very moment, Baltimore seemed like an alluring place. "I seem to be getting the hang of how to be a college student," he said. "It's not too difficult."

"And your studies?"

Alex winced at the word. "Studies" was too dignified for what
he was doing. "Well, I'm not going to major in sociology. That's all I
can say for sure."

"What's it like?" she asked.

"The dorms are pretty nice, but at night the only place to get
food is the candy machine." He paused for a moment. "The classes
are good, though," he went on, thinking she would enjoy hearing that.

Sloan was the first girl he had really gone out with in college,
and by extension, the first girl he had really broken up with. She
was a vegetarian poet who had her own place off campus, which
seemed like a very daring move in sophomore year. Her apartment
was just across the road, but the fact that it was technically off
campus made it seem illicit. They had gone out together for a few
months, but just before vacation Sloan informed him—or "reminded"
him, as she pointed out—that she had another boyfriend at home.

She told him that she felt she had to give that a chance. It was shaping up to be a miserable Christmas vacation, he thought.

His mother cupped her face in her hands. Her chin rested on the heel of each palm and her fingers were over her cheeks, framing her face. She was very pretty, and yet her happiest expression always seemed to have a tinge of sadness. His father had died of cancer nine years earlier, and Alex couldn't remember whether this look of gravity had come into her face after that. Perhaps being happy always reminded her of her loss. She hadn't remarried. She hadn't even painted the apartment. Alex looked into her liquid eyes and smiled. Then he escaped down the hall.

His room seemed different. Freshman year, he had scurried down to New York from Poughkeepsie almost every chance he got, and his first Christmas vacation had seemed like a reprieve. His room had welcomed him. His mother had welcomed him. The whole house had burst to life, as if it had been in suspended animation since the day he left. Coming home this time was different; he couldn't get over how strange it felt to be back. His room was just as he had left it, but it just sat there, inanimate, waiting to be occupied by whoever came along.

He went out into the early-evening light and walked over to a bar on Eighty-third and Amsterdam, the Jaunting Car. It was the last bar in his neighborhood with any charm, but today it was almost empty. He ordered a scotch and looked at himself in the mirror behind the bar. One of the better things he had acquired since going to college was a taste for scotch. Previously he had drunk only vodka, a habit he had formed at the age of fourteen when he had sampled all the bottles in his parents' liquor cabinet and had decided that vodka was the least unpleasant. His mother didn't drink, and hardly ever had guests, and it had sometimes occurred to him that the bottle of Wolfschmidt he was drinking from had probably been bought by his father. His first cigarette, which he had smoked at about the same age, had come from an ancient pack of Dunhills

he had found in a table drawer, in among a collection of broken sunglasses frames, pipe cleaners, loose buttons, and other artifacts of
his father's. It was an odd collection of items, the debris that comes
together only because there isn't enough of any one thing to require its own drawer. When he came upon it, four years after his father had died, the stash itself looked static, stunned with age. That
cigarette, Alex recalled now, had been rancid. The pack of Dunhills
was probably still there. The drawer was always shut.

~

He spent the first few days back from school mostly alone. He had
stopped frantically trying to touch base with friends from high
school, the way he'd done at this time a year ago. He thought
about Sloan, he walked around the streets at midday in the bright
high winter sun, and spent hours meandering around his house examining shelves and closets he hadn't looked at in years. The apartment, with its cracked and peeling paint, its rickety wooden chairs
with half-broken cane seats, was filled with books, among them
many dark green or maroon volumes with titles like *Textbook of Pa-
thology* and *Clinical Hematology,* and a huge book with the ominous title *Heart.* His father had been a doctor—a psychiatrist. Alex
perused the bookshelves with a peculiar interest, as if he were looking for clues. One set of twenty-four books in pale blue dust jackets
took up an entire shelf: the complete works of Sigmund Freud. He
took out *Totem and Taboo* and looked at the first chapter, "The Horror of Incest." He put the book back with the haste of someone who
had opened the door of an occupied bathroom.

Scanning for a lighter topic, he took out *Jokes and Their Relation to the Unconscious.* He opened to a random page and read, "It
is remarkable how universally popular a smutty interchange of this
kind is among the common people and how it unfailingly produces
a cheerful mood."

He returned the book to its place, and listened to the silence of the house. He and his mother lived in an apartment building, but all their neighbors were quiet. While he was growing up, the only noisy person in the building had been himself—he had once bounced a rubber ball so incessantly that the downstairs neighbors had called the police. He then took to throwing water balloons out the window. He was so intrigued by the way the balloons shimmered—like Jell-O, he thought—in their flight to the ground that he always forgot to duck his head back in the window in time and soon he got caught. He and his mother were nearly evicted, she told him. Again and again as he prowled around the house now, he was struck by the evidence of lives lived. It lay on the shelves, along the walls, stacked in piles on the floor.

Alex's college roommate, Milo, called and announced he was going to be in New York for an afternoon before he went skiing. They met in a coffee shop for lunch.

"You're bored," Milo said over a tuna fish sandwich. "You should get out of New York. Come skiing with me."

"I don't ski," Alex said.

"Come for the scenery."

"There's plenty of scenery here. I can see a little sliver of the Hudson River and part of New Jersey from my window."

Milo gave Alex an appraising look. "Come for the women," he said. "This place is going to be crawling with women. You need a distraction."

"I am distracted," said Alex. "I need to concentrate."

"You're concentrating on your distraction," Milo said. A little piece of food had lodged itself at the corner of his mouth. This completely discredited him in Alex's mind. The guy couldn't swallow properly; he wasn't someone whose advice was going to be helpful.

"All right, all right," Milo went on. "You're concentrating on Sloan, which is depressing you. Tell you what—work on it, and when you've got it perfected, give me a call." Then he neatly pinched the tuna speck from the corner of his mouth and flicked it at Alex.

"That was the problem with you and Sloan," he went on, with some satisfaction. "You were just an amateur at being depressed. Sloan was a pro. You couldn't keep up."

⁓

The apartment's foreignness had begun to wear off, giving way to something even more disturbing. It was familiarity, but not the kind that makes things disappear into the background. Now every detail jumped out and announced itself as significant, the way banal things became significant whenever there were guests in the apartment. Alex was his own guest now, he decided, a sightseer in his own home.

He began to realize that his house was submerged in books—hundreds and hundreds of them, in the corner bookshelf, on the bookshelf against the wall, or stacked in dusty heaps in a corner, spilling over everywhere. He noticed that some of the books held slivers of paper, which projected above the tops of the pages. He opened one such book and discovered faded pencil underlinings on each of the marked pages, with a word or two of comment here and there in the margin. Alex didn't know much about his father's intellectual life, but he had lately noticed that his father's haphazard handwriting bore a conspicuous resemblance to his own. He examined the pages more carefully, and the marginal notes seemed to confirm it. He went from book to book and eventually stopped at one and began to read. It was *To the Lighthouse* by Virginia Woolf—a book he'd never read.

The volume itself was old; its gray cloth cover was tattered at the corners, but the binding remained stiff and dignified. The pages were only slightly yellow and had a certain weight to them. The book had been published in 1927, five years after his father was born.

When had his father read it? He had arrived in America as a teenager sometime before the Second World War. So if he had read this in college, it would have been the early 1940s, and he would have been almost the same age as Alex was now, reading the same pages. But there was the possibility that he had read the book years later. Maybe even after Alex was born. There were no marks to indicate which, one way or the other.

He read on, turning each page in anticipation of another one of his father's marks. On page 99, a strand of pencil underlined a fragment of a sentence: ". . . she had known happiness, exquisite happiness, intense happiness . . ." It was not a line that would have jumped off the page at Alex, but seeing it underlined by his father disturbed him and moved him. The words "exquisite happiness, intense happiness" resonated above the whispery pencil mark that flowed underneath them. Alex stared at the pencil lines for a moment, as if they were completely separated from the writing. He was waiting for the lines to reveal something. The pencil was neither sharp nor dull. The lines didn't seem to have been drawn with a great deal of pressure, but they weren't too light, either. Had they been made in bed, or at a desk, or an armchair—or on a bus? He felt a pang of frustration, trying to imagine what his father had been thinking. It was a sharp twinge that made him shudder for a moment.

He was in the kitchen one afternoon, staring into the refrigerator, when his mother came in and sat down at the table expectantly, as if she wanted to have a conversation. He obliged, sitting down across from her.

She smiled, tilted her head a little, and said, "What are you thinking?"

"Nothing," he said. He wanted to say more but couldn't. It was always this way with his mother—the unwilling retreat.

"You have been walking around with a funny expression, as though something is bothering you."

"Nothing is bothering me, it's just odd to be back. You know, like, when you go away and then come back and it's, like—"

"Stop saying 'like.'"

"It's weird, then."

"I can tell something is on your mind. You have this cloudy look about you. I've been wanting to bring it up for some time now."

"I've only been home for three days."

"But before even. I've been worried about you." His mother had the rare but unmistakable expression she got when she was preparing to try to exert authority. She wasn't the authoritarian type, but in the absence of a father she had to take the offensive periodically.

"You seem very unfocused," she said. "As if you're drifting. There is a certain urgency lacking."

"What is there to be urgent about, Mom? It's Christmas vacation."

She looked at him some more, with her hazel eyes, which sometimes turned green. Her affection was discomforting, though he had never been without it, or even considered that he might ever be. He felt his cheeks warm up, and watched the corners of her mouth slowly turn into a bittersweet smile, as if she was seeing something that had not yet come into view for him.

⌒⁀

Another passage read: "He knew, of course he knew, that she loved him. He could not deny it. And smiling she looked out the window and said (thinking to herself, nothing on earth can equal this happiness)—" A dried piece of scraggly orangish paper—a ripped strip of it—had stuck out of the top of the book like a buoy in a channel, and when he got to it he found these words underlined in pencil.

He took out the shred of paper and examined it. He was sitting on the floor in a dusty corner of the study, next to a ragged brown armchair. It was a shred, all right—one of several torn up and placed, perhaps, in a pile, so they could be used over the course of a reading session. This shred was the first of several sprouting up from the top of the book, a grove of markers densely clustered in an area where his father seemed to have found interesting material.

The next marked page contained just one underlined sentence: "It's almost too dark to see." Very enigmatic observation, thought Alex.

Some lines were neatly drawn, but most had been made casually, almost sloppily, though they never ran over the words. They wavered. It was hard for him to gauge how much the pencil marks had faded over time.

The whole issue of time and dates bothered him. How old had his father been when he made these marks? Alex wanted to know. Another underlined segment he came across was itself in quotes and read: "And all the lives we ever lived / and all the lives to be / are frill of trees and changing leaves.'" How old would the man be who marked that?

⌇

He walked around his neighborhood in the daytime, looking at people passing, and wondering why they weren't at work. No one in the middle of the day in a residential neighborhood was in a rush, he realized. He scrutinized faces, searching for the anxiety of lateness, but only found people drifting into hardware stores, clothing stores, the corner market. What was their excuse? He had his and it comforted him: he was a student. Such an easy excuse—he wondered how long it would last. At this rate, he thought, an eternity.

He imagined calling Sloan. "I've discovered peeling paint on all the walls and I've walked around the apartment pulling pieces off the ceiling so it won't look as bad," he would say. "The house hasn't been painted since three years before my dad died."

"Maybe you should get the place painted," she would say. She was annoyingly pragmatic when she wanted to keep a distance between them.

"I thought maybe you weren't having a good time with what's-his-name and wanted to come up to New York," he would say. He imagined what she would say to a question like that. He decided he wouldn't want to hear it.

~

Amid a battalion of small photographs set up on his mother's bedroom bureau was a small snapshot of his parents. His father and mother were extremely good-looking—particularly his mother, who had high sharp cheekbones and thin lips and wore her brown hair in a bun. Her family was from Berlin; her grandfather had been an enormously wealthy banker who had shot himself just after the First World War, when he had lost all his money. Alex liked that detail of his family history; the combination of death and money had a certain glamour for him.

His father had been born in Vienna. He was handsome in the photograph, with dark hair and deep grooves in his face, particularly in the forehead. He had a certain monkey quality to him. The picture was a head-and-shoulders shot of the two of them, dressed up nicely, with their shoulders squared to the camera but their heads turned a little toward each other, each of them gazing at the other's face. His mother looked stunning. She was wearing a black dress that contrasted sharply with the string of pearls around her neck; her smooth skin caught the light and glowed. His father was merely handsome in comparison, and his smile suggested that he felt even gleeful at his good luck. But they shared a conspiratorial gaze, glimmering with hidden knowledge. Was it the secret of beauty? Was it the secret of happiness? Alex imagined the moment as intense.

The picture was small, not more than two inches square. His mother liked antique things, small things—frames and cameos in particular. The family history was suffused in a nineteenth-century ambience, completed by ornate silver embellishments and delicate wood carvings around the frames. The frames were precious, personal. He rarely saw them, though. Because of the sharp rays of the morning sun that flooded his mother's window, the pictures were all turned to face the wall. She had never managed to put up any blinds.

That the sun was fading the pictures was a discovery his mother had made somewhat late in the game, and most of the pictures had already lost a good deal of clarity, as if they were undergoing the development process in reverse. In one, he himself was walking on unsteady legs across the grass. He was chubby-cheeked but had a look of great purpose. But the photograph was now nearly a mirage, it had faded so badly.

His parents' good looks interested him, but not as much as their shared expression in the small picture. They had recently married. That was for sure. He was rugged and dark, and wise-looking, with his lined face. His mother looked like a goddess. Her eyes and his seared into each other's with deep meaning. Or was it just lust?

"Exquisite happiness, intense happiness." He looked at the words and then the scrawny pencil lines underneath them. The underlining was no more or less emphatic than elsewhere, but he still stared at it, trying to infer something more. When did his father read this? When did he make these marks? What was the proximity of the time of these marks to that of the small picture? To all the pictures? The day Alex had gone to the bureau and, in a rout of the established order, about-faced the whole group of photographs so he could look at them together, it had dawned on him that all the photographs of his father had been taken when he was an adult. He had reached a watershed in life that Alex had yet to get near. He had the look of a man whose twenties had never taken place, or, if they had, had somehow been lost. Where had his father been when he was twenty? What secrets had he learned between twenty and the time of the picture? What had prompted him to underline these words? What had he figured out?

An impossibility, an immovable wall, lay between Alex and the answer. He felt the strain of permanence in the situation and in everything that reminded him of it: the remaining cigarettes, the same paint on the walls, the stain on the headboard on his father's side of the bed. There was a secret in them that had clearly been lost. Gone down, away. It had descended beneath an impenetrable surface. Alex could only run his hands over it, searching for a subtle suggestion, a different kind of imperfection. He didn't feel sentimental about it. Just frustrated, like an archaeologist who has hit bedrock—no farther to dig. No more options. Except, perhaps, one. He decided to move laterally.

He began to scavenge the house for things obsolete, unexpected. He took a pack of the old, yellowed cigarettes and marched out into the day with it. Broadway glistened in the stunning white light of noon. It had been remarkably clear weather since he got back. Walking down the street with an ancient and unlit cigarette between his fingers, it occurred to him that he wasn't depressed at all. If anything, he was buoyant. He had this thing, this business about his father and his secrets of happiness, that he couldn't figure out. The challenge was dredging him up out of his self-pity about Sloan, and he took this to be a good sign.

He wasn't depressed—he was merely mystified. He was looking for something between the lines. Enjoying this state, he lit the cigarette and took a few lung-scorching puffs. Awful. He held it between his thumb and index finger, felt its warmth. He liked it in his hand. It was his father's cigarette—one of the last few in a pack that he had never had a chance to smoke. They'd been stranded.

~

Alex was reading *To the Lighthouse* with a dual diligence. He was watching for his father's markings but at the same time the book was captivating him in its rhythm, like a boat that rocks subtly, and whose rocking sensation persists even when its passengers have disembarked.

Then on page 193, he made a starling discovery. Between the pages he found a business card. Clearly meant as a marker, it had slipped down, so it hadn't been visible. The card was yellowed, and on it was his father's name, "Solomon Fader, M.D." In the lower right-hand corner was his father's office address and telephone number, with the exchange spelled out: "TRafalgar 9–3072." Alex picked up the card and turned it over in his hand for a moment before realizing the full significance of the find. His father was at that office for only the last nine years of his life. It meant that he probably knew he was dying as he read *To the Lighthouse,* for his illness, Alex knew, had lasted more than eight years.

Alex suddenly thought about a spring walk in Central Park that his mother had once told him about. The day was warm and sunny and his parents had gone out for a stroll at lunchtime. Things were going well for them, by any standard. Except during that particular walk the man in the picture informed his wife that he was dying, and things were no longer going well. By any standard. The words "She had known happiness, exquisite happiness, intense happiness" sprang to Alex's mind again. Then came the image in the photograph—that secret but happy gaze his parents shared.

Did his father read the book just before he found out he was dying of cancer, when things were going so well? When he had a ca-

reer and a wife and a baby boy—or just after, when all such perceptions would be influenced by this new knowledge? Or had dying
caused some kind of purified state of emotion, something that
heightened everything? Was imminent death a magnifying glass
through which the heat of life was intensified—enlarged and sharp-
ened into a prism point of misery and joy?

He went out again and walked down the street, preoccupied
with his thoughts. His gaze was fixed on the pavement in front of
him. Then he lifted his head and saw his mother just down the
block. She was holding a plastic grocery bag, but it was a light load,
probably only a carton of milk, maybe some oranges, some bread.
His mother, when not in a celebratory mood, lived frugally.

But it was her expression that stopped him. She too was engrossed in something, and had her head down as she scrutinized
the ground in front of her. Her face looked concerned, even old,
and it struck him that his mother was aging. Not that the idea was
such a shock, but it jarred him to see how different the face he was
looking at just then was from the taut, angular, smooth-skinned
face that looked so coolly into the smiling monkeyface of his father,
in the photograph. This face—her face now—wore an expression of
mild confusion, as if she were trying to remember where she had
left her keys.

He stood still as she approached him on a direct collision
course. She was oblivious. The face that had so often warmed his
looked a little gray. It came nearer, a visage, and only when she was
only five or ten feet away did she look up abruptly, as if she had noticed his shoes standing still on the pavement. Alex had been smiling as she came nearer, and he was looking forward to the prospect
of surprising her. But when she suddenly looked up, she had such
an expression of alarm and shock that he felt his own face freeze.
Her expression was completely unfamiliar. She was wholly surprised,
off guard. Her mouth was slightly ajar, her eyes wide, her face a
little slack around the edges. She blinked a moment, composing her-

self, registering that this was her son in front of her, and then started to smile.

But it was too late; he was upon her, hugging her. Something had come over him at the sight of her disorientation and he had leapt forward to embrace her, as if he were catching her in midfall. The leap was urgent—desperate even—and when he got to her he put his arms around her and squeezed her tightly to his chest, as if he were afraid that she might drop something or lose something, or as if some secret which only she knew would slip away.

What My Boss Is Thinking
Art Grillo

You sit there at your desk knowing you are just here for the summer and that you will never get your skirts dirty—if I can use such a metaphor—while I get my skirts dirty all the time, although as you know I don't wear skirts, I wear pants. I wear *the pants*. You sit in judgment from your fine position as outsider. To you I am many things: cop, corporate grunt, semiliterate Republican airhead. Mostly, I am Dominant Woman. You go home and fantasize about being handcuffed to the desk where you sit and do so little for the ninesomething per hour you get from the temp agency. You fantasize about being raped. And these fantasies are comfortable for you, given the glorious escape hatch of September. You smile at the irony of being a Ph.D. candidate in labor history who answers the phone at Pinkerton Investigations. You think someone like myself with a bachelor's degree from a commuter school knows jack squat about the Molly Maguires. You think you're the only temp in the world who knows that our great founder Allan Pinkerton was himself a labor militant back in Scotland before he wised up and came to America, where a man could get rich being a private dick and screw the rest of the unwashed masses who came over with him.

Still, don't think I don't like you. I like hearing your sweet male voice answer the phone and seeing your fat male fingers type an occasional letter or fumble with the coffee filters. You are simply a paragon of manly resilience, temping for me because you couldn't get a summer teaching assistantship, poor baby. You tell your friends you're playing secretary to a woman who wears false eye-lashes and chews gum and was once married to a trucker. Right, once married, as in not married anymore, as in divorced, as in no ring on the fourth finger, something you noticed right away. I saw you look. Yes, I'm available, if not quite suitable, but don't get any ideas, because I'm one of those *trés passé* bosses who avoids office entanglements, even with temps who will be gone before the leaves change color.

I must admit, however, I was thinking of you last night at the strip joint, a fitting haunt for a woman who grew up in a trailer park, right? Well, listen professor: I happened to be working last night on a surveillance case. A workers' comp scam. This guy who not long ago worked for the county roads department was claiming complete disability. Claimed he could not lift ten pounds and he could not bend over. Walked with a cane. Funny thing, though: Said Claimant, as yours truly found out, happens to be a featured dancer on ladies night at the Club Paris, a job that may not require much lifting but does require you to bend over now and then. I was sitting at a table by the stage when he picks up the microphone stand (there's your ten pounds) and starts riding it like a little hor-sie. I'm capturing the whole performance on a video camera the size of a quarter. The camera is hidden inside the casing of a beeper. The "beeper" is clipped to the side of my purse. The camera lens is three-sixteenths of an inch in diameter. I could go on, but I'd only be fetishizing technology and fetishes are your thing. I've seen you staring at my purse, for instance, as if it were a repository of un-speakable feminine power and judging from last night you are maybe not so far off base. I held the thing in my lap and tilted it up-ward as he danced for me and I nailed him good. There's enough tape for a bachelorette party. And let me tell you, I derived from the evening a tremendous feeling of power, realizing the case would be open-and-shut and that this stud's free ride was coming to an end. But do not assume the feeling was erotic. Do not think I fantasized about having a penis and sticking it up the you-know-what of the dancer. I was just doing my job and enjoying it. I derived no more erotic pleasure than you would finishing one of your little scholarly papers, or giving one of your freshmen an F. Or maybe those things are erotic for you.

And still you ask why you were on my mind last night. It's because I know you think you've got a hot body. You think you could be a male dancer. I've seen you gazing at yourself in plate glass windows and department store mirrors during your lunch hour. Right, I've tailed you. I've seen you flexing your biceps in the changing room at Marshall Field's (we've got the place wired).

And I've seen you do other things.

I've seen you at the magazine stand down in the lobby, ogling *Glamour* and *Cosmo* and even *Good Housekeeping,* gaping at women and women's clothes, at ads for lipstick and bras and everything else you wish I'd make you wear to work. And let us not forget the pulpy, forbidden *Variations;* how your dear face reddened when you found the item about the lady exec and her submissive male secretary! Remember, you are under surveillance at all times. "We never sleep," is the Pinkerton motto. Plus, I've eyes in the back of my head, just like your mother.

All of this is thrilling for you and scary only in the manner of a good horror movie. Go ahead—fantasize. Make me into whatever you wish. Put words in my mouth. Put thoughts in my head. Just remember—someday it might be more than just a fantasy. A person need not subscribe to the *Chronicle of Higher Education* to know the academic job market is dismal, especially for humanist chumps like yourself. What if you can't find a job after your New Historicist take on the Molly Maguires is all finished and defended and unpublished? You said you'd never be a part-time lecturer—too exploitative. Well, you type fifty-five words per minute and you answer the phone nicely and you make okay coffee. We offer full health benefits—no need to be pulling any workers' comp scams around here, not that you'd get away with it for one second. There'll be a place here for you as my underthing (as in garment, as in pantywaist, a term you've come across during your scholarly strolls through the nineteenth century). You'll no longer be my temp. You'll be my permanent (as in something you get at a beauty parlor). You'll be in my control for good. I'll take off your pants; you'll have to stay at your desk and work and not be getting up every five minutes to seek the pleasures of the coffee machine and the men's room and the magazine stand. Then we'll see what you think.

Fraternity
Dan Chaon

Cal used to be president of the fraternity. But then he was in a car wreck. Cal and Hap and a group of boys from the fraternity house had been out to the bars, and they were on their way home. Afterward Hap often pictured Cal dipping his hand into a cooler of beer, letting the water run off the can, popping the tab. Cal's head was tilted back, Hap could see him in the rearview mirror, and it was when he looked back to the road that he saw the parked truck. Hap remembered, or thought he remembered, someone screaming, "Mom!"

John wasn't hurt that bad. He was in the hospital for a few weeks, but then he didn't come back to school. He was still at home, working in his father's auto parts store. He didn't drink anymore, he didn't go out. Talking to him, Hap remarked to people, you'd think he was middle-aged.

Stephen wasn't injured at all, but he graduated early—finished up his major and got out of school and their fraternity as quietly as possible, packing up like a swindler without even saying goodbye.

It was Cal who got the worst part of it. He'd ducked down at the last minute and covered his head, but it was his side of the car that was crushed. They had to cut him out of the wreckage, where he was pinned between the car door and the seat.

Cal was in a coma for nearly a month, and all that time they were expecting him to die. He woke up one morning, but he wasn't the same person. There was brain damage and he had to go to a re-habilitation clinic.

Hap had been driving the car. He wasn't drunk, and in fact he took a Breathalyzer at the site of the accident. All he could remember were the faces peering out of the slow-moving cars, and the whirlpool of red and blue lights from the police cars. He passed the test. He'd had a beer or two, of course, but he was definitely within the legal limit. It was an accident. And it wouldn't happen again: he didn't drive anymore.

Not that anyone ever blamed him. Still, he sometimes noticed how their eyes darkened sidelong when he reached for another beer. He noticed how their faces suddenly tightened when he was in a good mood and got to laughing. It was as if, he thought, he'd turned for a second into something unclean.

Hap had tried to put everything back in order. They'd held an emergency meeting when they found out Cal wouldn't be returning, and since Hap was vice president at the time, they told him the presidency was his if he felt up to it. And so he'd stood there, with bandages on his head and hand, talking in nervous circles, saying how life had to go on, how Cal would have wanted it that way.

A few months after the accident Hap began to pass out in unusual places. The first time it happened was for real: he woke in the hall-way, with no idea how he got there. Magic Marker was scribbled across his face and belly, as if he'd been trying to write himself a message.

After that first time it became an act. On mornings after parties, his fraternity brothers began to find him in the foyer, curled up among the discarded advertisements and catalogues, or in the shower fully dressed, with the water running, or outside under a tree, his hands caked with dirt as if he'd been digging. At first they thought it was funny. They joked that Hap ought to have bells tied to his heels before he was allowed to drink a beer. Some of the incidents became amusing anecdotes.

He planned things in advance, considering which place might be most surprising, most ridiculous. One night he'd squeezed onto a shelf on the trophy case, twisted around gold statuettes of basketball players and wrestlers and the engraved plaques. Even in that precarious position they couldn't tell he was faking. He opened his eyes with a start, and sat straight up. One of the trophies fell clattering onto the living room floor.

Often he'd wait a long time before anyone found him. He'd get frustrated, sometimes, and decide he was just going to forget it and go on up to bed. But then he'd hear voices and his heart would pound and his mind would begin to whir like a fan. He could feel the shape of them as they moved closer, slow, hovering, and he'd open his eyes to find them leaning over him like surgeons. Once this pre-med named Matsumura reached down and took his pulse. The pressure of his finger had run through Hap like an electric shock. He jerked up, and everyone laughed, circled around him, shaking their heads.

But the novelty began to wear off. "Oh brother," he heard Charlie Balbo say one morning. "Look who's passed out again." Balbo pulled on Hap's arm. He was in ROTC and always woke up early to do exercises. Hap could hear Balbo sighing through his nose. "Rise and shine, buddy," Balbo said, and when Hap fluttered his eyelids and moaned, none of them were smiling. Hap figured they were all thinking about the accident.

~

Cal's mother called. Cal was back home, she told Hap, and she hoped some of his fraternity brothers would come for a visit. It had been six months since the accident.

Hap wondered how she'd gotten his number. He hadn't met her, really, just shook hands with her once during parents' weekend when Cal pointed them at each other and said, "Mom this is Hap, he's one of my best pals," or something like that, quick and stilted; that was the way he talked. Later, after Cal had gone to the clinic, Hap sent a get well card to his home. He'd never visited the hospital, though he told people he had: "Cal's doing real good," he said. He'd called the hospital a number of times, and that's what they told him. "Under the circumstances," they said, "he's doing well."

As the visit approached, Hap would feel a wave of panic pass over him, and he was desperate to call Cal's mother and make some excuse. But what? He couldn't think of any excuse that wouldn't provoke disbelief. He would think of it from time to time, when he wasn't expecting to. That Saturday, a week before he was to go, it was like a rushing at his back.

There was a party that night, and Hap had been downstairs long before anyone else, organizing guys to clear the furniture and push it against the wall, directing the football players to lift kegs of beer into ice-filled trash cans, hurrying to get the tap or the strobe light. There were certain things Hap did that he felt no one else could do quite so well. He was the one who liked to put up decorations and make up themes for parties—putting red lights in the windows and taping up orange and yellow poster board in the shape of flames, so the house looked afire; lining the dance floor with old mattresses and balloons; setting up elaborate spreads of dips and vegetables and so on. He played the music, building up to the best dance songs, urging the crowd into a kind of frenzy. He'd stand on the window ledge and look out over their heads, calling out chants which the crowd would repeat. It was almost as if this was his fiefdom, for one night at least.

Cal used to shake his head. "Geez," he used to say. "Take a Valium." Hap remembered one night they'd gone to this place, Elbow's Room, where they didn't card. It was a dim, hazy bar, with country

D a n   C h a o n

music on the jukebox, and they went in before a party. Hap was anxious to get back; he didn't want to miss anything. But Cal was in no hurry. Hap was telling him that he was going to miss the fraternity when they graduated, that it was one of his main reasons for staying in school, and Cal stared at him. His face was lit by the fireplace glow of neon, made spooky and dark by it. Hap was hoping he'd say, "Me, too," or even, "Yeah, when we go that place is dead." But all he said was, "Christ, I can't wait to get out. You're crazy, Hap." He shrugged, and Hap felt something clench inside him; it was like Cal was abandoning him.

That was one of the things that stuck in his mind that night. The dancing had died down early, and Hap was making his way upstairs to his room. There were four girls on their way up to the ladies' room when they saw Hap rubber-legging up the steps. He nearly fell over them, and they caught him, laughing. It was what he did, sometimes, he wasn't sure why. He liked to act more drunk than he was. The girls wrapped their arms around his shoulders and guided him toward his room—someone in the hall directed them. Hap kept his eyes closed, and shortly he felt one of the girls sliding her hand in his back pocket to get his keys. "I can't believe I'm doing this," she said breathlessly, and another whispered, "Is he out?" He wasn't, of course. But when their grip loosened he slumped to the floor, and another girl said, "I guess he's out." They carried him in and put him on the bed, but he didn't sleep. The more he lay there, the more awake he became, listening to the music pulsing through the floor. A couple stood outside his door, thinking they had privacy, and murmured urgently—he couldn't tell if they were arguing or making out. When he was sure the party was over, nearly five in the morning, he went downstairs. He planned to pass out again, this time sprawled on the pool table. It was a gray morning: it could have been dawn, or dusk again. When he passed the window in the stairwell a heavy bird lifted from the sill and blurred into the fog. It startled him, and he felt suddenly that there was some-

Fraternity

127

one watching him. He wondered if the house was all closed up. Often after a party he found the front door hadn't been bolted or one of the fire exits was slightly ajar, or a window on the first floor was open, crepe paper streamers trailing off into the breeze. Sometimes it was hard to feel safe.

Everything seemed to pause, waiting. He peered in on each floor. All the doors were closed, lined up as still as motel rooms. Long shadows stretched in the dim hallways. He felt as if the place had been abandoned.

When he went downstairs the living room seemed thick with haze. No one had cleaned up after the party. The furniture was all cleared out still, and there were plastic cups cluttered on every surface. From across the room he could hear the wind blowing through an open window. He squinted in the pale half-light. For a moment he was certain he saw the shape of someone standing there, a figure by the window, with the curtains fluttering around him.

"Hello," he called, and his voice rang hollowly in the empty room. "Hello? Is someone there?"

And then he turned and ran up the stairs to his room. He bolted the door and put on the radio. He wanted to wake someone up, just to prove he wasn't alone in the house. He kept turning the stereo louder, until at last Doug Cohn in the next room began knocking heavily on the wall between them. Hap turned off the stereo and sat there in the bed until it was light enough to sleep.

⁓

There were times, lots of times, when it seemed like everything was back to normal. Hap would go downstairs before dinner to find a group of guys standing around the pool table, tapping balls into the pockets with the palms of their hands, and the talk was all easy jokes and gossip. Mornings, he'd walk into the bathroom, where a line of people from his floor were all at sinks shaving, and move in beside them without a hitch. Even the day after the party, when he woke, there was a moment when he imagined himself shrugging to Doug Cohn, he heard himself chuckling, "Hey, thought I saw a ghost last night, Doug. Scared myself shitless."

But later, when he saw Doug Cohn on his way out the front door with his bookbag, it seemed that the things he planned to say were frivolous and artificial. He drew back, acting as if he hadn't noticed Doug, and he decided that it was probably best not to mention anything at all. After that, the day didn't seem like it would cruise along so easily. There was always some little snag to send him spinning.

The early evenings were the worst, after everyone had gone off to the library or their girlfriends' rooms. He flipped through channels in the television room, one after the other so the voices and music and yelps of white noise melted together in a collage, an abstract code he could almost recognize. Or he'd end up back in his room, listening for someone to come down the hall. He made lists: party ideas; things he planned to do tomorrow; friends, in ascending order of closeness. He'd number things from one to ten. It was calming to mark things down.

~

Sometimes he thought he would just give in, that he would let himself spend the whole day brooding about Cal. But he found he couldn't. He tried to remember something specific about Cal, some significant conversation they had, the special things they used to do together. But his mind would go blank. Or rather, he'd remember how once someone spray-painted ELIMINATE GREEKS on the outside of their house. They'd circled the A in ELIMINATE, and there was a picture of Cal in the campus newspaper, standing in front of the big red A in his Greek letter sweatshirt and grinning. He recalled the time he and Cal came up with a way to combine philanthropy and

Fraternity

partying. They planned to get a bunch of organ donor cards from the Department of Motor Vehicles and use them as admission tickets to a huge bash. They were going to have T-shirts that said: Lose Your Liver—donate an organ/have a beer!

It seemed to Hap that all these memories were grotesque, like the old photos he'd found once in his basement at home, pictures half-eaten by silverfish. He wondered if something was wrong with him. He believed that if things were the other way around, Cal would remember him better—that Cal would have fond stories of the night they pledged or the time they were both elected officers of the fraternity; some recollection that would make everyone laugh.

∽

He didn't know what the others were thinking. At the chapter meeting on Monday night, he announced as if effortlessly that "a group of brothers will be visiting Cal Fuller this Sunday," and then went on with the other items on the agenda. When he scanned their faces he couldn't read anything. Even the other three guys who planned to go to Cal's house didn't seem to respond. Eric sat staring at the textbook he'd opened on the table in front of him; Charlie Balbo rocked back in his chair, balancing on two legs; Russ, Cal's freshman-year roommate, traced his index finger across his palm.

He didn't know what he expected. But he didn't like it when Balbo patted him on the back, and said, "I hear you made it to bed Saturday night, for once." He didn't like his own reply: "Yeah, your girlfriend showed me the way." He gave a short laugh, and the sound of it made his face feel pale.

∽

There was no party that Saturday and the house was unnaturally still. Yet he felt too edgy to go out. In the distance, up and down the fraternity quad, people were calling and laughing, on their way to other parties. Any other Saturday night Hap would be out there with them, on his way somewhere to unwind. He'd melt into the heat and flex of crowded rooms, nodding at acquaintances, easing into casual conversation with girls, just letting the smoke and alcohol work through him. There might even be a moment, late at night, when everything seemed perfect—like the time he and Cal had sung "Papa's Got a Brand New Bag" on their way home, very slowly and with melancholy, and there had been a few bars of clear harmony, echoing against the walls; or the time an enormous raccoon had regarded him from a rain-soaked lawn, standing on its haunches, holding an apple. Heavy clouds of steam were rising from manholes, drifting low to the ground, all the way down the sidewalk.

Hap could see his reflection in the window, staring in at him. The ivy was thick across his window so he couldn't see who was laughing outside. All he could see were twisting vines, the shadows of leaves showing through his reflection like an X-ray of something, he wasn't sure what. This was what it was like for Cal, he thought—floating as people passed below you, as if you'd levitated out of your own body.

When Russ knocked on the door, Hap was staring out the window and feeling as if he could lift out of his skin. He hoped there wasn't an edge of desperation in his voice when he said, "Come on in, buddy. Have a beer with me."

"I was just stopping by to let you know when we were going to leave in the morning," Russ said. He glanced around as if he were entering a room full of strangers. When Hap handed him a beer, he sat there considering it. For a moment, they sat not saying anything, both moving their heads to the music that Hap had playing, constantly.

"So anyway," Hap said at last. "It'll be good to see Cal again, huh?"

Russ shrugged. "I guess," he said. He moved his mouth as if to say more, but then took a sip of beer instead. He swallowed. "I mean, you know," he said.

"Well anyway, they say he's doing pretty well," Hap said. "It'll be cool. We'll just sit around, shoot the breeze for a while. No big deal."

They nodded at one another. Russ had never been easy to squeeze conversation out of; some people used to say that if he hadn't been roommates with Cal freshman year, he never would have gotten a bid. He'd still be in the dorms, studying his Saturday nights away.

Yet it used to be easier to talk, even to Russ. Hap used to believe he could connect with most any of them, that they would all get together in twenty years, like the old paunchy alums who came back every spring to drink together, to tell old stories and sing songs. Hap had seen that as part of his future. He used to imagine that his fraternity brothers would think of him from time to time for the rest of their lives. Some little thing—an old song on the car radio, a face glimpsed as an elevator closed—would startle them, and they'd think suddenly: Hap! What's he up to these days?

Russ lifted the beer to his lips; when he set it down, a droplet of moisture trickled slowly down the side of the can. Russ seemed to be waiting for him to say something. But all he could think of was small talk, trivia: sororities, classes, sports teams. It made him cringe. Outside, the wind came up. Hap could hear the muffled buzz of a motorcycle speeding down a faraway street, someone showing off.

"I don't think it will be so bad tomorrow," Hap said.

Russ nodded slowly. "Yeah," he said at last "It should be okay. I mean, I'm sure you'll do fine."

Hap said, "Hey, I'll be sober at least"

Russ looked down and shook his head. "Yeah," he said softly. "No big deal," Hap told him. "It won't be any big deal."

~

Cal's home was in a new development called Stone Lake Estates. It was at the far edge of the suburbs, and some of the streets weren't marked clearly on Russ's map. No trees had been planted yet, so the rows of houses stood bright and unshaded against the clear sky.

The boys were all still as they circled through Stone Lake, so quiet that Hap could hear Charlie Balbo in the backseat, breathing through his nose. Every time they passed a street sign, Russ slowed and gazed at it uneasily. At last, he pulled into a driveway. "This is the place," he said. Hap saw him cast a quick look at Charlie Balbo. None of them seemed to look at him, though if they had he would have simply smiled firmly.

Cal's mother came to the door, but she didn't open it right away. She peeked through the curtains, and they waved at her uncertainly. Hap could hear the bamboo wind chimes that hung from the porch, the deep hollow tones as they rustled in the breeze. Then they heard the lock being turned, and she stared at them through the half-open door.

"Hi boys," she said.

"Hi," they echoed. They stood for a moment on the threshold, and she took Russ's hand. He'd stayed over with them one Thanksgiving, and she spoke lightly: "Good to see you again, Russ," she said. Then she turned expectantly to the rest of them. Eric and Charlie introduced themselves quickly, and they shook their hands, too. "Welcome, Charlie, Eric," she said. Then she smiled at Hap.

"I'm Hap," he said. "We talked on the phone."

"Of course," she said. "I believe I met you once at a reception."

She had dark eyes. They seemed wet and glittering as Hap took her hand. Hap thought maybe she was wishing the same thing on him, wishing him crippled or dead, though she held his hand for a long moment, tightly. She was always angry with Cal, Hap remembered, she always complained that he spent too much time socializing and not enough preparing for his future. Hap wondered if she thought it was he who led Cal astray. He wished he could tell her that everything, everything had always been Cal's idea.

"You're very lucky," she said softly, and dropped his hand.

She ushered them past several framed photographs of Cal: as a baby; as a long-haired high school boy; another that Hap recognized as the one Cal had taken for the fraternity composite when he was elected president. They walked into a living room, and it was then that they saw him. He was sitting cross-legged on the floor, watching an old black-and-white television series. He didn't move. He had his face turned away from them, and his mother seemed not to notice him.

"Can I get you anything to drink?" she asked, and it sent a shiver through Hap as if it were an accusation. "Coke? Milk? Water?"

As she went toward the kitchen, Cal looked up, and Hap lifted his hand hesitantly, as if to wave, or to shield his face. But Cal let his eyes drift shyly over them, then turned back to the TV. He didn't recognize them, Hap realized. Their stares made him shift bashfully. He leaned toward the television as if to be swallowed up by it and vanish. None of them looked at one another, or spoke. Hap just watched the screen, thinking that all of them were sharing the same images, at least.

The curtains had been drawn, so the TV was brighter. The sleepy dimness of the room reminded Hap of winter, of childhood sicknesses. Everything was muted. In the next room, beyond the cheerfully artificial voices of the TV characters, he could hear ice cubes being cracked from their trays.

Mrs. Fuller came in, carrying their drinks on a tray. Cal continued to watch television until she said, "Cal, honey," very firmly. Then he looked up at her impatiently. Hap tried not to glance at him. He held tightly to his glass, staring down into it.

"Do you see your friends?" Mrs. Fuller said. "Look who's come to visit you!"

"Hi," Cal sighed, and Hap's hands began to throb. He wasn't the same person, Hap thought. He tried to put on a polite smile, but he knew it looked false. All he could think was that Cal must be in that body somewhere, but sleeping, or maybe only vaguely aware, like someone drugged; he imagined the real Cal was submerged somehow, curled up like a fist, struggling to break out.

"How's it going, Cal?" he said brightly, and Cal gazed up at him. Russ and Eric and Charlie were lined up on the long sofa that faced the television, and Hap was a little apart from them, in a high-backed easy chair, his hands clasped tightly in front of him. Everyone was watching him. "Good to see you!" he said, but Cal didn't answer. He glanced back at the TV show.

"Cal," Mrs. Fuller said, in her calm, stern voice. She got up and shut off the TV, and Cal's head turned as she went, noting each movement wistfully. "Look, Cal," she said softly. "Who are those boys?"

He hung his head. "My friends," he whispered.

She was close to him, avid, bright-eyed. She lifted her finger suddenly and pointed at Hap. His heart leapt. "Who's that boy, Cal? Who is that?"

Hap caught his breath, stiffening, but Cal was silent. The quiet stretched out like a long shadow, and Hap felt that all of them were waiting for him to do something. He stood up. For a moment, he just wavered there, awkwardly, as if he'd been asked to give a speech, but at last he began to move forward a bit. He nodded encouragingly at Cal. "Who am I, Cal?" he whispered, so soft he could barely hear himself, and Cal closed his eyes. He slumped down, and for a moment Hap thought he'd fainted. But then his eyes snapped back open.

"I don't know," Cal said.

The room seemed to darken. Hap kept inching forward, holding out a hand to shake, though he could see that Cal didn't quite trust him; he drew back a little, the way a child would when a

stranger's friendliness seemed false. "Hey," Hap said. "It's me, Cal."
He raised his voice. "It's me—Hap."

Cal sat there on the rug, his legs tucked carefully under him,
and Hap just hovered there, looking down on him. He thought
maybe he ought to crouch down on the floor, too, so that Cal could
see him face to face, but before he could Cal stood up and walked
over to his mother. He sat down next to her, leaving Hap alone in
the middle of the room. He faced all of them.

Mrs. Fuller put her arms around Cal, and he leaned his head
against her shoulder. "When he came out of the coma," she said—
Hap standing there helplessly, as if surrounded—"When he came
out of the coma, he didn't even know who I was." She smiled ruefully. "He was like a baby again: couldn't dress himself, feed himself,
anything. But he's come a long way." She couldn't look up. They all
watched her, hypnotized, as she spoke in a slow, sweet voice, as if
to Cal. She told them how happy she'd been when he'd drawn a
circle on a piece of paper, when he played a game of Chutes and
Ladders with a nurse. "Who knows what he remembers?" she whispered, her mouth close to Cal's ear. "He'll look at those pictures
from your fraternity for hours. He's just fascinated. And sometimes
he'll say something and he'll sound almost like himself."

She sighed. "But you can't think of it that way," she said. "He's
a new person now. And we have to love him in a different way than
we used to. Not any less," she said. "Just different." She laid her
hand on Cal's cheek, and he nuzzled against her. There was a long
silence, and at last, the spell broken, Hap edged back to his chair.
That was it, he thought. Cal was gone. He imagined a sudden bright
flash burning the person who had been Cal away, leaving only a
blurry whiteness, a hiss of static. He saw it so clearly that for a minute he felt as if the chair were tilting underneath him. He held to
the arms, tightly.

"Of course, he'll always need to be taken care of," Mrs. Fuller
said at last. "Like a little boy." Then she was quiet again, stroking
Cal's hair, watching the movement of her hand as if mesmerized.

"Do you see how his forehead is scarred?" she murmured finally. A kind of thrum went over Hap's skin as she brushed Cal's bangs back to reveal rows of reddish, rounded strips. "It's hard to believe, isn't it? That's the pattern of your car seat. And he was pushed forward with so much force that the imprint is still there." She was moving her hand slowly through his hair, as if thinking of something far off, but her eyes were fixed on Hap. He couldn't meet her gaze; he could only look at Cal, who was enjoying the touch of his mother's fingers over his brow. He had his head tilted back, his expression relaxed, staring up as if he were star-gazing. And for a moment, Hap felt as if they were seeing the same thing, up there in the distance, a meteor shrinking into the stratosphere, layers sloughing off in fiery husks until it was just a speck, plunging into the dark. They stared up toward some distant point and it seemed, it was almost as if Hap or even Cal himself were about to remember something important. Something he'd forgotten. But then it was gone.

No more than a few words passed between them as they drove home. They each took a corner of the car, each tilted in different directions. Russ held the steering wheel in both hands, staring out at the signs, the road. Eric turned his face away from Hap, resting his head against the window, pretending to be asleep.

It was almost as if it were late at night, and the world was calm and dark. But it was still daylight, and when Hap closed his eyes, orange flashes beat irregularly against his closed eyelids: the sun, flickering through the trees.

On the very edge of sleep, Hap could feel the shape of a dream. It was a party, and Hap had just joined the fraternity. He could see someone moving toward the dancing crowd, clapping, shouting. Everything began to stop: the music faded, the lights came up. One after another, the dancing couples separated, began to clap in rhythm, and the men from the fraternity emerged out of the dark. Then he felt himself being lifted. He was up above their heads, carried on a rippling of dozens of hands. Their chanting echoed beneath him as they poured out into the open air, under the night sky. He was floating, and when he looked down he saw a boy waving at him, at the end of a long tunnel of people. Cal! he thought.

He started up with a laugh.

PART TWO
The Faculty

Professors
Tom Whalen

The first professor possessed, as it were, smugness. "Heh, heh," he said looking at me over his bifocals, crinkling his harelip, stroking his beard. "Heh, heh." I exited his office backwards, clutching my books across my bosom.

~

The second professor said, "I would like to stroke your thigh with my slide rule." I said my thigh was too young to be stroked, it was only seventeen, almost as old as I, and a good half-dozen years younger than he. He said he would write problems only I could answer. "Like what?" I asked, thumbing through the section of the catalogue that spelled out the math requirements. "A young technician in a yellow blouse and cream-colored skirt," he said, "has to monitor a flow meter in order to study the variation in the flow rate which is essential for passing her Introduction to Experimentation course. She starts out by taking readings every minute and her first ten readings are 36.0, 49.7, 56.0, 45.9, 41.1, 51.1, 53.6, 45.9, 47.0, 48.9. If she falls asleep after the first ten minutes, will her professor say she was taking her readings frequently enough, or too frequently? Will he accede to her pleas to let her pass his course if she is willing to spend extra hours at the microscope and surface coating?" "I've found it," I said. "Yes?" the professor replied, fingering the slide rule magnetized to his belt. "This course isn't required for graduation," I answered, and thanked him for his time.

⌒

The third professor took me into the woods and said, "Feel this tree." I felt it; its back was vertically ridged and solid cork, its needles soft and blunt. "Do you know what kind of tree this is?" he asked. I looked at his thick, dusty boots, his broad waist, his mountain beard, his bald head. "No," I said. "This is *Pseudotsuga taxifolia*," he said, "the Douglas fir, the highest expression of tree greatness of our time. Look at the three-pronged tongues sticking out between the cone's scales." All around me the tall, straight trunks of the firs stood close together, letting hardly any of the noonday light through. The professor put his arm around my shoulders and whispered in my ear, "Would you like to hold one?" "A fir tree?" I asked. "Well," he said. The forest darkened even more. Not even a breath of wind stirred the soft nettles. "I think I'll skip botany the first year," I said. "Could you point me to the cafeteria?"

⌒

In the office of the fourth professor I was taken by the hand and led to a telescope, the ceiling opened a crack, the lights were dimmed. "Now tell me what you see," he said in a deep, gentle voice. I saw a streak of white, like the quick stroke of an abstract painter, across a backdrop of stars. "Is it a comet's tail?" I asked. "That's right," he said, and placed his hand at the base of my spine. My knees went all soft and buttery, but I held tightly to the telescope. "Some tails," he continued, "reach lengths of more than 100 million miles. Three forces effect the material that form a comet's tail; a radial force ejected from the nucleus of the comet when it nears the sun and heats up; a repulsive force moving radially away from the sun; and the gravitational attraction of the sun which causes the molecules of a comet's tail to move in an orbit." My heart was beating so fast I thought he might hear it. "A steady flow of cometary material is ejected outward by the radial force away from the head of the comet. I shall demonstrate for you now the material's angular velocity . . ." But by then I had stumbled in the darkness to the door and escaped into the hallway. Goodness, I thought, I never even saw what his face looked like.

The walls of the fifth professor's office were covered with prints of nudes by Rubens, Velázquez, Rembrandt van Rijn, Watteau, Boucher, Ingres, Chavannes ("The Toilette"), Marées ("Horsedriver and Nymph"), Pascin, Modigliani, Balthus, Delvaux, and Bellmer.

The sixth professor was also the president of the college and taught French poetry. He poured me a cup of tea. "Cream?" he asked. "Please." We were sitting in newly upholstered, antique chairs on a glassed-in porch—the day room, he called it. Beyond the glass, September roses bloomed at the edges of his manicured back lawn. "Any problems so far?" "Well," I said. "Good, good," he replied, stirring with a silver spoon his tea. He was a short man, late forties, I guessed, and in good trim. He wore a sky-blue shirt, white shorts with a cloth belt, white socks pulled up almost to his grass-stained knees and a pair of mouse-gray slippers. "You know," he said, setting his cup delicately on the serving tray, "my wife died last year and now I have this huge house all to myself. I've many spare rooms." He turned his head away from me and stared casually out at the lawn. "You could, if you wanted, and if you were willing to do a few odd jobs for me here and there about the house for your keep, stay with me for free." "That's awfully nice of you," I said. "I'll think about it," and left my tea unfinished.

~

"What can I do for you?" the seventh professor asked me. He looked a lot like the first professor except he didn't have a harelip or beard. His office was small and windowless and his desk was a clutter of academic journals and books. "Could you tell me about your department?" I asked. "Philosophy?" "Yes." "You're looking at it," he said. "Oh." A three-speed Schwinn was propped against one wall and in the far corner stood a clothes tree covered with three raincoats. "What's your specialty?" I asked. "Wittgenstein," he said, then added, "an Austrian philosopher." "What did he believe?" "Well," the professor said, laughing a little and rubbing his hand over his gray hair, "he believed that all philosophical problems have the form: 'I don't know my way about.'" I thought about this for a moment, then pulled out my registration card and asked him to sign it.

Hartwell
Ron Carlson

This is about Hartwell, who is nothing like me. I have sometimes
told stories about people, men and sometimes a woman, who were
like me, weak or strong in some way that I am or they shared my
taste for classical music or fine coffee, but Hartwell was not like me
in any way. I'm just going to tell his story, a story about a man I
knew, a man not like me, just some *other* man.

Hartwell just didn't get it. For years he existed, as the saying
goes, *out of it*. Let's say he wasn't alert to nuance, and then let's go
ahead and say he wasn't alert to blatancy either. He was alert to the
Victorian poets and all of *their* nuances, but he couldn't tell you if it
was raining. This went way back to when he was in college at the
University of Michigan and everybody was preparing for law school
taking just enough history, political science, things like that, but
Hartwell majored in English, narrowing that to the Victorians, which
could lead only to one thing: graduate school. As a graduate student, he was a sweet guy with a spiral tuft of light hair that rose off
his head like fire, who lived alone in a room he took off campus and
who read his books, diligently and with pleasure, and ate a steady
diet of the kind of food eaten with ease while reading, primarily
candy.

When I met him, he had become a sweet, round man, an asso-
ciate professor of English, who taught Browning and Tennyson,
etc., etc., and who brought to our campus that fall years ago his
wife, Melissa, a handsome woman with broad shoulders and shiny
dark hair cut in a pixie shell.

I say "our campus" because I too teach, but Hartwell and I couldn't be more different in that regard. I know what's going on around me. I teach rhetoric and I parse my students as well as any paragraph. My antennae are out. I can smell an ironic smirk in the back row, detect an unprepared student in the first five minutes of class, feel from the way the students file out of class what they think of me. Hartwell drifts into his classroom, nose in a book, shirt misbuttoned, and reads and lectures until well after the bell has rung and half the students have departed. He doesn't know their names or how many there are. He can't hear them making fun of him when they do it to his face while handing in a late paper, whining his name into five sarcastic syllables, *Pro-fess-or Hart-well,* and smiling a smile so fake and sugary as to make any of us avert our eyes. He is oblivious.

This was apparent to me the first time I met him with Melissa at the faculty party that fall. The effect of seeing them standing together in the dean's backyard was shocking. Anyone could see it: they wouldn't last the year. As I said, she was attractive, but as she scanned her husband's colleagues that evening it was her eyes, her predatory eyes, that made it clear. Poor old Hartwell stood beside her, his hair afloat, his smile benign and vacant, an expression he'd learned from years alone with books.

Melissa shopped around for a while, and by midterm she was seeing our Twentieth-Century Drama professor, a young guy who had a red mustache and played handball. It took Hartwell the entire year to find out about the affair and then all of summer session to decide what it meant. Even then, even after he'd talked to Melissa and she to him and *he'd* moved out of the little house they were buying near the college, even then he didn't really wake up. The students were more sarcastic to him now that he was a cuckold, a word they learn as sophomores and then overuse for a year. Watching that was hard on me, those sunny young faces filing into his office with their million excuses for not being present or prepared, saying

Ron Carlson

things that if I heard them in my office would win them an audience with the dean. Things I wouldn't take.

I, however, am not like Hartwell. There isn't a callow hair on my head. I am alert. I am perspicacious. I can see what is going on. I've become, as you sense, a cynical and thoroughly jaded professor of rhetoric. My defenses are up and like it or not, they are not coming down.

It was in the period just after Melissa that I became friends with Professor Hartwell. Our schedules were similar and many afternoons at four-thirty we fell into step as we left the ancient Normal Building where we both taught. Old Normal was over a hundred years old, the kind of school building you don't see anymore: a red block structure with crumbling turrets, high ceilings, and a warped wooden floor that rippled underfoot. I'd walk out with Hartwell and ask him if he'd like to get a coffee. The first time I asked him, he said *what* and when I had repeated the question, he looked at me full of wonder, as if I'd invented French roast, and said, "Why, yes, that sounds like a good idea." But, of course, with Hartwell that was the way he responded every time I asked him. He was like a child, a man without a history. His experience with Melissa certainly hadn't hurt him. He thought it was odd, but as he said one day, over two wonderful cups of Celebes Kolossi at the Pantry, about the drama teacher, "He had vigor." But we primarily talked shop: semantics. Hartwell was doing a study of Gerard Manley Hopkins, and I offered my advice.

I wasn't surprised during this time to see him occasionally lunching with Melissa. He was the kind of man you could betray, divorce, and then still maneuver into buying you lunch.

But our afternoons together began to show me his loneliness. He was as seemingly indifferent to that feeling as any man I'd ever met, even myself in the life I have chosen, but more and more frequently during our conversations I would see his eyes narrow and fall upon a table across the room where a boy and a girl chatted over their notebooks. And when his eyes returned to me, they would be different, and he would stand and gather his books and go off, a fat fair-haired professor tasting grief. He never remembered to pay for his coffee.

~

Then the next thing happened, and I knew from the very beginning what to make of it. When you fall in love with a student, three things happen. One: you become an inspired teacher, spending hours and hours going over every tragic shred of your students' sour deadwood compositions as if holding in your hands magic parchment, suddenly tapping into hidden reservoirs of energy and vocabulary and lyric combinations for your lectures, refusing to sit down in class. Two: the lucky victim of your infatuation receives a mark twice as high as he or she deserves. Three: you have a moment of catharsis during the denouement in which you see yourself too clearly the fool, a realization that is probably good for any teacher, because it will temper you, seal your cynicism and jade your eye, and make you sit down once hard and frequently thereafter.

The object of Hartwell's affections was a girl I kind of knew. She had been in my class the year before, and she was a girl you noticed. Ours is a small midwestern college and there are a dozen such beauties, coeds with the perfect unblemished faces of pretty girls and the long legs and round hips of women. These young creatures wear plaid skirts and sweaters and keep their streaming hair in silver clips. They sit in the second row and have bright teeth. They look at you unseeing, the way they've looked at teachers all their lives, and when one of these girls changes that glance and seems to be appraising, you wear a clean shirt and comb your hair the next day.

That was what gave Hartwell away: his hair. I met him on the steps of Normal and he looked funny, different. It was the way people look who have shaved beards or taken glasses, that is, I couldn't tell what was different for a moment. He simply looked *shorter.* Then I saw the comb tracks in the hair plastered to his head and I knew. He had been precise about it, I'll give him that. After a lifetime of letting his hair jet like flame, wildfire really, he had cut a part an engineer would have been proud of and then formed the perfect furrows across the top of his head and down, curling once to disappear behind the ear. If you'd just met him, I suppose, it didn't look too bad. But to me, god, he looked like the concierge for a sad hotel. He had combed his hair and I knew.

There were other signs too, his pressed shirt, the new tie, his loafers so shiny—after years of grime—that they hurt the eye. He was animated at coffee, tapping the cover of the old maroon anthology of Victorian poetry with new vigor, and then the *coup de grace*—one afternoon at the Pantry, he picked up the check.

Hartwell was teaching a Hopkins-Swinburne seminar at night that term and the girl who was the object of his affections, a girl named Laurie, was in that evening seminar. When Hartwell began to change his ways, I simply noticed it. It was none of my business. One's colleagues do many things that one doesn't fully appreciate or understand. But Hartwell was different. I felt I should help him. He had not been around this particular block, and I decided to stay alert.

I could see, read, and decipher the writing on the wall. This shrewd pretty schoolgirl was merely manipulating her professor to her advantage. I knew she was an ordinary student from her days in rhetoric, an officer in Tri-Delta sorority who wore a red kilt and a white sweater and who spent more time choosing her blouses than studying verb phrases, and now she was out for poor Hartwell.

I changed my office hours so I could be around when his class broke up, which was about 9 P.M. Tuesday and Thursdays, and I saw her hang around my old friend, chatting him up, always the last to leave and then stroll with him, and that is the correct word, *stroll,* down the rickety corridor of Normal, the floor creaking like the fools' chorus. She would laugh at the things he said and toss her hair just so and squeeze her books to her chest. And Hartwell, well, he would beam. From the door of my office I could see the light beam off his forehead, he was that far gone.

In most cases these things are not really very important, some passing infatuation, some shrewd undergraduate angles to raise his or her grade point average, some professor's flagging ego takes a little ride, but I watched that term as it went further and further for Hartwell. The shined shoes were a bit much, but then at midterm that spring, he showed up one day in gray flannel slacks, his old khakis and their constellations of vague grease stains gone forever. And I could tell he was losing weight, the way men do when they spend the energy necessary to become fools.

Melissa, his ex-wife, now uneasily married to our drama professor (who had since developed his own air of frumpiness), came to my office one day and asked me what was going on with Hartwell. I hadn't liked her from the beginning, and now as she sat smartly on the edge of the chair, her short carapace of hair as shiny as plastic, I liked her even less, and I did what I am certainly capable of doing when required: I lied. I told her that I noticed no difference in her former husband, no change at all.

I knew with certainty that there was danger when one afternoon in April he leaned forward over his coffee and withdrew a sheet of type paper from the pages of his textbook. It was a horrid thing to see, the perfect stanzas typed in the galloping pica of his office Underwood, five rhyming quatrains underneath the title "To Laurie." It was fire, it was flower, it was—despite the rigid iambic pentameter—*unrestrained*. It was confession, apology, and seduction in one. I clenched my mouth to keep from trembling while I read it, and after an appropriate minute I passed it back to him. He was eager there at the table in the Pantry, beaming again. He had begun to beam everywhere. He wanted to know what I thought.

"It is very, very good," I told him quietly. "The metaphors are apt and original, and the whole has a genuine energy." Here I leaned toward his bright face. "But Hartwell. Don't you ever, under any circumstances, give this to a student."

"I knew it was good," he said to me. "I knew it. Do you see? I'm writing again."

"Do not," I repeated, "give this to Laurie. You will create a misunderstanding."

"There is no misunderstanding," he told me, folding the poem back into the old maroon book. "It is a verity," he said. "I am in love."

As everyone knows, there is nothing to say to that. I stirred my coffee and saw from how high an altitude my friend was going to fall.

~

April is a terrible month on a campus. This too is a verity. Every pathway reeks of love newly found and soon to be lost. It is one of the few times and places you can actually see people *pine*. The weather changes and the ridiculous lilacs bloom at every turning, their odor spiraling up the cornices of every old brick building in sight, including, of course, Old Normal. Couples lean against things and talk so earnestly it makes you tired. Everywhere you look there is some lost lad in shirtsleeves gesturing like William Jennings Bryan before a coed, her dreamy stare a caricature of importance. This goes on round the clock in April, the penultimate month in the ancient agrarian model of the school year, and as I walked across campus that spring, I kept my eyes straight ahead. I didn't want to see it, any of it.

~

Of course, Hartwell and I couldn't be more different. That's clear. But I had a sensation after he'd left that afternoon that reminded me too strongly of when I had my troubles, such as they were. Years ago, a lifetime if you want, a student of mine became important to me. She wasn't like Hartwell's Laurie—at all—her name isn't important, but it wasn't a pretty name and—in fact—she wasn't really a pretty girl, just a girl. She came to my notice because of an affliction she carried in her eyes, a weight, a sorrow.

This is not about her anyway, but about me in a sordid way. I saw what I wanted to see. What I needed to see. She was frail and damaged somehow and I was her teacher. Well, who needs details? It was the same story as all these other shallow memories, some professor off balance and a young person either willingly or unwillingly the victim or beneficiary of it all. My student, this strange girl, received an A for B work, and I waited for her to pick up her term paper a week after the semester ended. Let me explain this to you: there was no reason for me to be on campus, sitting in my office in Normal Hall, no reason whatsoever. I had my door cracked one inch and I waited. Tuesday, Wednesday, Thursday, Friday. On Friday afternoon I was still on the edge of my chair. Just having her paper (which I read and reread, held in my lap as I waited) was enough, and undoubtedly, it would have powered me through the weekend. I am the kind of professor who is in his office more Saturdays and Sundays than he will ever admit. On Friday evening, when I was preparing in my routine way to leave and go home, she came. I heard a step on the stair, the first step which was not the janitor's step, and I knew she was coming. How long could it have taken between the sound of those beautiful footsteps and their pausing at my opened office door? Twenty seconds? Ten? Whatever the time, it was the eon between my young and my old selves. I had a chance, as the old scholars put it, to know my tragic flaw. Not that I'm any more than pathetic, and certainly not tragic, but I came to know in that short moment that I was a fool and that I was about to join a legion and august company of the history of all fools. The girl came to my door and paused and then knocked on the open door. She acted surprised to find me there. She acted as if she expected to retrieve her paper in a box outside my door. I told her no, that I had it. I handed it to her, still warm from my lap. She nodded and averted her eyes and said something I'll never forget. "This was a good class for me," she said. "You made it interesting." And then she turned and touched the rippled floor of Normal Hall for the last time. Without her paper and with no reason to be on earth on Friday night, I became a fool, and in a sense the guardian of fools.

Like Hartwell.

But what could I do? This Laurie was as shrewd as any I'd seen come along. She not only accepted his poem—she'd commented on it. I'd quizzed him on what she had said, but he'd just smiled until his eyes closed, and shook his head. He was so far gone that I had to smile.

But Laurie hadn't stopped there. With no reason whatsoever, she had invited him to the Spring Carnival. There was no reason to do this. She'd already won her victory. Hartwell was absolutely incandescent about it. He was carnival this and carnival that. I should come, he said. Oh go with *us,* he said. It was as if they were engaged. I told him no. It was a sunny spring afternoon in the Pantry, too hot really to be drinking coffee, and I told him no to go ahead, but for god sakes be careful. If you want to know the meaning of effete, just say *be careful* to a fool in love. My advice didn't get across the table.

The Spring Carnival on our campus is a bacchanalian festival. It is designed with clear vengeance: victory over winter has been achieved and this celebration is to make sure. Years ago, it was held on the quad and consisted of a few quaint booths, but it has grown, exploded really, to the point where now every corner of campus is covered with striped tents, and the smell of barbecued this and that clouds the air. I haven't been in years.

But. Hartwell's invitation was tantalizing, and then it was all tripled by something that happened the last week of classes. I was packing my briefcase in my office in Normal when the door opened.

There wasn't a knock or a hello, the door just swung open and Hartwell's Laurie was hanging on it, half out of breath, her blond hair swinging like something primeval. "Oh, good," she said. "You're here. Listen, Downey," she said, using my nickname without hesitation, "Hart and I are going to the carnival and he mentioned you might like to go. Please do. You know it's Friday. We're going to eat and then take it all in." Hartwell's Laurie looked at me and smiled, her tan cheeks not twenty-two years old. "It's going to be fun, you know," she said and closed the door.

Well, an interview such as that makes me sit down, and down I did sit. I took the old old bottle of brandy out of my bottom drawer, a bottle so old my father had bought it in Havana on one of his trips, and I had half an ounce right there. Downey. I was jangled. So she and Hartwell called me Downey, when they called me anything. The prospect of being talked about set part of me adrift.

To the carnival I went.

But I didn't go with them. I told Hartwell that I might see him at the carnival, but to go ahead. It was the last week of classes and I had a lot to read. Friday afternoon I was plowing through a stack of rhetoric papers when—outside my window—I heard the Gypsy Parade, the kazoos and tambourines that signal the commencement of festivities. A feeling came to me that I hadn't had in years. I had heard this ragtag music every spring of every year I'd been in Normal Hall, but this year it was different. It called to me. I felt my heart begin to drum, and I put down my pen like a schoolboy called outside by his mates. It was the last Friday of the school year and I was going to the carnival.

Part of all this, naturally, was a sympathetic feeling I had for Hartwell. Laurie had invited him to the carnival, after all. I was—and I'll admit this freely—happy for him. At the corner I stopped and bought a pink carnation and pinned it to my old brown jacket and I thrust my hands into the pockets and plunged into the carnival. The crowds of shouting and laughing merrymakers passed around me in the alleyway of tented amusements. It was just sunset and the shadows of things ran to the edge of the world, giving the campus I knew so well an unfamiliar face, and I had the sense of being in a strange new village as I walked along. Bells rang, whistles blew, and a red ball bounced past. I saw Melissa, Hartwell's former wife, on the arm of one of our Ph.D. students, eating cotton candy. By the time I'd walked to an intersection of these exotic lanes, I had two balloons in my hand and it was full dark.

I bought some popcorn and walked on beneath the colored lights. Groups of students passed by in twos and threes. They didn't see me, but I know that I had taught some of them. I felt a tug at my arm then and it was Laurie, saying, "Downey. Great balloons!" She had Hartwell by the other arm.

"Yes," I said, smiling at both of them and tugging at the two huge balloons. "They're big, aren't they?"

Hartwell was in his prime. He looked like a film actor and confidence came off him in waves. He wore a new white flannel jacket and a red silk tie. "They're absolutely grand!" Hartwell said. "They're the best balloons in this country!"

Laurie pulled us over to a booth where for a dollar a person could throw three baseballs at a wall of china plates. The booth was being managed by a boy I recognized from this semester's rhetoric class, though he wouldn't make eye contact with me.

"I want you two to win me a snake," Laurie said, pointing to the large stuffed animals that hung above our heads.

"Absolutely," Hartwell said, reaching in his pocket for the money. Hartwell was going to pitch baseballs at the plates. It was a thrilling notion—and when he broke one with his final throw, that was thrilling too.

"Well," I said. "If we're going to ruin china, I'm going to be involved." I paid the boy a dollar and threw three baseballs, smashing one plate only.

We stayed there awhile, acting this way, until on my third set,

Hartwell

I broke three plates, and the boy, looking as shocked as I did, handed me a huge cloth snake. It was pink. Hartwell was right there, patting my back and squeezing my arm in congratulation, and I imagine we made quite a scene, Laurie kissing my cheek and smiling as I handed her the prize. I'll say this now: it was a funny feeling there in the green and yellow lights of the carnival—I'd never been patted on the back before in my life. I am not the kind of person who gets patted on the back, which is fine with me, but when Hartwell did it there, calling out "Amazing! Magnificent!" it felt good.

We floated down the midway, arm in arm after that, until I realized we had walked all the way down to Front Street, which is the way I walk for home. I said good night to them there, Hartwell and I bowing ridiculously and then shaking hands and smiling and Laurie kissing my cheek lightly one more time and calling, "Good night, Downey!" I turned onto Front Street and then turned back and watched them walk away, Laurie tightly on Hartwell's arm. They stopped once and I saw them kiss. She put her hand on his cheek and kissed his lips.

As I moved down Front Street, the noises of the carnival receded with every step and soon there was just me and my two balloons in an old town I knew quite well.

It is not like me to enter houses uninvited. I have never done it. But I was in a state. I can't describe the way I felt walking home, but it was about happiness for Hartwell and a feeling I had about Hartwell's Laurie. I had begun to whistle a lurid popular tune that I'd heard at the carnival. This should tell you something, because I do not whistle. And when I came to Old Tilden Lane, where all the sorority houses are lined up, I turned down.

I'd been to all of the Greek houses at one time or another. Each fall, the shiny new officers invite some of the faculty out to chat or lecture or have tea in the houses, and we do it when we're younger because it counts as "service" toward tenure or we're flattered (we're always flattered), and I had done my canned "English Department" presentation at Tri-Delt years ago.

I found Tri-Delta, halfway down the winding street tucked between two other faded mansions. It was almost ten o'clock. The lights were on all through the house and the windows and doors thrown open. I walked up the wide steps and into the vestibule. Everyone was at the carnival at this hour and I felt an odd elation standing in the grand and empty house.

This was among the strangest things I have ever done as a college professor—wander into a sorority house. But I did. I went through the living room and up the wooden stairway to the second floor and I went from door to door, reading the nameplates. The doors were all partially open and I could see the chambers in disarray, books scattered on the beds and underthings on the floor. The hallway smelled musty and sweet, and the doors were festooned with collages of clippings and photographs and memorabilia so that many times I had to read the notes to discover whose room it was. It was kind of delicious there in the darkened hallway, sensing that hours ago a dozen young women had dressed and brushed their hair in these rooms.

At the end of the corridor, on a dark paneled door, there were several sheets of white typing paper, and I saw instantly that this was Laurie's room, even before I went close enough to read any of it. It was, of course, Hartwell's poetry. The poem I had seen was taped there, along with five others he had typed and not shown me. Now, however, each was scrawled with red-ink marginalia in the loopy, saccharine handwriting of sorority girls. Their comments were filthy, puerile, and inane. Obscene ridicule. My heart beat against my forehead suddenly, and my eyes burned. Through her open door, I saw Laurie's red plaid kilt on the floor next to a black slip. I felt quite old and quite heavy and very out of place.

I fled. I rattled down the stairway, taking two steps at a time, and across the foyer and back into the night. A couple, arm in arm, were coming through the door. They were drunk and I nearly knocked them over. I recovered and hurried into the dark of Old Tilden Lane, where I found something on my hand, and I released the two balloons.

I am a man who lives in six rooms half a mile from the campus where I teach. I like Chopin, Shostakovich, Courvoisier, and Kona coffee. I have a library of just over two thousand books. After these things, my similarities with Hartwell end. He has his life and I have mine, and he is not like me at all. We are lonely men who teach in college. I'll give you that.

The Wife of the Indian
Lucia Perillo

She sees the clown standing in the drainage ditch at the strip mall, wearing one of those Phyllis Diller neon rainbow-colored wigs on its head and a kabuki face that looks like it's been drawn with eyeliner and lipstick. He's waving like a madman, like maybe an accident involving circus trucks has just taken place, his big red mouth gumming around phrases that she can't quite lip-read driving past at fifty.

Hey but no, there's no accident: it's just a clown.

The first time she sees him there's also a storm moving in from the west, lightning bolts shooting across a sky that's as dark and silvery as pencil lead, and each time the flashes arc she can see the clown cower, raccoonlike, pawing his face with his gloved hands so they get streaked with gray and pink. He has the word "Carnival" appliqued across his chest and the same word reversed across his back, so she can read it rightways in the mirror when she passes. She thinks maybe he's advertising some local fair, but she doesn't see a ferris wheel, no Tilt-a-Whirl or Swiss Bob peeking up from behind the berm separating the strip mall from the road.

After a few days of driving by she finally figures out what he's mouthing—Pull Up! Come in!! Hey Kids!!!—not something rational like *why am I standing here in the pissing wet?* This is how curiosity lures her into the Festiva Town Center, which is what they call the strip mall to dress it up a bit, where she discovers that the clown's no more than a shoe store's advertising gimmick. Carnival *Shoes,* for God's sake. Inside she finds a battleground for warring themes—circus, safari, gymnasium, disco. In the center of the store there's a fiberglass elephant roaring up on its hind legs, its front paws or claws or whatever youcallzems forming a hoop that's suspended over a bin full of basketballs painted with the fur patterns of the various great cats. A young man with a microphone stationed in an elevated cage is trying to whip the hordes into a frenzy: *That's right, shoppers, for the next five minutes only we're running one of our carni-value specials on ladies' clogs! Every pair of ladies' clogs slashed to half the ticket price for the next five minutes!* His enthusiasm seems misplaced and possibly threatening, since she's the only person in the store and stands not ten feet from his feet.

"Why don't you get that clown off the road," she whines.

"You don't like the clown?" Suddenly, the boy looks genuinely injured. Like most people in town, she realizes, he's one of the college kids, paid five bucks an hour to stand in the shoe store dressed in a referee's uniform. She wants to ask him something more abstract and intimate, but he will not speak to her except over the microphone.

"In about five minutes it'll be pouring," she says. "Every day I see that clown get soaking wet."

"He's got an umbrella."

"All the clown is doing is freaking everybody out. He's about to cause a major collision, trust me on this." Outside the sky has dimmed to a fearsome color, same as every afternoon she's been here.

"You'll have to talk to my supervisor when he gets back from his break. I don't have any authority over the clown." The kid's voice garbles from a burst of static, which tells her that any minute now the sky is going to plug itself in and start playing like Jimi Hendrix.

Something weird about this town, like right away she suspects that somehow the clown is one of Tony Domenici's handmaidens. *Easy to get spooked when you hear a giggle coming at you from the other side the abyss* is what Tony has to say on the matter, Tony being the kind of guy who would bribe the abyss just to prove himself right. She has to drive down to the strip mall to get the food that Tony eats, mainly little pizzas shaped not like pizzas at all but like miniature egg rolls and if you don't monitor your microwave settings the filling'll sear the roof right off your mouth. There's even a warning on the box, like the surgeon general's warning—*Caution: filling may be hot.*

The frequency of these kinds of warnings makes her think that the world has started clicking together in unsettling ways, though Tony argues that these clicks are just the cosmic tumblers tailing into place here. *Here* being this rinky-dink college town where Tony has scammed a job teaching art. Not 100 percent scam, because the one thing Tony can do besides conning people is paint; even when he's acting like a dickhead she will admit it, though he has no papers that will witness to this fact (she *is* his witness). What papers he needs he's culled out of thin air—a bogus M.F.A. degree, three nonexistent articles about some artist, she forgets who, the one who paints the pope and meat. The résumé looked good Xeroxed on a kind of ivory-colored vellum, and when it didn't work he added one more thing.

Surname Drowningcreek.

So now Tony Domenici is Tony Drowningcreek, born to Nevada's Lovelock Paiute nation. Colleges ate it up like candy and spat it out in perks. Bidding wars. House-hunting trips. She came along as Mrs. Drowningcreek and still can't stop herself from answering the name with "hunh?" The secretaries gaze at her with pleasant but frightened looks, as though she were a woman from a National Geographic magazine walking around with her breasts out.

"Mrs. Drowningcreek?"

"Hunh?"

"You just have to sign here to be eligible for the tuition waiver that extends to all of Professor Drowningcreek's family. You're entitled to up to fifteen credits a semester."

Right. Why not? While Tony performs his voodoo exegesis about the man who paints the meat, she'll take a degree in . . . something. He's pulling down so much money that they can afford to drink cognac and imported bottled beer, goodbye flip-tops, goodbye twist-offs; when they can't find the opener Tony pries the cap off with his teeth. He teaches his seminar on Wednesday nights, so there's nothing to keep them from having sex when the slope of daylight makes her dizzy, Tony scooching her around on the hardwood floors until her bare ass tingles from the splinters. Tony couldn't believe what seven hundred bucks would get you in a mining town that's been depressed for years. Four bedrooms, two acres. "I don't know why we didn't think of this sooner," he says, "For seven hundred bucks in New York you can't even buy the roaches any elbow room."

Best of all, Tony has an excuse to wear his black hair long and ratty without somebody breathing down his neck. They get invited to parties where people show up wearing interesting ethnic clothes, bearing hand-thrown clay pots full of interesting ethnic foods, and when she and Tony get loaded on the free booze their behavior is chalked up as merely interesting and ethnic.

But it's not yet Thanksgiving when this very pleasant small-town life autodestructs, after the department chair makes some pointed phone calls to the Lovelock Paiutes. It isn't the quantity of Tony's body hair that tips him off, not even Tony's Brooklyn accent or his lectures—in fact the students can't get enough of his anecdotes about the men who paint the meat and what they'd snorted and who they'd coupled with in Fire Island discos in the seventies, although the administration wishes his focus were a bit more . . . *multicultural?* No, they never would have stuck a fork in Tony's

Lucia Perillo

scam if he hadn't gotten into an argument with a geography professor at one of those parties where up until then they'd all been having *such* a good time. In and of itself, acute intoxication would not have been cause for anyone's wrath (in fact the men felt obliged to keep pace with Tony to prove they were in touch with their inner "wild man") except that in this case Tony's insisting that Las Vegas is the capitol of Nevada because Las Vegas is the only place Tony has ever *heard* of in Nevada. But this guy keeps lobbying for Carson City until Tony's left with no way of salvaging his own authority except to sock him. And when the chairman, who's seen the whole argument go down, makes his unfortunate little phone call he finds out there are no Drowningcreeks on the tribal registry.

"Damn," Tony says, "I should have known not to pick a name with creek in it. Nevada's got no creeks. How could you let me fuck up everything on a such a tiny detail? I could have called myself Tony Desertleaf."

"No leaves in the desert, Tony," she reminds him.

"Tony Cactustree, Tony Mountainpeak. Something. And where the fuck is Carson City would somebody please just tell me that?"

In the end, Tony makes the best of the fact that his days in this town are numbered and turns scofflaw with a $10,000 car loan from the credit union and a student of his named LeAnne Skylor, a girl who, like certain pro b-ball players sporting the continent of Africa on their scalps, wears a silhouette of her home state as a crew-cut patch on her otherwise shaved head. Unfortunately, it's Wyoming, and when people ask why she's got a square on her head she has to correct them: "It's not a square, it's Wyoming." One day Tony Domenici is talking about this girl with a note of derision in his voice and then the next day he's on the lam with her in his Miata, driving east with the top down (she imagines) while a gray rind of frostbite threatens to engulf Wyoming from all sides. This is Tony's way of getting even, since by not leaving quietly at the semester's end Tony knows he'll make the department scramble for his replacement, and quite possibly the chair himself will have to pick up Tony's lectures. *Then* everyone'll see what a tough act Tony is to follow. What a void he leaves behind him in his wake.

At first, when she found all three pairs of his Levis missing, she couldn't believe it—that Tony would leave her stranded here amidst the mysterious yellow fields of "sorghum," the heartland's equivalent of Soylent Green—while he hightails it one midnight. Back to New York, most likely, where a checkerboard-bald girl and a hairy sleazebag old enough to be her evil uncle would fade into the background just like fuzzy wallpaper. Then later, after she's had a chance to think about it for all of five minutes, she can believe it; in fact, this abrupt getting out of Dodge is eerily familiar from when Tony's real wife was trying to serve *them* with a subpoena. So she knows that there's no use going after him, that he will have already made himself invisible. Shazam, and once again Tony Domenici has bribed the abyss—into narrowing for him while his Miata sails across.

For a couple of days she goes down to the Dollar Store at the strip mall and buys these glasses with decals of Tweetie Bird that make a sound she happens to find consoling when she lets them smash against the floor. And glass by glass she also forces herself to list the items in the plus column. Like that living with Tony meant getting used to black hairs everywhere, in the sink and in the food, which is one of the reasons why she went along with the egg roll pizzas in the first place. And no more girlie underwear turning up in the car, no more chronic migraine from living in her own turpentine stink. Because not just metaphorically he'd used her—after roughing her in as a series of (usually ochre) trapezoids he'd dip her hair in a gallon of oil-based kitchen paint and use it to swab the shadows on her form. And no matter how much rinsing she did, when it was dry her hair always turned into a splay of long stiff spikes. Put that in the plus column: no more madwoman hair.

So in the end when she adds the columns up, she decides just to hang tight. To finish the classes she's started—a scattershot of subjects ranging from Etruscan Art to Scandinavian Literature in Translation. She's old enough to have lodged herself at the top of the pecking order in these classes and easily talks her way out of taking tests. *Mrs.* Drowningcreek. The wife of the Indian. Because they're afraid the laziness that lies behind their preference for the multiple choice quiz will come to light, none of the professors dare to challenge her contention that tests based on rote memorization have sucked the blood from higher education. Instead she writes papers, using the computer that the college threw in as one of Tony's perks, scrolling through page after page while she's flying on these all-night espresso-powered highs. If she speaks a language they cannot understand that's their tough luck; she will not apologize for making a mincemeat of their Eurocentric discourse. The words run like wildfire in her brain, her touch is golden, she doesn't understand a word she's saying yet the professors always give her As because they are afraid of her, that she will file a grievance over anything less. Mrs. Drowningcreek, victim of the Lovelock Paiute diaspora (out of embarrassment, the affirmative action office has kept Tony's predicament hush-hush; there's even a rumor going round that he's at a Mexican Laetrile clinic)—victim of the pogrom instigated by the sons of Rushmore, which has turned the country's rightful owners into permanent wanderers on this earth.

~

After she complains, the clown is history. At the Festiva Town Center, a position near his former post is taken up by Will Work For Food, an older chunky man with a cardboard sign and coveralls. He has the same reddish cast to his skin as the sweet potatoes that the region is chiefly known for now that the coal is gone; she'd never tasted anything like them in New York, but how much of an economy can you stake on sweet potatoes? Will Work For Food made his appearance a few weeks before LeAnne Skylor's, right before Tony was defrocked of all his shtick; every time she's idling at his stoplight, Will Work For Food looks like he's about to burst into tears. She wonders what kind of food he would work for, how much food he would work for, and how come if he's so hungry he's not thin?

These issues become more pressing after the landlord shows up one day, barging into the house without even knocking. At the time she was curled up on the floor in a nest of papers, the computer screen glaring in the as-near-to-darkness as she could get it with the shades drawn in the middle of the day.

"I don't mean to be rude, but the lawn looks like shit, Mrs. Drowningcreek."

"Hunh?"

"The lawn. You and your husband are responsible for raking and mowing."

"I didn't know that."

"Your husband knows it. I was very clear with Professor Drowningcreek."

There's a bad marriage somewhere in Landlord's past that's made her bitter, but neither woman wants to get into it. Landlord has retaliated by moving to some city that her ex-husband cannot spell, like Cincinnati or Chillicothe, and she only comes to town every once in a while to check with the realtors about how the house is doing. Tony Domenici had struck a deal that he'd show the house to potential buyers, but houses stayed on the market in this town for years and the few people who came were scared off when Tony, clad in his underwear and bespeckled with paint, opened the door with his rendition of the greeting *How!*

"My husband's a busy man." She gestures around the empty room as though this will explain Tony's absence. And the absence of everything: they'd never gotten around to buying furniture. When Tony skipped town she put his paintings in a storage locker, fearing that he'd return and steal them back, her only asset besides the seven hundred dollar deposit that will be coming her way so long as she doesn't get too wired and do something stupid and expensive, like put her fist through the sheetrock.

But Landlord's a wind-up toy, still running: "I can't make an eight-hour drive every two weeks just to make sure the two of you are keeping up the lawn. This place looks like a disaster." Blah blah blah blah blah: Landlord is trying to sound like the kind of person who cannot be pushed around. Opting for the same defensive strategy employed by snakes and possums, she lies on the floor until the landlord leaves.

Actually she'd tried to mow the lawn with the rusty push mower Landlord deigned to leave behind. But she has arthritis in the big toes of both feet, which doesn't sound like that big a deal until you consider that every second of every moment of your waking life hinges on some diplomacy on the part of both big toes. Even in bed, the weight of the blanket pressing on them is so unbearable she has to stage a pillow down around her feet. As a result, she walks with the eensy-tiniest bit of a shuffle, which she suspects Tony Domenici has long held against her, her clumsiness stacked against his new nymphet, who is sulky in a Mr.-T-goes-Weimar-Republic sort of way but at least she's agile enough to prance around in platform shoes. Mowing, raking—let LeAnne Skylor perform these chores for Tony Domenici!

But the resounding note left after Landlord's visit suggests that Landlord is serious about this yard thing. Serious enough that she begins to worry whether "bad lawn" would be reason enough for Landlord to withhold the seven hundred dollar rebate. So the next morning, when she's at the Festiva Town Center getting some chocolate Pop Tarts and a liter of Mountain Dew for breakfast, she stops the car in front of Will Work For Food.

The Wife of the Indian

"I have work for you," she calls out.

Will Work For Food does not look excited about the prospect of her charity. In fact the squeaking of his quickened breath stops when she gets out of the car. He says nothing, but looks down at his pudgy hands.

"What's the matter? I'll give you better than food, I'll give you money. All I need is some lousy yard work."

"I don't like yard work," he says quietly.

"Well, what kind of work do you like?"

He shrugs. "Usually they just give me money. Nobody ever wants me to work."

That does it—suddenly she feels whatever normally separates her body's different cavities bursting as her lungs spurt down into her stomach. "Well buddy," she snaps, "this isn't going to be one of those drive-by, fork-over-some-cash deals. This is America, where Lee Iaccocca used to be a household word. And either you're getting into the car or I'm telling the cops that you made a threatening gesture at me."

"What threatening gesture?" The man's lips are aquiver.

She holds up her fist with the thumb poked through. "The fig," she says. "In Sicily this'd be enough to get you killed."

For the short drive home, the man is squeaking again while liquid runs from his eyes. "I didn't know about the fist," he says, "I swear." She tries to console him by saying "Lighten up, I'm telling you it'll be easy" and "I've got pizza" (spoken with cheery ascending notes) and "I'll pay you five bucks an hour, which is ninety cents more than minimum wage in this goddamn state." But when they get to her house, she realizes how big the yard is and curses Tony Domenici for sticking her with the house. The dropped leaves have congealed into a thick mat with the smell and texture of a roadkill after several weeks of rain.

She gets a rake out of the shed and shoves it into his hand. "Just see what you can do, that's all I'm asking," she says apologetically. "If it doesn't work out I'll take you back."

She goes into the house while Will Work For Food makes a few tentative swipes across the ground, the leaves wet enough to ball up on the tines. Inside she finds the bottle of Remy Martin and pours some for herself, thinking *This is what Tony Domenici has reduced me to, drinking cognac from a Tweetie Bird glass.* She lies down on the cool wood of the living room floor and thinks about the old days—two weeks ago—when sex with Tony Domenici had left its splinters in her haunches. He was her hairshirt, her lumbering sasquatch, her Sitting Bull, her spaghetti western. When she curled against him the fur on his back was thick enough to throw off sparks . . .

She isn't sure how long she's asleep, or even if she's asleep or only daydreaming, but suddenly she becomes aware of the missing *screech screech screech* that's not coming from Will Work For Food's rake. In a benevolent mood, she half-fills a tumbler with cognac for him and makes a sandwich out of ham. These she brings outside, where Will Work For Food is dozing on a small pile of leaves.

"Here," she says, nudging him with her foot. "Remy Martin. See what the Protestant work ethic can get you?" He gulps eagerly from the tumbler and makes the sandwich disappear in three easy bites.

"Thank you ma'am." He wipes his mouth with his shirt sleeve and hands her the tumbler.

"Don't call me ma'am."

"Okay," he says.

"Call me . . . " She realizes that Will Work For Food is disinclined to this exchange of names. "Call me Mrs. Drowningcreek."

"Haw haw," he laughs. "Haw haw haw." With a handkerchief from his pocket he's mopping up his face.

"What's funny?"

His face goes slack when he sees she's irritated again. "Nothing," he says. "I just never heard of a name like that."

Once Will Work For Food is back on his feet, she goes inside again and refills his tumbler and drinks from it without even wiping the rim. The floor is the only place to lie down, but even if she had other options it'd be the place she'd pick because it makes her feel connected with something hard and therefore permanent. She'd go outside and lie right down on the ground except that Will Work For Food would be able to see her drinking. Then she realizes that he wouldn't *care* if he saw her drinking, but he'd want to drink too— that's the democratic spirit. And then Landlord would be back to blow more hot air up her ass, and if Landlord ever got off her jag about the lawn she'd be on to other topics, like where *is* Tony Drowningcreek anyway and who *is* this guy in the backyard and why *is* the house completely empty? Actually, she decides, it's better empty: the memory of his paintings disturbs her, to think of how cavalierly she'd exposed her breasts. She remembers his big hands on the base of her neck and how erotic it seemed at the time, though now she considers the harshness of his grip as he steered her head around the canvas. And when he released her wasn't it always with a little shove, a small act of violence like breaking the brush to signal the painting's finish? So his exodus with LeAnne Skylor meant more than the usual trading-up for younger snatch; it also signaled a sea change in his technique. He would get a new sort of smear from her smooth skull, another from the crewcut Wyoming patch. It would be like having the Doublemint twins at his disposal: two, two, two women in one.

Now there's no screech-screech-screech outside, and when she looks out the window she sees that Will Work For Food has once more fallen asleep on his pile of leaves. "Jesus," she says, and this time goes outside without her offerings of peace. "Hey," she says, wishing that they had exchanged names after all when she realizes that his color is off. A kind of gray verging on indigo. She doesn't even have to get close to him (he smells, not bad but bad enough that she is grateful for the leaves) to figure out that he's not breathing. In his pocket—she tells herself she's looking for a wallet, someone to call—she finds a wad of bills that she can't quite stop herself from counting. Ones mostly, a few fives, the occasional twenty—all together it adds up to over four hundred bucks.

She puts back a few of them and feels like someone leaving coins on the eyelids of the dead.

~

After calling 911, she brushes her teeth, gargles, washes the Tweetie Bird glass and puts the bottle of cognac in the cupboard along with what she imagines is the whole of Will Work For Food's estate. The cop, who arrives first, turns out to be one of those young men whose athletic build looks a bit too aggressively worked at, and in his voice she detects the kind of muted hostility that comes from being blue-collar in a college town. Still, he is cordial to her, and when he gets to the part in his filling out of forms where she's required to give him her name, she has to spell it.

"Domenici," he says. "Is that Italian?" He pronounces it the way most people do around here—eye-talian—and she nods her head, considering the necessity of covering her tracks. They're standing in the yard waiting for the volunteer ambulance to show, and fortunately Will Work For Food has expired with his eyes closed, so neither of them has to touch him beyond the cop's verification, using the wrist pulse, of her assessment that the man is dead. She doesn't even have to give the sob story she's prepared about Will Work For Food's demise—turns out the cop knows him. Not well enough to know his name, of course, but occasionally the cop had to go out to the Festiva Town Center to tell Will Work For Food to move along. Now the cop smells the liquor on the man's breath and shakes his head. "These people. You'd think someday they'd realize that their lives'd be a *whole* lot easier if they just went out and got themselves a job like you and me."

In Loco Parentis

Gillian Kendall

For months afterwards, I had the sense that I was being questioned
by reporters, or addressing a judge: *For the record, Your Honor, the
accident was not my fault. I plead not guilty. . . . And I was not in
love with her!*

First of all, I could not have fallen in love with Laurel. Besides being too young, my student, and not (or not yet) a lesbian,
she was not my type. With her round face, her long twiddles of hair,
and compassionate eyes, she seemed like a nun.

The engraved numbers on the headstone look symmetrical
and silly: 1978–1998.

Laurel was not the type I am at thirty-five, the type of professor whose face is perpetually sunburned, never tanned, whose hand-
outs emerge from the printer askew, whose voice-mails go unan-
swered. Nor was she the square-shouldered, forward-looking,
strong-cheekboned type of women I struggle across dance floors
for, place personal ads in search of, and talk too much about after
they have left me.

Laurel could not leave me. Being a double major on honors
scholarship at the rich kids' college where I teach the paltry wom-
en's studies offerings, she had to take my classes nearly every term,
for what should have been a neat four years. But during Christmas
break in her senior year, while housesitting for me, Laurel attempted
to drive my car over hail-slick streets to her boyfriend's house, and
by the time the EMTs, police, and firefighters reached her body, her

beer-diluted blood had seeped into her daypack and stained the up-
holstery. Empty Rolling Rocks lay in the back seat. The bottles,
along with Laurel, had come from my house.

Laurel was survived only by her father, whom I had met the
previous spring. I had been summoned to the dean's office, where
Laurel's father, Mr. Anderson, sat leaning forward in the good leather
chair, stomach spread between his legs. Clumps of grizzled hair
grew over his ears, which stuck out from his papery, old-man skin.

When I walked in, his coarse eyebrows shot up: apparently I
was not what he'd been expecting. No army boots, no crew cut, no
visible tattoos (he couldn't see the orchid twining on my left shoulder). I should have lipsticked a big lavender *L* on my forehead, I
suppose.

The dean—a neat, long-closeted little man who had his soft
red hair cut in a way that made him look younger, and he knew it—
had sent me a heads-up e-mail. Now we were meeting for the requisite "candid talk." After the preliminaries (we remarked about the
decibels generated by two juniors playing drums on the quad, and
ruefully discussed the poor soundproofing of old buildings) we
came to the opening arguments.

Mr. Anderson breathed through his nose, gathering pressure.
"I am grateful," he began, as flatly as possible for a Southerner, "for
the time you have given my daughter. She tells me that you have
taught her more history than she acquired in all of high school. You
know she went to Rosemount."

I hadn't known—Laurel didn't brag—but I nodded to show
that I was impressed.

He continued. "I have read some of her papers—when she
shows them to me, you know." A contrived chuckle and fraternal
nod to the dean. "I thought her paper on that woman abolitionist
was very good. Not that it's my field, of course." He sighed. "But it's
just that . . ."

Sensing the onset of sincerity, I tried to listen well.

"She has told me that she is aware of certain aspects of your personal life, your . . . I don't recall what word she used."

"*Orientation?*" the dean offered. I looked over to see if he might wink at me, but the man made seventy thousand a year.

Relieved, Mr. Anderson nodded. "And I am concerned."

His face turned to me, heavy and flaccid, and I looked back hard, seeking evidence of love for Laurel, seeking connection. His eyes were tight gray stones, but sometimes stones crack.

"I know very little about higher education," he went on, "but I know better than to question the integrity of the professors here." A pause.

Into the silence, I murmured, "That's good." It didn't seem the right response, somehow. I crossed my ankles but forced my arms to stay open. "I'm sorry that you're uncomfortable. How can I . . . What can I say that would make you feel more . . . comfortable?"

He wheezed, and a hoarse, tobacco-scented cough came out of him. He looked and sounded ancient, but he wasn't: Laurel had recently mentioned his sixty-fifth birthday. I felt embarrassment for him, almost pity. He raised to his mouth a clean linen handkerchief—the same kind that Laurel brought out whenever someone was crying. This man had wiped her tears, fed her oatmeal, paid fees for the private school that helped her win the scholarship to the college. He clearly wanted what was right and good for her, as he saw it.

"Mr. Anderson," I said, "your daughter is the best student at this college. I'm sure you know how brilliant she is. It's an honor to have her in my classes. She's a leader, she's wonderful in class discussions, and her papers are so good I use them as examples for other students. She and I do have an unusually close relationship; it's true. But please—" I sounded desperate. I leaned forward, feeling foolish in front of these significant men. "I hope you don't think for a moment that anything improper has gone on. I would never, ever do something like that. I am Laurel's *mentor.*" I thought, *Please,*

please, don't take her away. Pretty often she is the reason I get out of bed in the morning.

The dean shifted in his chair, suddenly alert. "I believe Mr. Anderson is concerned about Laurel's need for a role model," he said, cryptically.

"I don't understand." I looked from the dean to the older man. Did he think queerness was contagious? "What are you hoping I will . . . model for her?"

Southern distaste for being explicit showed in Mr. Anderson's face. "I would like for you to model the Christian values we have tried to teach her." He looked at me, pausing, waiting for me to agree.

I could neither confirm nor deny my ability to model Christian ideals. "How would you want me to go about doing that?" I said, as politely as possible. "I mean, it's a little late for me to pretend I'm married."

He leaned back, and I felt I had won a point. If the dean had led Mr. Anderson to think I'd crawl further into the closet, produce a finacée, or fake a conversion to the Baptists, well, he'd been disabused now. My loyalty to the college and my desperation for a job didn't extend to telling lies, especially not to students I cared for.

The dean flattened his palms against the wooden desk. "Perhaps there is a win-win solution here," he said. "I think there was another concern that we hoped you could help with, Libby." Turning, deferential, impeccable, to Mr. Anderson, he said, "Would you like to mention that other matter?"

Mr. Anderson drummed the arm of his chair. Finally, he said, "I assume you are familiar with the young man Laurel keeps company with." Sighing through his nose, he continued. "It isn't that I dislike the boy; it's just that, in my opinion, she is too young to be spending so much time with him. I have reason to believe she sometimes spends the night at his apartment, off campus." His thick fingers tapped silently. "Her mother would not have wanted it. Laurel won't listen to me, but her mother would have convinced her not to do that."

Her mother. Of course, I thought. Raising Laurel alone, he worried about the lack of feminine influence in his daughter's life. He wanted me to guide Laurel, the way her mother would have. He wanted me, as the state would have it, *in loco parentis.* In place of parents. Or in this case, in place of Mama.

"Would you like me to talk to her about that—about staying at her boyfriend's?" I asked. It certainly wasn't in my job description, not even under the loosest interpretation of "advising," but if Mr. Anderson wanted me to warn Laurel against heterosexual coupling, I'd oblige.

~

Your Honor, ladies and gentlemen of the jury, I thought I was doing everything right. Even the time some students came to my house for an end-of-semester dinner, and Laurel stayed on after the others had left and told me that she had kissed a girl, another student, both of them drunk, on a dare—even that time, despite our both having had some wine, and even though she ended the story with, "It wasn't a very good kiss for me. . . ." leaving the silent suggestion hanging in the air that I, being older and smoother and softer, could offer her a better one, one with all the lesbian womanness of real adult women kissing—even then I refrained. Despite the Merlot and her glimmering look and the suddenly romantic candles, I looked at the tablecloth (not at Laurel's mouth) and said lightly, "So, how was it for her?"

Laurel laughed and said the other girl hadn't even remembered it the next day. Then she went on to discuss hangover cures, and the moment had passed.

I never even fantasized about her.

At the end of the fall term of her senior year, Laurel strolled across the creek from the dorms to faculty row, where I lived, carrying a paper plate full of warm chocolate-chip cookies from the school cafeteria.

"When I used to housesit for my parents," I told her, "I always had parties. So, it's all right with me if you have people over. Just keep it small and quiet, OK?" Laurel was leaning on the kitchen island, watching me pack the espresso filter with fine black coffee grounds.

"Sure," she said, "I wouldn't want to scare the kitties."

"Or the neighbors," I added, wrestling with the long-handled filter until it clunked into place. I would give Laurel a few dollars a day to baby-sit Hope and Glory, my two spoiled domestic shorthairs, but even without payment she'd have preferred spending her Christmas break at my place to the isolation of her father's farm. He lived on 150 acres of peach trees several hours out of town. Besides, Laurel didn't trust her decade-old Volvo, Rusty, to lumber up and down those hills very often.

"Where are you going?" Her grainy voice seemed to belong to someone older. Perhaps the Marlboros she smoked were deepening her tone. But her voice lilted, too, as if she had once lived in the Scotland of her ancestors.

"Chicago," I said. "But it's a secret. I'm interviewing for another job—please don't tell anyone."

"Another job!"

I peered at the stream of black coffee pouring into the espresso cup. "Oh, it's no big deal. Probably about eight million people applied. They're interviewing finalists on campus. I doubt I'll get it." I had been visualizing the move to Chicago so hard I could taste snow and real scholarship. I was ready for wind and winter and a respected women's studies department. I wanted to live where queers outnumbered Baptists. I'd sent résumés out to any city with decent gay bars; anywhere without churches looming at every intersection, anti-Halloween movements, and landlords who sent part of my rent to the radical right. I missed coffeehouses, independent

bookstores, vegetarians, and liberals. I hated greens and grits, barbe-
cue and beer.

*I kept beer in the house for guests, Your Honor. She was al-
most twenty-one!*

Laurel shook off her jacket, pulled a rumpled ponytail from
her collar, and pushed up her sleeves. In the cool months, she wore
layers of clothing—turtlenecks and overalls and flannels several
sizes too big. I kept to myself the fact that she dressed like a New
England dyke—the kind with an organic herb garden, too many
cats, and a long-term girlfriend in a wheelchair.

She leaned against the microwave, chin on hand. "I can't imagine this place without you—the college, I mean."

Too pleased to reply, I opened the freezer and took out a plastic bag that rattled with frozen coffee beans. "I stocked up on your
drug of choice. I even got you some of Jamaica Blue Mountain.
Ever had it?"

She shook her head. "They don't serve that in the cafeteria."

"It's even better than Kona, and slightly cheaper." I closed the
freezer and opened the fridge, displaying a bottom shelf full of six-
packs. "I also got Rolling Rock. I know that's what you live on when
you're here: beer and coffee."

"Oh, I ate some of your chocolate last time. It was good."

I handed Laurel my extra car key, an indication of trust. "In
case Rusty goes into one of her periods of decline, you can use the
Honda."

"Hey, thanks," she said. "That's a relief. She's been having a
little transmission problem. I've been in denial about it, but Devon
drove her the other day, and he noticed it. But I won't use your car
unless I have to."

"No problem," I said, feeling almost maternal, and began
steaming milk for her latte.

In Loco Parentis

Having spent nearly three hundred dollars on my charcoal gray suit, I spent another forty to have the Chicago Midway Marriott stylist arrange my hair in a professorial bob, neither rigid nor sexy. At 9 A.M., dressed up, made up, and tense, I took a taxi to the campus.

The women's studies department occupied an old science building that retained the chemical aura of objectivity. A metal sink filled the corner of the secretary's office, and the walls were a cool, flat green. Sitting in a vinyl chair, waiting for the head of the department, I held my stomach in and prayed.

Dr. Hudson opened her office door at ten after ten. She was plump, tall, and ungainly. Despite the presence of a wedding ring on her finger, I liked her immediately, maybe because her office looked worse than any I'd ever seen. Piles of papers on the floor towered higher than my head, like stalagmites. We had to weave through them to reach her desk—actually two desks, placed back to back, both overflowing with mounds of folders, flyers, and books. "What You Need to Know about Breast Cancer" peeked out from a stack of purple brochures on queer studies. My kind of woman.

A phone rang, and Dr. Hudson's lips parted as she looked around. "Oh, I know who that is. I need to get it." Dr. Hudson wedged the receiver under her chin, saying, "I'm so glad . . . What? . . . Oh, I'm sorry to hear that." She held a fountain pen in one hand and a huge planner in the other.

I leaned back and breathed, visualizing dropping by this office and leaning in the doorway to ask a question or make a witty observation for which she would never be too busy. If I got this job, what a good, community-building, team-playing, academic lesbian I would be.

Dr. Hudson hung up, wrote something down, and then came and sat by a stack of newspapers on a love seat. Smiling across about two hundred books, she said, "I'm so glad to meet you in person." She said she knew the college where I taught, and wondered why I'd want to leave it.

I'd discussed this issue on the phone, but this time I came nearer the truth: "I like my job where I am—at least, I love the students. I love my classes. But Montgomery is . . . I'd like to teach and work in an atmosphere that's more liberal and open-minded." Did I need to add, state, scream, *I am a dyke! I need out of the closet?*

Dr. Hudson praised a paper I'd given the year before, then asked about pedagogy. I sat up straight and answered smartly. I looked right into her eyes and talked lesbian theory. "My students have trouble with some of the French stuff," I said, "but everyone likes Adrienne Rich."

She smiled. "Where would we be without Adrienne?" She pronounced the name the way I had, the French way. I took it as a sign.

The interview lasted all day, after which I returned, limp but optimistic, to my hotel. As I was packing for the flight back to Alabama, I called work to check my voice-mail. The first message was from campus security.

～

Usually when I arrived home from a trip, all the booze in my house would be gone, and in its place would be a three-page note in Laurel's eccentric, curlicued handwriting, containing among flowery observations on life in my home, apologies and offers to pay me back. To make amends, she left pints of Ben & Jerry's, sometimes partially eaten, always chocolate.

I imagined that, in my absence, my house saw little parties where Laurel would forget about her glass of chablis, while the young men who hung around her like satellites guzzled. I hoped she drank sanely, perhaps a beer in the evening while she perused my journal, which I hid uncarefully in a sock drawer. The few times she had eaten dinner with me, she had drunk exactly as much as I: not much. Sometimes her own journal entries—written for class and turned in for a grade—referred to hangovers and wild parties, but few students' didn't. Should I have worried? Could I have known? *Your Honor! I would never have let her drive after drinking!*

⁓

When I got home, I was surprised not to see my Honda in the driveway—then I remembered. It had been totaled, thus creating an insurance nightmare as well as limiting my transportation options, but at least I would never have to see the car Laurel had died in. I imagined a mess of twisted metal, the pungent stains of human debris, shards of windshield, shards of bone, shards of dark green glass.

I had stocked Rolling Rock because I was too cheap to buy imported beer, which she might have drunk more slowly. My cheapness, along with my indulgence, had killed Laurel. My beer had killed Laurel; there should have been no alcohol in the house. (If I had not left beer, though, she would have brought in tequila.) My stupid little car killed Laurel. If I'd driven a Volvo, like the one her father had bought her . . .

My dining-room table held a jumble of clean, unfolded clothing. An inside-out black sweater lay curled like a cat on the couch, and on it she had left her reading glasses.

I picked up the glasses and looked through the frames where her eyes used to be. Those tortoise-shell ovals made me see her whole face behind them. In class, I could always turn to her for a thoughtful answer. When silence filled the room, she would speak. And when someone else was talking, she'd listen, looking through those glasses, giving the person her full attention.

My answering machine had recorded part of a conversation. A male voice said, "Hey, Laurel, are you there? If you're there, pick up the phone. Come on, I know you're there. I'm just going to keep talking and talking—"

Laurel's voice cut in, sleepy and struggling: "Hello. What? Oh. Hey."

"Are you asleep? It's only nine o'clock. I thought you were coming over. You want me to call back later?"

"No, I have to get up. I shouldn't have fallen asleep, I—" The machine clicked off, and I wondered whether I should save those inches of tape, for a time when the timbre of her voice would have left my memory.

As I moved through the house—unpacking my garment bag, doing the few dishes she'd left in the sink—I kept expecting to turn around and see her, perhaps coming from the shower wrapped in my robe, or shading her eyes to peer in through the screen door. It felt as if I needed to return the basil plant she'd brought from her dorm room, or call her to come and collect the books and CDs she'd left.

On the night table lay a novel by Charles Bukowski. Indulgently, I had let Laurel do a paper on him—specifically, his implied attitudes toward women's sexuality. Had that book made her think that she, the five-foot-two girl who went without food, the air-child, fey little Laurel, could drink as that horrible, hulking man had done? I hated Bukowski more than ever, now that he'd killed Laurel.

~

The funeral happened fast, only two days after I got home. Alabama's despicable sun shone as if for a spring wedding, and nearly every member of the faculty—more than a hundred of us—and scores of students interrupted their Christmas breaks to attend. Dozens of Anderson relatives and friends crowded the big Baptist church, as well. The gaudy white lilies and chrysanthemums, the tailored black and navy everyone wore, and the preacher's deep, down-home voice all seemed ungodly foreign to me, something Laurel would have written ironically about in her journal.

I had not wanted to go to the viewing the night before, to see little Laurel laid out, but I had gone anyway, thinking I would simply speak to her father and then leave. But I arrived so early that almost no one was there, and it would have seemed rude to ignore her. So I had to walk by the pale blue coffin and peer through blurred vision at Laurel, who looked neither asleep nor peaceful, but very still and made up.

A solid throb rose from my chest, blocking speech and making me flush. The ache felt all the worse for being secret. No one, I thought, could know how much I had adored Laurel. It was unseemly and inappropriate to think so highly of a student, yet I would never give up the sweater she had left at my house. I looked forward even more to leaving the college, because there was no point in being there without Laurel.

I was sitting at the back of the room, trying not to let my crying become vocal, when Mr. Anderson loomed over me. I had already shaken his hand and murmured sincere condolences. What more could he want?

"I wonder if you would have dinner with me one evening," he said quietly. "I know that our last meeting was somewhat unfortunate, but I would appreciate it if you would be kind enough to enlighten me about a few things."

Oh, god, I thought. *He's going to have me arrested for giving beer to a minor. He's going to have me fired, then tortured and killed. He thinks—he knows—that it was all my fault.* "Of course," I choked out, tears drying on my cheeks. "I'd be happy to."

⌒

A week later, Mr. Anderson and I met at a restaurant I could never afford: the Montgomery Inn, an old hunting lodge remodeled in "Ye Olde" style and settled smugly into the side of the city's best hill. As I drove into the entrance, the rearview mirror revealed a slice of the black-and-silver cityscape below, twinkling and empty.

Battalions of mums lined the Inn's driveway, at the peak of which BMWs halted and valets in ill-fitting caps relieved patrons of the chore of parking. Brake lights flashed red in the cramped lines of traffic snaking up the slope. I parked my rented car on the sidelines.

Standing by the hostess's table, I watched well-heeled Montgomerians bundled against the fifty-degree weather totter in to spend inherited money. I waited for Mr. Anderson the way you wait after being pulled over for the police officer to belly up to your window and demand your license. Red and white lights flashing, flashing, flashing.

The flashes were coming from a Christmas tree. It wasn't a real holiday tree, with boughs bearing Santas and angels; just a potted ficus strewn with little white bulbs. They flickered; that was all. The red was coming from outside, from the flashing brake lights. Brakes plus ficus equalled Merry Christmas, no more Laurel. Was I losing my mind?

Mr. Anderson pushed through the doors chest first, kitted out in an old, fur-lined coat. Laurel had been vegetarian. Usually I forgot, and left food containing meat in the fridge for her; I'd come home to find ten-day-old chicken tortellinis rotting in the Tupperware. She wouldn't even eat mushrooms in case fungi were sentient.

Despite the mink or muskrat around his throat, Mr. Anderson looked frozen, his cheeks pink and stiff. *Perhaps the heater in his Caddy doesn't work,* I thought, and then mentally slapped myself. This man could use some comfort, and, for all his flaws, he had raised Laurel. After he removed his gloves, I shook his frigid hand, trying to press back, but his palm engulfed my own. Too late, I considered kissing his cheek, dutiful and daughterly.

"Nice to see you, Elizabeth," he said.

Try "Libby." No one uses all four syllables. I started to say it was nice to see him, then thought of complimenting his ostentatious outerwear. What came out was "Nice to see your coat. Fur, isn't it?"

Something sparked in his eyes, but Southern politeness prevented him from laughing. Nodding, he patted my arm and told the hostess, "I'd appreciate if you would get us seated as soon as you can."

Was he anxious for predinner drinks? If so, then it might indicate that he was an alcoholic, or at least someone who managed tension with drink, and thus I could blame his genes and him, not myself—*in loco parentis* though I might have been—for Laurel's habit. But when the waiter asked if we cared for anything from the bar, Mr. Anderson passed, saying he'd have wine with dinner. Although I wanted a gin and tonic, I requested seltzer. After the waiter left, I kept my eyes down, studying the pink linen napkin I was twisting into knots below the table. *This is ridiculous,* I thought. *Breathe. Look at him.*

Mr. Anderson was gazing out the window, not focusing on anything. It was the most uncomfortable silence I had ever endured. Everything I could think of to say was inane: *Chilly night, isn't it? Sure is dark out there. Do you miss Laurel?*

Then I remembered a trick from teaching. At the start of a new class, when you ask the first question, there will be silence as the students wait to see if you really want them to answer. The silence will last a long time, and it will seem longer to you than to them. To resist breaking it, you count inside your mind. And so I began counting. I got to thirty before Mr. Anderson spoke:

"I'm sorry," he said, "if I appeared ungrateful the last time we met, at the college. I hope you can understand that, as Laurel's only parent, I have made some mistakes. I never expected that I would become my child's sole guardian. In my day, fathers were not involved in child-raising. When my wife died, I thought of sending Laurel to live with her aunt, because I felt supremely inadequate." He set his hands—large, clean, and white—at the sides of his plate. "But I couldn't, Elizabeth. She was so bright, so dear, that I wanted her near me. And so I have muddled through the last ten years without a mother for her. She has never seemed to me to be permanently damaged by the loss."

It was an odd place to stop speaking, but I realized that he was seeking reassurance. "She seemed very stable and well adjusted," I said, although I knew that, at times, Laurel had visited the dark land of despair. Most students went there occasionally, but she had gone further than most and had stayed longer. Still, I thought she'd done so with grace. Her emotion at those times had not been depression, but a pure grief, like that of a little girl missing her mother. "She was very healthy."

When the bread and my drink arrived, we moved into the safe territory of praising the dead. He asked me to tell him about his daughter. "Anything," he said, loudly enough that the couple at the next table turned their heads, thinking he had addressed them. "I would like to hear any details you can give me, even the most mundane. I'm sure that sounds foolish."

"No, it doesn't," I said. "I understand. You want to be in touch with as much of her as you can be." I sounded too counselorish, too much like an advisor seeing a freshmen through a crisis—but, freshman-like, he nodded, the rims of his eyes red.

Since Laurel had been about my favorite human being on earth, certainly in the southeastern United States, it was easy to remember anecdotes. As I spoke, Mr. Anderson neither acknowledged nor attempted to suppress the translucent streaks descending his cheeks. They were like breathing.

I dipped a crust into a glossy plate of olive oil and told him how I had first encountered Laurel:

One of the fraternities on campus held an annual festival called "Southern Splendor." For a month or so beforehand, the members had to grow beards. In class, they'd slouch in their chairs, their blank, rather stupid faces temporarily distinguished by Lincolnesque whiskers.

Their dates would come to the big weekend bringing corsets and long plantation-style gowns. For two days the partygoers would listen to an all-white band play Dixieland. They'd roast a pig, smoke cigarettes, and drink. They drank Jack Daniels, kegs of Bud,

cases of Heineken, bowls of lightening blue punch made with grain
alchohol, and frozen margaritas. They had tequila shots with lemon,
vodka Jell-O, and glow-in-the-dark shooters. The empties piled up
in hills beside the house, and the girls tried not to stain their grand-
mama's gloves with crème de menthe or pork grease.

The festivities peaked on Saturday night with the Plantation
Ball. The girlfriends dressed in pastel-colored gowns, and their
beaux bought corsages that matched. Extra booze would be
trucked in from a cider press in Georgia, and someone's brother
flew in from Ohio with sweet corn, still in green sheaths, picked that
morning.

The exhausted undergrads would twirl each other around the
living room in dances their parents had paid good money for them
to learn a long time ago, before the girls had come out, before the
boys had mustered erections.

They used to hold a "slave market," auctioning off kidnapped
professors for charity, until the college—mainly the faculty, pissed
off at losing a weekend evening—stopped the practice in the name
of civil rights and good taste.

Three years before, I told Mr. Anderson, at the height of
Southern Splendor, some thirty students savvy enough to make
their own friends *sans* ersatz fraternity had rented Union uniforms
from a theater company. They assembled themselves into ranks and
marched down frat row in formation, slim blue bodies straight,
steps synchronized.

A few other professors and I stood on the creek bridge and
watched. The pride I felt, hearing the drum move that squadron toward the raucous ball, equalled, I was sure, that of the proudest parent watching her offspring slam-dunk a basketball or play in a sym-
phony. For the liberals on campus, this was Homecoming, and
history said that we were going to win.

The blue-uniformed students marched closer to the "plantation," their expressions humorless and adult. When they reached the

fraternity yard, one of them blew a whistle and called an order; the troops executed a quarter-turn, and the party band stopped. Bearded boys and long-gowned young ladies crowded onto the front porch and balconies, juleps in hand. The two sides stared at each other. Then one of the soldiers stepped forward, unrolling a long scroll of paper, and began to read.

The voice was clear, low, and feminine. Laurel, her hair tucked up under her cap, got halfway through the Emancipation Proclamation, her voice rising as the frat boys threw beer bottles, before the Confederacy rushed the Union Army and tore the paper away.

Sick and scared, I watched frat boys cream peaceniks. In seconds, we went from the Civil War to Vietnam. Some of the professors waded into the fray and started shouting, but history said that we would lose. After the campus security guards arrived, I went home.

❧

Mr. Anderson's tears came heavily, and he pushed away his salad. I felt terrible, wondering whether I should have told that story. The waiter came back to see if everything was all right. Did we want anything? I looked up, unable to focus on his face, and thought that everything was wrong, and that if I wanted anything, it would be to go home to find Laurel's mess and men and a small party in progress.

Mr. Anderson ordered an entree—not because he expected to eat it, I supposed, but because if you invite a person to dinner, you order a meal. "I'll have the same," I said, through a tight, sore throat, and the waiter, embarrassed but sympathetic, left us.

"I don't think anyone really got hurt," I said to Mr. Anderson. "No one hit her. If I had it to do over again, I'd have gone in there and defended her. I didn't know her then, but now, if anyone tried to lay a hand on her . . ."

Of course, now no hands would be laid on Laurel in any way, not in violence or affection, warning or blessing, passion or praise.

"You must hate me," I said miserably. "If I were you, I'd blame me. I mean . . ." I felt Northern and awkward, unable to say a graceful word. "I just want you to know that I know I should never have left beer in the house. It was a terrible thing, but . . ."

I paused, hoping he would interrupt, but he simply narrowed his cold gray eyes, made more human and more desperate by the red streaks.

". . . she drank anyway," I fumbled on. "They all do. I just never thought she'd be foolish enough to drink and drive. She was so young. I overestimated her judgment. I trusted her, but she was too young."

Mr. Anderson nodded once, and let his chin rest near his chest. "I see," he mumbled, and cleared his throat.

He didn't see. I couldn't make him see. I fled to the ladies' room and honked into a coarse paper towel. The evening was turning into a morass of bodily fluids and guilt. This decent man's daughter had died due to my lack of judgment. I pressed my cheek against the gray marble divider between the stalls and opened my jaw wide, screaming silently. A few feet away, people's wives and mothers applied lipstick. If you are a loving person, and lonely, and a teacher, it is easy—and not always wrong—to channel your feelings toward a remarkable, affectionate student. But to let that bond alter your perceptions of that student is a terrible mistake, in this case tragic. I had loved Laurel passionately, beyond reason. And if I had not, she would be alive.

Back at the table, Mr. Anderson was waiting for me to return, and when I did, he picked up his fork and wearily began eating. He would go on, I saw, doing the right thing, the responsible thing, growing peaches, keeping his appointments, sleeping and waking in the farmhouse where his wife and daughter had chattered and cooked and argued and made up; he would go on trying to live a life that no one would want.

"I think about Laurel every day," I said. "Not just every day, but many times a day. You must think of her all the time." *You must think constantly about losing people. You must carry death not on your shoulder but in front of your eyes, like a lens.* I wondered whether I would do that from now on: see every student, friend, student's parent, and enemy through the magnifying, softening spectrum of loss. If I'd known, that day in my kitchen with the coffee and cookies, that it was to be my last conversation with Laurel, would I not have listened more carefully, made her laugh more, and lingered in our hug?

Later, absently, politely, Mr. Anderson asked me, "Where was it that you went—on your trip?"

"Chicago," I said. "To visit another women's studies department." I didn't say that I had been looking for another job, because suddenly I was not anymore. The job in Chicago was not for me now, whether they offered it to me or not. What mattered was the place I was in, the moment I was living through. I knew that I would stay in this town, at this college, and would get to know this man and other students who might one day give me a reason to get up in the morning.

"Let's get dessert," I told a surprised Mr. Anderson. "Something chocolate, that Laurel would have liked. Let's get coffee." What I meant was, "Let's talk."

He smiled for the first time that I had ever seen. "Hell," he said, "Let's get brandy. We've done so much goddamned mourning I can hardly think anymore. Let's celebrate something—Laurel liked to celebrate things."

He knew that! "She did," I said. "Let's drink to your daughter." As I heard my words, I was afraid I'd said something terrible, ruined the brief camaraderie.

But Mr. Anderson was waving towards the waiter. "I think Laurel would approve," he said. "She liked you a lot, I know."

He went on talking. I was looking at him through a lens.

Free Writing
Sondra Spatt Olsen

September 28

What am I doing here, trapped in a grammar class? It would be worse if I weren't the teacher. Students bent over your ragged notebook paper, do you know who you are, and where we are going? Free writing means writing whatever comes into your head. Don't let those pencils slip off your damp little scraps. Don't stop; don't think. If you get blocked, just repeat the same words till you break through.

Free writing will set your creative juices flowing. That's what Mildred, Director of Composition, said. And even if it doesn't, it takes up ten minutes of this interminable remedial hour. Wastes ten minutes, that's what I say, me, Fortune's free-writing fool—eleven years of experience teaching my guts out, but not the Director of Composition, no, not me. Many are called but few are chosen. We also serve who only sit here 'til ten o'clock at night in this windowless building. Teaching the Unteachable. Reaching the Unreachable. It's OK if you really want to do it. But I don't really want to do it.

Must keep busy scribbling, though. Theme paper, smooth, white, available at any stationery store. It's the third night of the term, for god's sake, and how many students made it to a stationery store? Two out of twenty. My brain cells are popping one by one, and if I find free writing hard, how are you faring, poor bastards?

May Mildred be smashed with heavy thesauruses, smitten with

semicolons, crushed by colons. If I get the chance, I'll wring her shallow chicken's neck. False, smug, self-righteous, hypocritical. Oh for a stream of icicles freezing her face! Oh dull housewife with a duplicating machine! She brags like a horse. She's teaching Romantic Poetry tonight in this very building, upstairs where there are snot-green industrial carpets, very chic, while I labor in a bare room, formerly an animal laboratory, drain in the middle of the floor, air conditioning booming off the formica like Victoria Falls.

I fancy I hear Mildred's grating voice through the ceiling, shredding the Odes. Faint melodies are sweet but those unheard are sweeter. I fast, I faint, I die, I try. If you don't like my harmonica, don't blow it. If you don't like my harmonica, don't blow it.

Stop this nonsensical parody of the only world the world has ever known. Get on with your class, Miss Thirty-Two-Year-Old Free Writer. Start the semicolons rolling.

September 30

Now, ladies and gentlemen, ten minutes ago I was crying in the toilet of the East Science Facility. Would that interest you if you knew it? Spinster schoolteacher, tough old birdy, meets long-lost lover in dim corridors of the East Science Facility. Almost knocks him over, in fact, since she, always buxom, has gotten very tubby in her loneliness and frustration, and he, always on the small side, has gotten weedy thin in whatever sick situation he's creating nowadays. Separation obviously isn't good for either of these birds, but after two years do they fall into each other's arms and cuddle, crying, "Well-met, well-met," all hugs and kisses and echoes of old ecstasies?

No, sirs and mesdames, they are cold. "How are you, Ivor?" Cold, cold. "Teaching one course while working on your dissertation?" Fine, good. Still working on your bloody dissertation. Too much screwing; one's vital juices stop flowing. (You told me *I* was preventing you from finishing your dissertation, dog, remember?)

"You, Helaine? Still working on your novel?" Sure, pal, would you like to see it? I've got it here in my back pocket. Just dash it off by candlelight after teaching four overcrowded composition courses. A chapter a day keeps the doctor away. Beats masturbation.

Do we exchange confidences? Relive old frolics? Review lusty quarrels and juicy brawls? No, we chat coldly. You look as distinguished as ever, Ivor. Do you still wear tattered underwear? Still shower with a cap on, like a girl? Still thrash around in your bed like a sardine? Publish essays in the *Pisspot Review?*

Perhaps you saw me crying, sisters. Through the mile-wide crack in the toilet door. I was in the cubicle that locks, sobbing into the corrugated toilet paper. I saw you, Charlene, standing in the spot of peril by the mirror (miraculous gray hair detector), getting cracked by the door each time it opened. You gave me a searching anthropologist's look. Some tribes would rather be seen peeing than crying. I pretended to have a heavy cold, my stiff upper lip like a handball court.

Oh Ivor, why didn't you just put your hand on my cheek and say, "There, there, old duck. If you lose some weight, you can hold out another fifty years"? Or why didn't I just silently kiss your hand?

We want to be happy, but how are we going to do it? My class wants to be happy, but how are they going to do it? We want to be loved, but how are we going to do it?

These questions ask themselves.

October 5

Awake, sluggards! Cast off your multiple choice exams. Throw your textbooks out the window. (But there are no windows here—no matter.) Anoint yourselves with salad oil. Put on your royal bathrobes; the feast of meaningless mistakes is about to begin.

How I wish I had a little cookie to nibble on, meanwhile. To compose myself as I compose. Make little announcements. See all those sleeping, swaying heads bounce up.

"Class, I'm taking next week off to be with my lover. We're locking ourselves in the slop closet with a twelve-pack.

"I'm planning to set myself afire. Forget about the theme paper. Please bring unleaded gasoline.

"No, better, I'm planning to set your assignments afire. If you want the ashes, you must give me a stamped, self-addressed envelope by Thursday night."

Peter Heinz is absent tonight. Peter Heinz is absent; so is José Pereirra and John Incremona. I don't think you can pass the course, young man. Why not, sir or madame? Because you're stupid.

Where is my plagiarist? There he is, slumped in the back row under the coats. A weedy blond. Butter wouldn't melt the scoundrel. Did he think that I'd believe those fine, sensitive moments occurred in *his* childhood? And that sublime final image, the blue rubber ball disappearing into the cloudless sky never to be seen again. A bit of poetry in English 1.5. David Gold with the golden hair. A long history of thievery, I'll wager. Absent from the first impromptu essay, clever dog, and planning to be absent from all future impromptus. A strong, solid style, a little better than Orwell's. A maniac's handwriting. Absurd technical errors (like missing capitals) unimaginatively sprinkled here and there. I'll track this plagiarist down if it's the last thing I do. Catch him inky-fingered. Nail him at the Xerox. I will not be tricked by a stripling. I'll try Orwell first. Haunt the libraries. Leave no stack unturned.

"How pleasant it is at the end of the day / No follies to have to repent / But reflect on the past and be able to say / My time has been properly spent."

October 7

Full Professor, step right in; take a seat in the back. My guardian and my observer, observe me, yes. An amazing display of talent—no relaxation but lots of nervous tension and anxiety to make you feel at home. I'd strip myself naked for you, Stranger, but how will you get it in your Evaluation Report?

"We generally do ten minutes of free writing right at the start to let the creative juices flow, heh, heh, heh."

Such tact! Such wit! Fly with me to the blackboard and see how we go. The true thrill—grade a paper with me. Watch me stalk sentence fragments, pounce on wordy constructions, disport myself among awkward tenses, linger on those ever-loving concrete details. I want to caution you about one thing, however. I always put observers on my Death List.

He looks pretty bored, my keen observer, lolling in the back row, playing with his pencil. No learning takes place here, Buster. Why don't you try an auto school?

October 14

Walking to school from the bus stop today—unspeakable happiness. I floated! I sang! And why?

Because David Gold is alive. He walks, he talks, he exists on this planet. He is sitting before me now, holding his head in his hands, not free writing a bit. All I can see is a grubby green sleeve and some golden hair.

Dear boy. You are my booster cable. I thought my heart had gone dead long ago, but for good or bad, you recharged it for me.

It was his turn for a conference. He sat sideways by my desk, with his lanky legs folded twice over, staring at the blackboard. He had been late; he didn't seem to be listening. I couldn't mention his plagiarism until I had some evidence, and in my frustration I let my contempt show too plainly.

"Losing that rubber ball must have left a big hole in your life," said I scornfully. "Do you always omit capital letters at the beginning of sentences, or do you do it just for me? Have you ever thought of attending Handwriting School?"

He looked straight at me for the first time, flushing, and one bright tear rolled out of one eye. At that moment the rest of the class came piling into the room. "I'll talk to you about this later," I said, turning toward the others. "We're going to write impromptu tonight," I told them impulsively.

They shrank back with well-known groaning noises. "It's not fair. . . ." "Why didn't you tell us?"

"Then it wouldn't be impromptu." I smiled encouragingly. "Don't be afraid. It's only one paragraph." Only your native language. I hurriedly wrote a topic on the board.

Meanwhile David moved back to his seat, turned his plastic chair around to the wall, tucked his head down to his chest, and sat in that furious hidden posture until I called for their work. All the while I sat there, watching him, half-suspecting his paper was going to be blank.

As soon as the classroom was safely cleared, I plucked his impromptu from the pile. One and a half closely scribbled sheets. Describe a concrete object concretely. Almost impossible for a remedial student. I was a sadist to assign it.

David described his Harley-Davidson so crisply I could see it shining before me on the sidewalk. (Still no capitals, but editors can always fix up that sort of thing.) I thought—perhaps he had this magnificent paragraph up his sleeve, would have written about motorcycles no matter what the topic. Perhaps he had assorted plagiarisms stuffed in all the pockets of his jeans. Then I remembered the single rolling tear and his scarlet, vulnerable face, the fury in his hunched-over neck. I read the paragraph again, savoring it. I felt an unfamiliar yet well-known stirring in my chest. (All great things are clichés.) I felt joy swelling up, or perhaps it was pain. Felt something, anyway, instead of dead. I remembered the last time I felt my heart move. I was sitting in the front seat of Ivor's car, parked for a long time in the snow. "You don't seem to understand. I'll put it more plainly," he said. "I don't want to see you anymore."

I will purify myself for David's sake. I will better my life. David Gold exists. For no other reason, I rejoice.

October 19

A class of five. Five little blackbirds sitting on a branch. My brilliant one is not among them.

George, your work has not been good. Achilles, your work has not been good. Everyone else, your work has not been good.

Nobody's work is any good. Except for my darling.

I had today:

2 cups coffee with real milk
1 toast with diet butter
1 midget bagel with peanut butter
1 cup Bran Buds with skim milk
1 roast beef sandwich with lettuce & tomato & a cup of tea

That's not too much. A penitential menu. When I come home, I will have:

1 cup decaffeinated coffee with real milk
1 piece of deskinned chicken, broiled

That will truly be delicious. That's not asking too much. Who am I to ask too much?

He has a girlfriend. How could I have not noticed it? She waits for him every Tuesday and Thursday evening right outside in the hallway beside the elevator. She is short, size three, I'd say, young and nondescript. When he emerges, she falls comfortably into place at his side like his hunting dog, and the elevator closes slowly upon them. They never speak. They are shy. Their utterances are too significant for the general public. She is a deaf mute. How will I ever know what the answer is? Why do I want to know in the first place?

They are probably necking in the backseat of a car right now, her head pillowed on his grammar. No, I am hopelessly outdated. They are screwing.

I am glad he has a girlfriend. I am glad he is screwing.

Face it, Helaine. Don't be a fraud. It's not just that he is a fine student with a good mind whom I will be glad to recommend for the Nobel Prize. Not that he's shy and humiliated and at my mercy. He also has rosy skin and long muscular legs in tight pants. He is a beautiful, desirable young man. And I desire him.

October 21

All you can eat and doughnuts, too. A steaming cup of hot coffee and a cracker. A bowl of chili, reddening your mouth. Plenty of fresh milk and cookies. Sesame crackers and small kegs of beer. Tree-ripened pears with russet flecks on them. Cider and doughnuts. Hot tomato soup with six oyster crackers tumbling on the surface. A bacon, lettuce, and tomato sandwich crunching crisp, especially the lettuce. No soggy greens, please. Two mugs of fresh coffee with cream. A peppermint stick ice cream cone. Twelve cinnamon buns with jelly inside. A hogshead of cream cheese, one-half pound smoked Scotch salmon, and two dozen bagels. Chilled caviar, black ripe Greek olives. Dainty little cucumber sandwiches with the crusts cut off. Rum mulled with cider. A barrel of pickled herring with fresh onion curls. Carrot sticks as a refreshment. Cold Heineken beer, oysters, beets with pickles, a bit of salami and cold tongue on fresh bakery rolls with onion and a quarter pound of sweet butter. Freshly scrambled eggs and toast and a very tiny little bit of ketchup. I give up all of these for you, my chicken.

October 26

I can't help thinking someone is out to get me.

Could it be me? Am I out to get me?

This time I arranged our conference better. Little seminar room not used at this hour. Thirty minutes before class time so we won't be interrupted. I have emptied my papers on the table to give the little cell a homier look. I have muted the air conditioning. I have put his last essay with a big red A in magic marker on top of the pile. Everything to put him at his ease.

He is not at his ease. He does have a pleasant sweet odor about him, which I can't quite place. He has crossed his legs more gracefully this time, but he's still looking at me as though I'm about to take a bite from his rosy flesh. He thinks I am a meat-eating dinosaur—ferocious tyrannosaurus rex—when I am really a shy, love-sick brontosaurus—huge vegetarian with a marshmallow heart.

"You are a talented writer," I begin. "What are you doing in this remedial class?"

"I failed the proficiency exam. Do you think I'm taking this class for fun?" He is still angry with me. He speaks in a thin, waspish, bratty young man's voice. "I failed it three times, if you want to know."

I try not to be insulted. I hate English 1.5, too, so why should I be insulted? Am I teaching it for fun? "You must get terrifically nervous, then," I say kindly.

"I don't know."

"Well, there must be something on your mind when you take the exam."

"I think it's because my mother works here."

Oh, I think. I visualize the refugee daughter of a great philosopher, scrubbing floors in the library. Blond braids pinned upon aristocratic head. All hopes pinned on her son. "Does your mother expect you to do very well? Is that why you're nervous?"

"*You* know my mother. She teaches in this department." A petulant smile tweaks his mouth for an instant before he drops his dynamite. "Mildred Gold." Director of Composition. Administrator of proficiency exams.

The son of Mildred. In a flash I understand everything. Omission of capital letters is, after all, a reasonable act for the son of Mildred. He does pretty much what he wants. Revenge is his reason for living. Does poorly in school because it irritates her. Is lazy. Has gotten everything he's ever wanted. Psychologically unsteady. Poor boy.

Also oddly, in the same flash I understand something about myself. Humiliation is the root of the attraction, but it's *my* humiliation, not his. Humiliating for a grown woman to care about a boy. And now that I know whose boy it is . . . I feel self-disgust oozing up.

He lives in the home of my enemy. Empties her garbage. Shovels the snow on her front walk. Walks her poodle. I've lost all respect for myself. How can I care for the fetcher and carrier of Mildred's petty household domain? Her bootblack.

He was once a speck in her ovaries; he passed down through her birth canal, squeezing her bladder. She wiped his baby ass for him, and he vomited over her when he was sick. These sordid custodial details notwithstanding, he now has the power to hurt me, that is, I now love him desperately. I am helpless and angry, but my fine old poker face does not betray me. From outside I appear calm and beneficent, not even very much surprised.

"It must be hard for you to study a subject your mother teaches, in a program she directs. Why don't you switch to another school?"

"She won't allow it. It's inconvenient."

"What about your father?"

"My stepfather. He does whatever she wants. She's a very powerful woman."

Admiring (spurious) smile on both our faces. Mildred. What do I really know about her? She is always rallying others to her causes. Collecting money for the Big Chairman's wedding present (third marriage, why bother?). Appeals and posters clutter her office. *Sauvez les Trésors de la Nubie. Rettet die Schatze aus Nubien. Salvad los Tresoros de Nubia.* Prevent new coal gasification plants in Navajo Territory. Save our Football Field. Ban the Bomb. Robert Frost's sappy face beams over her shoulder. None of this good work seems native to her. Everything's a front. She works hard to seem

good-natured. Her hostile, stupid eyes twinkle from behind her avia-
tor frames. For some reason, she hates me.

"I could speak to her about it. You really don't belong in a remedial class. You must know it."

He gives me a blank look. A marble-eyed look of elegant
Greek statues. Antinoüs, the Emperor's favorite, whom I also fall for
once at Olympia.

"Of course, I'm very glad to have you in my class," I say
warmly. "I like brilliant people."

Whatever made me think he was diffident? He accepts my declaration with bland indifference. His royal due. "I was thinking of going out west," he remarks.

"Next summer?"

"Next month."

"Oh, please, David. Don't do anything precipitously."

"I'm going by motorcycle. If I go, I have to do it before it's
too cold."

"Does your mother know about this?"

He gives me an "Are you kidding?" look.

"How are you doing in your other courses?"

He looks pleased. Glad I asked. "I'm failing two, math and sociology, and an A-plus so far in the other, in Ivor Braun's class. He
wants me to major in comparative literature. And I don't know
about your class."

"C," I say, just to shake his self-image a little. Exactly like Ivor
to give out A-pluses at midterm, then let you down hard at the end
with a B. Did the same to me once. "You deserve an A, David, for
content and general style, and an F, of course, for punctuation. But
if you sat down for twenty minutes and read your grammar book
. . . Why didn't your mother tell me about your problem? I see her
every day."

"She wants me to be independent."

"I'll bet."

I say it out loud, sarcastically. He doesn't flinch. He doesn't blush. His eyes are green and filled with contact lenses. I hate to mention how long his eyelashes are.

"Don't speak to her about it, please," he says seriously. "Just pass me. That's all I need."

"How old are you, David?"

"Twenty-one." He grins, ashamed.

"So old?" Only eleven years between us. Dr. Johnson's wife was at least twenty years older. He was inconsolable when she died, but kept right on writing his dictionary.

"I dropped out once before, when I was in high school." He leans forward a little, as if telling a secret. I'm enjoying his lovely fragrance. "My mother got me a job with Scribner's, as an office boy."

I think more about Mildred, what it must be like to live under her benevolent direction. I can't imagine what it must be like.

Mildred wears a lot of makeup. She articulates poorly. One of her mimeographed notices began, "Due to a lack of examination booklets . . ." I guess you could say she is vulgar for an academic or academic for a vulgarian. She takes a housewifely interest in paper clips, envelopes, and exam books. She is the chatelaine of the supply closet.

At the end of each semester, Mildred collects a set of essays from one student, chosen at random from each class. They must be submitted in a lightweight, soft-covered binder with metal fasteners. She reads through the papers and makes some trenchant comment. Last term mine said, "Fine!" The semester before that, there was no exclamation point, so I guess I've improved. A few years ago, I taught Creative Writing, which I rather enjoyed, but Mildred thinks I do better with Composition. "We need good people in Remediation," she said good-naturedly. She likes to be chummy. When I stopped seeing Ivor, she said, "I see you've stopped seeing Ivor." When I lost the office key, she said, "Do try and be more careful with this one. I know you're an artist and have published a book, and all that, but . . ."

It's 9:30. The class is looking at me a little bit cross-eyed;

they're tired of writing. David is smiling at me from way back there, flirtatiously peeking at me from under his hands. It's a kind of sweet blackmailing smile, a buddylike smile, most unsuitable for student-teacher relationships. I know you know I'm a gem, that smile says. I've revealed my true identity, like Billy Batson. What are you going to do for me now?

I will close up shop. One final thought occurs to me: the ultimate humiliation. That pleasant, sweet odor I liked so much was, oh help, bubblegum.

October 28

Tonight an unusual show: Ivor and David together. Standing together at the front of the lunchroom, they canceled out each other's good looks. Ivor, of course, seemed much older; next to David's bright head his gray hairs suddenly stuck out stiffly, like brush bristles. He seemed worn, stained, as though seen through a muddy filter. David, on the other hand, without Ivor's authority, looked white and pasty, like a pie taken out of the oven too soon.

I had a clear view but couldn't hear at all. They seemed to be speaking pleasantly enough, but urgently. Why were they all standing up? This was no passing chatter. At one point David thrust out his hands in the incongruous shrug of a Yiddish peddler. He couldn't account for something. What the hell was it? I was torn by curiosity but kept flicking my eyes back and forth mock-casually and, desperate to see, purposely blocked my vision with my upthrust coffee cup. It occurred to me, as it often does, that someone else in the lunchroom might be watching me. I determined to betray nothing to the unknown watcher but felt on reflection that I must look like a frantic bunny, my head swiveling, eyes swimming, my mouth still chewing wildly my already swallowed food. But of course there was no one looking and nothing to be seen.

Oh yes, I forgot to mention that David's girl was present throughout the colloquy, standing silently at his elbow. She impressed me as usual as being very short (She always seems only to come up to David's elbow. His elbow stands out in these scenes.), very dowdy, and vaguely nice. Naturally I never focus on her, as my eyes are engaged elsewhere. I would not recognize her alone.

When the conversation, which took about three minutes, was over, David and the girl walked briskly out of the lunchroom. Now something strange happened, which I have read about in books but never experienced before. Either David put his arm around her as she trotted along at his elbow or else he didn't. I, an alert type, watching with the fixed seriousness of a UN observer, am uncertain. Perhaps they flowed along so smoothly, so adhesively that it looked as though they were connected by an arm, and I seized on this false dramatic detail to remember. Or perhaps there was an arm, and even as I looked at it (this is what I have read about in books), I was unwilling to see it.

November 4

I am not even on campus. I am on Main Street in front of the public library, at least three miles away, when I hear the zoom of a motorcycle. The chances that this will be David are 7,000 to 1, but these days I am thrown into a frenzy by the sight of any motorcycle. It's the ambiguous figure of the helmeted, goggled rider that throws me—the masked rider of the plains. This time the figure I imagine is David *is* David. It must be, because the rider in back is Mildred.

The bike pulls up to the curb for a moment, and she hops off, spry as you please in her denim pantsuit. She's a pretty high kicker for a woman her age; you have to give her credit. Goes to the health club three times a week and steams herself to a pulp. Takes yoga, too. I saw her chuffing away in the lunchroom once, noisily demonstrating how to expel poisonous, used-up air from the lungs. She sent a little poisonous stream my way.

As David roars off, I try melting back against the library wall, but she's spotted me. She hails me excitedly. I wonder whether to bring up David's problems, but, as usual, subtlety is not a requisite with Mildred.

"Well, are you going to pass him?" she asks.

"Mildred," I say diffidently. "Why don't you send your son to another school? It can't be good for him to study under your shadow, so to speak."

Her powerful carbon-arc eyes shoot me a furious look through her glasses, but her mouth continues smiling benevolently. "He's not failing, is he?"

"Mildred," I begin again, "I won't fail him unless he forces me to do it. The trouble is—he's stopped doing his assignments. How can I pass him if he doesn't write anything?"

"Well, I thought if anybody could handle him, you could, Helaine. I can't make him write. I haven't been able to make him do anything since he was toilet trained." She laughs raucously. "What he does and when he does it are a mystery to me. He has his own apartment over the garage. He has his own transportation, his own stereo. You don't know what it's like to have a teenage son these days."

"If David doesn't like college work, maybe he should just be cut loose. He's not really a teenager anymore, is he?"

Mildred is really furious with me now. Or is she in pain? Her face has creased badly in a spasm of some emotion; it's hard for me to tell.

"We've tried that already. He quit a good job in publishing to work at a soda fountain."

The image of David in the guise of a soda jerk is as painful to me as it is to Mildred but for different reasons. Perhaps he has waited on me in a comic-book cap, and I've thought him negligible.

"Helaine, Davey is beyond my control. That's what I'm trying to tell you. How will he get along without his diploma? He can't stay in my garage forever. And he used to be such a bright, cheerful kid." Mildred's voice is breaking. She is actually weeping, her eyes glazed over. She is metamorphosing before my eyes from department tyrant to bereaved parent, and I resent it. Dammit, Mildred, stop sniveling. Stalin worried about his teenagers, too, perhaps.

November 9

He did not come for our conference tonight. He did not give me any assignments. He entered the room all tousled, rain-bedraggled, his jeans soaked up to the knee. Perhaps he'd been stuck on the highway. "David," I called out cheerfully. "You look as though you waded to class." He stalked past my desk, avoiding my eyes.

I rather expected it. Screw you, he's saying. You claim to be my admirer and friend. Prove it. Pass me no matter what I do. Fail me, and I'll go west. Go ahead, wreck my academic career.

I had a fantasy about him the other night. A daydream, that is, I was controlling it. I dreamed he came to my apartment for tea. I dusted especially for him. I bought two cakes from the Dumas Pâtisserie, and I took my Tabriz carpet out of hock.

He brought grass, special high-quality Acapulco Gold, and we sat on the carpet, sharing a joint. In my dream he wore a fuzzy woolen sweater of an unusual orange, something pumpkinlike but more pleasant. All colors were sharp because of the imaginary grass, and I felt myself leaning imperceptibly toward him, till I felt the sweater fuzz against my bare neck. We were listening to Chopin, *Valse Brilliante.*

You think this was prelude to an erotic fantasy? He stroked my neck, I slowly unbuttoned my blouse, my nipples popped out, he unzipped his pants. You are wrong, quite wrong. You know me very little. In my dream I never forgot he was David. In my dream we simply sat in a deep passionate calm; Arthur Rubinstein was doing all the work. Then David said solemnly, "Thank you, Helaine, for a very happy moment. Don't get up: stay with the music." He left the package of grass on the table and went away, and I never saw him again.

He is absent again. He is not here tonight. He is absent again. He is not here tonight.

Freewriting freewriting freewriting because I'm so afraid. I have to hold my face together.

She came in, the girl, just now while I was writing, and said, "Here are David Gold's assignments. He's sorry they're so late."

I stare at her. "Where is David?"

"He said please excuse the handwriting. He was nervous; he had to write them on his wedding day!"

"His wedding day!"

She giggles. "We were married this morning at City Hall and tomorrow, if he finishes his paper for Comp. Lit., we're going to California." She giggles again, a cheerful young girl.

I stare at her harder. She looks wholesome, a nice friendly face, too nice for him. She's wearing a useful gray jumper. She should be wearing alençon lace with a bouquet of stephanotis and sweet peas. From the back of a motorcycle she hurls her bouquet.

I hold the envelope steadily in my hand. "You're going by motorcycle?"

"No, by plane. His mother gave us the tickets as a wedding present. We were going to go at Christmas, but we decided not to wait."

The people in the front row have stopped writing and are looking at us curiously. Up till now I have never let anyone, not even my observer, interrupt my free writing.

"Now that he is up to date . . ." She has a soft voice. Her enunciation is very good. "David wants to know, can you please give him an Incomplete grade? We'll be back next semester."

The result of this question is that I begin shaking from the waist down at my desk, as if I have palsy. My legs are trembling so violently, I have to keep shuffling my feet, as though something unpleasant has stuck to my shoes. I can also feel myself blushing, but to my astonishment, the girl doesn't notice a thing. Of course. The desk has a little skirt around it for modesty's sake.

"Why doesn't David come and ask me himself?"

"He can't. He's writing this paper for Comp. Lit. And I think he's embarrassed."

Now that I look at her, I recognize her from the front desk of the library. She has checked me out many times. I wish to say, "It is highly irregular to give the grade of Incomplete except in cases of serious illness or a death in the family," but the words seem like bullets, and I can't mouth them. Instead I put the envelope in my briefcase, and I nod, smiling. I clear my throat, I croak a little, I say, "Have a good time." As she exits, smiling, I see she is taller than I had thought. I still don't know her name.

This happened one minute ago. I already feel a little remote from it. I am planning to resume my normal life. My mouth has already frozen back to its normal shape. My legs have stopped trembling. No one could tell how I feel.

How I wish I could start all over again as a tadpole. Something small swimming around in a sea. Something squirreling along.

I don't know what to do. I don't know what to say. I don't know where to go. The door is blank. The wall is blind. The floor has a drain.

The mouse lurks in the pantry. Garbage roots in the backyard. Birds fly in the circular sky.

Don't relax for a minute. Make sure you sleep at night. Give a knock if you exist. No knock if you don't. Nod your head if you can breathe. Forget me. Forget me not.

Another opening, another show.

Another opening, another show. Another opening, another show.

Another opening, another show. Another opening, another show.

Another opening, another show. Another opening. Another show.

The Rhythm of
Disintegration
Marly Swick

All winter, from his office window in the Humanities Annex, Marshall has looked out over the frozen lake—Mendota or Monona, he can never remember which. All he knows for certain is that this lake is not the one in which Otis Redding's plane crashed. That was the other one, over by where his ex-wife lives in a large white cuckoo-clock chalet—the window boxes ablaze with healthy geraniums, like a travel poster of Switzerland. The beautiful and spacious house is so far from the rickety lower duplex Hannah and he shared in Berkeley it is as if she has been reincarnated into her next life while he is still living out his first. And in fact, when they talk—or try to—they are like two strangers who knew each other in a past life, a past life that he remembers and she chooses to forget—a willful amnesia that insults and saddens him. He has the sense that if it were not for Tilden, their nine-year-old daughter, his one living shred of proof, Hannah would cease to recognize him altogether. He wonders if it is something personal or if Hannah would treat Charlie, her new husband, with the same blank detachment were they to divorce someday. Of course *their* divorce would of necessity be more complex, a more substantial dissolution—houses, cars, antiques, a stock portfolio. Not like six years ago when Marshall remained in the duplex with the stereo, what passed as furniture, and Stokely—their aging black Labrador, while Hannah moved back to Madison with their daughter, 1971 Datsun, and thousand-odd dollars in savings. At the time, Marshall consoled himself with the thought that she would regret it. Marshall regrets most everything he has ever done. He is a man full of regret, riddled with regret, but since returning to Madison, he has had to face the fact that Hannah not only does not regret, she does not even remember. Or so it seems. Or so she *wants* it to seem. Marshall's curse is that although he sees what's what, he always leaves the door ajar for hope.

The sun is shining, fierce against the large windows of his office, and the lake—Mendota or Monona—has nearly thawed, overnight it seems, into a surprising dazzle of blue. And now, after only a week or so of spring, Marshall finds that he can barely recall the long and brutal months of snow and subzero windchill about which he, a patriotic Californian, complained so relentlessly to whomever would listen. Already he doubts that the winter was really as bad as all that. It must be like labor pains, he thinks, looking at his watch. At noon he is meeting Hannah for lunch at the Memorial Union. It occurs to him to ask her whether she can remember her labor pains or whether it is simply another old wives' tale, but then he remembers she barely remembers *him,* their twelve years together, so it is unlikely she would remember anything so elusive as physical pain.

He has chosen the union over other more sophisticated restaurants because he hopes the familiar setting will jar something loose inside her. One sip of Rathskeller beer, and she will remember, suddenly *remember,* all the good times they had here, before the not-so-good times in Berkeley, and she will thaw, right before his eyes, like Lake Mendota or Monona. As he grabs his jacket, locks his office door behind him, and waits for the elevator, he feels hope fluttering its wings inside him, springing eternal, even though he knows that Hannah has only agreed, after some undignified wheedling on his part, to meet him today because he is leaving next week, his one-semester visiting lectureship ended, back home to California. The lunch is his reward for disappearing.

Keep it light, he lectures himself as he lopes down Langdon Street, past the tables full of jewelry from Nepal and thick bright sweaters from Colombia—just like Berkeley, like how Berkeley used to be before it went both downhill and uphill in the '80s. Today, walking past the tie-dyed T-shirt and candle vendors on his way to meet Hannah, he feels he has slipped into a time warp. He whistles and slings his tweed jacket over his shoulder, rolls up the sleeves of his pale blue shirt, imagining himself twenty years younger, knowing what he knows now, with an American Express card in his wallet.

Inside the union he weaves his way through throngs of students, gaudy and exuberant in the first heat of spring. A couple of attractive female students from his Historical Methods seminar call out his name and motion for him to join them. Flattered, he shakes his head, making a sad face and pointing to his watch as he continues on toward the terrace. Some days Marshall thinks becoming a professor was the most boorish choice he has ever made; other days it strikes him as a wonderful scam to get paid to monopolize the conversation, beautiful bright young women scribbling down your every word, the summers off.

He catches sight of Hannah sitting at a small table close to the lake. She answers his extravagant wave with a discreet nod and pulls her pocketbook tighter against her stomach, as if she expects him to make a grab for it or the sight of him makes her nauseated. He hopes that maybe she is just a tad nervous—butterflies—which would suggest that some atavistic memory is at work inside her, the place is working its magic. From a distance she does not look like her old self. Any number of girls sitting there in blue jeans and long straight pale hair look more like how she used to look back then. But as he threads his way toward her through backpacks and dogs and discarded trays, smiling self-consciously, he sees her face more and more clearly, her familiar distinctive expression, and he feels as if he is flipping the pages of a photo album backward. You would think up close the ravages of time would be more apparent, but in

The Rhythm of Disintegration

Hannah's case, somehow the opposite is true, as if she were just going through the outward motions of aging so as to fit in with Charlie and his crowd, who are considerably older, fiftyish, and obsessed with fitness. Once when Marshall brought Tilden back early and no one else was home, he'd persuaded his daughter to lead him on a tour of the house. The two things that most impressed him were the sunporch converted into a Nautilus home gym and the bookshelves full of crisp hardbacks at twenty dollars a shot, books that Marshall coveted in the bookstores but could not afford to buy until they came out in paperback. This was the straw of affluence that broke Marshall's back, and he'd left feeling depressed, a failure—angry at a society in which a cardiologist who never reads anything except the morning newspaper and the occasional best-seller on his annual vacation in the Bahamas can afford to stock up on hardbacks as if they were so many cans of soup.

Hannah has a half-eaten salad and a half-drunk glass of iced tea on the table in front of her. As Marshall sits down, she slides on some black sunglasses with mirrored lenses the color of oil slicks. The fact that she has not waited, that she is already halfway through lunch, irritates him. The message is as clear as if she'd spelled it out in salad dressing on the table. So much for his idle hopes of a lazy romantic lunch, the afternoon sun sinking into the blue lake as their conversation finally plunges into the past, the two of them as deaf to the hubbub around them as two sleek fish suspended, gliding in a shimmering deep-sea silence.

"Why are you frowning?" Hannah says, frowning herself.

"You could have waited."

She shrugs.

He jogs back inside the cafeteria, grabs a prewrapped sandwich and a bottle of beer, pays for them, and returns, breathless, to the table where Hannah is single-mindedly working away at her salad. As he unwraps his sandwich, she starts chatting about Tilden's new teacher, Mrs. Gorman, as if he has never met her, even though she knows perfectly well that Marshall has spoken with her on several occasions during the past four months when he picked Tilden up after school. As he listens to her rattle on, his fingers squeeze the cold sweaty glass of the beer bottle tighter and tighter, and he begins to make little revving noises in the back of his throat, which she ignores. The way her fork jabs at her lettuce reminds him of those clean-up guys who walk through public parks with sharp poles, stabbing at candy wrappers and used condoms.

This lunch was a mistake, he thinks, looking out over the water. He wants to interrupt, to say, Hey, remember the time we rented the canoe and capsized it? Remember this, remember that? But somehow it is not possible. Listening to her brisk small talk, he feels like a climber attempting unsuccessfully to find a toehold in a towering mountain of slick, hard ice. The air is thin, hard to breathe. He finishes off his beer and wants to go inside for another but is reluctant to leave even for a minute, afraid she will take this as her cue to make a swift and graceful exit. So what? What does it matter if she stays another five, ten, even twenty minutes? he asks himself, as he morosely peels the label off his beer bottle. What could possibly happen? What is it he wants to happen? He has a life in Berkeley, a fine life—tenure, a lover, a much-coveted apartment on Panoramic Way with a view of Alcatraz. He is even thinking of marrying again. In California he rarely gives Hannah a second thought. For the past couple years, he hasn't remembered their anniversary until long after it has passed. A phrase of Toynbee's from this morning's lecture—"the rhythm of disintegration"—suddenly lodges itself in his brain. He sighs and says he'd like another beer, can he get her anything?

Hannah shakes her head and says, as he predicted, that she really should go. He sighs again, more deeply, as she abruptly flings her napkin into her salad bowl and snaps, "What is it you want from me?"

Although this is the very question he's been waiting to answer, Marshall is rendered mute by her brusque exasperation. The tone is all wrong. The words crowd his brain, stampeding each other to get out, but his mouth is jammed shut, some sort of electronic failure of nerve. Finally he stammers, "I want you to take off those sunglasses."

Behind the mirrored lenses she glares at him and yanks open her large handbag. Marshall flinches, imagining for a moment that she is about to fling a handful of money at him, as if he is some persistent, pitiful beggar, but she extracts a piece of sunny yellow construction paper, folded in half, and hands it across the table to him. "From Tilden," she says. "A Bon Voyage card."

Marshall opens it and reads, printed in multicolor crayon: THIS SWISS MISS WILL MISS YOU. LOVE, HEIDI. He smiles and shows it to Hannah, who for the first time, it seems, smiles back.

"Those are my pet names for her," he says, a bit sheepish, "because she lives in a chalet."

"I know. She informed Mrs. Gorman she wants to be called Heidi from now on." Hannah shakes her head and laughs. They laugh together for an instant, Marshall stopping a beat too late, but in that instant he thinks he glimpses that tiny toehold.

"What I want from you," he says, leaning earnestly forward, "is a recognition of history, our history. You make me crazy the way you refuse to talk about, to acknowledge the past. I want to shake you. I want to shout. I want to drag you back there and make you see it." From the alarmed expression in her eyes, he can tell he is going too far, losing it. He lowers his voice and leans back in his chair. "A sense of continuity," he says more calmly. "That's all I want." Then, on an even lighter note: "You know how we historians are."

Hannah removes her sunglasses and studies him with narrowed eyes, as if to see less of him, or maybe she is just squinting in the bright sunlight. "I'm remarried. I have a new life." With an impatient flick of her wrist, she shoos an aggressive wasp away. "There's no room in my life for continuity if it means sitting around mooning over some romanticized version of the past with ex-lovers."

"Husband," he corrects her. "Ex-husband." As he says "ex," he sees himself sitting there, crossed out by a big red X.

She shrugs and snaps shut her handbag, a signal that she is about to leave. "Think of me like a house you sold. Someone else lives there now. You can't just barge in whenever you feel like it."

"You just don't get it, do you?" He sees her bristle, but the pedant in him blunders on. "Life is a process of accumulation, not substitution." He slumps in his chair, his posture an admission of defeat, waiting for the sound of her chair scraping against the concrete as she rises to go. At this instant he could kill her, barehanded, without a shadow of remorse. She is like some willfully dense student who tunes him out, twists his words, refuses, out of spite, to understand. A fortress of vengeful, cold, unreceptive insensitivity. He can't believe he ever loved her, not for a single night. He closes his eyes, the sun battering against his eyelids, and tries to call forth a single heart-wrenching image of Hannah from the past, but there is nothing there—blank—like a tape that has been accidentally erased. Hannah says his name softly, nervously. He opens his eyes, blinking in the harsh light, and sees her shadow hovering over him, a dark avenging angel. If he stretched out his arm, it would slice right through her, through air, encountering no physical resistance, no corporeal reality. She is no more present in the present than in the past.

"Are you all right? Hey." She prods his foot with her toe as if he were a dead snake she fears might rouse itself for a final posthumous strike.

He nods untruthfully, dispirited, thinking he must find a new profession, which won't be easy at his age, forty-one. He sees himself, a defrocked priest of history, attempting to explain the reason for this career change to an executive headhunter. "I'm tired of looking backward," Marshall can hear himself saying. "The past is all washed up. I think maybe something high tech, something cutting edge." He will sublet his quaint apartment and move to some ahistorical condo in Silicon Valley. He will divest himself of the past, never eat leftovers, speak only in future tense. *Yea, though I walk through the valley . . .* He thinks of the quote from Lucretius he is using for the epigraph to his new book: *This is the sentence that has been passed upon the World; this is the law of God; that what has been must die, and what has grown up must grow old.* Suddenly he is trembling, shuddering, misfiring like a car with dirty plugs. Hannah touches a fingertip to his eyelashes and then says, "You aren't crying, are you?" as if she wants him to deny it.

"Go," he says. "I'm okay. I just want to be alone." His voice quavers, sullen and pitiful as a child's.

Hannah sits back down.

"I said I want to be alone," he repeats more firmly. He clears his throat, sits up straighter, stares Hannah in the eye. "You can go. Class dismissed."

But now there is no getting rid of her. She opens her handbag again, rummages around for a Kleenex, and holds it out to him, a little white flag fluttering in the breeze. The symbolism is not lost on him. He ignores her. She sets the Kleenex on the table, where it promptly blows away.

"I'll get you another beer," she says, all conciliatory.

While she's gone, he thinks about leaving. He sees himself standing up and walking out, stopping to chat wittily with the two female students from his seminar. He doesn't know why he doesn't. He really doesn't. A few feet away, two Middle Eastern students dressed like PLO terrorists are going through the periodic table, no doubt quizzing each other for final exams. KBr, NaCl. One corner of his brain translates wacky acronyms. Killers for a Brighter Rehabilitation. National Association of Chastened Lovers. Out on the pier, a black man is playing the saxophone, a small white dog snoozing royally in the purple, velvet-lined case. Sun, water. An academic resort. The antidote to education.

In the distance, he sees Hannah walking toward him, a beer in each hand, and he thinks maybe the lunch can still be salvaged, maybe there's still time to get what he needs from her, although he doesn't know what more he can say. Or do. And already he regrets everything he has said or done thus far. Hannah sets the two beers on the table and then tidies up, moving all their trash to an empty table, wiping up some spilled salad dressing. A fit of wifely domesticity.

"Now"—she places her elbows on the clean table, leans toward him, lowers her voice conspiratorially, maternally—"tell me what's really the matter."

Marshall takes a long swig of beer and looks out over the lake, the sun glittering, a sea of jittering diamonds. Later, looking back, he will think to himself, half-joking, it was the sun, the sun made him do it, like Camus's Stranger—the sun, the saxophone, the Middle Eastern chant of the basic elements, the abrupt, dizzying shift from winter to spring, the bright beam of Hannah's sudden solicitude.

"You really want to hear?" he says.

She nods.

It is entirely unpremeditated. At first he has no idea where it even comes from. All he knows is that he opens his mouth and next thing he knows he is sitting right there listening to himself telling her this story, listening along with her, just as curious and moved as she, just as anxious to find out how it ends, more anxious, since it is (supposedly) his life, his love, his grief. Her sympathetic clucks and nods spur him on. When he sees tears glinting in her gray eyes, he feels so tender toward this fragile, bruised self he has created that he thinks he cannot bear it. The sadness is a thick, viscous liquid, sweet like maple syrup, drowning his lungs; congestive heart failure, the cardiologists—Charlie and his pals—would call it.

The story he tells her is this. About a year ago, after many years of living alone, Marshall saw a woman at the Café Med on Telegraph Avenue. A beautiful woman, naturally, as in most stories.

She was drinking café latte, staring into space. Pale skin, huge dark eyes shadowed by dark circles. Marshall watched her for several minutes, transfixed, as he savored his espresso. Then suddenly, as if astrally projected, he felt himself drawn inside her. Never had he felt such grief, like an iron girdle squeezing his vital organs, every breath an intense effort. And then, just as suddenly, he was expelled—dizzy, buoyant with relief. As soon as he regained his composure, he stood up—without thinking, almost without volition—and walked over to her table. He waited. It took a moment for her to look up at him, then to bring him into focus, as if she were seeing him from a long way off. Looking into her eyes, he felt he was staring into deep water—anything could be down there—sunken treasure, shipwrecks, bloated corpses bedecked in pearls and coral. When he had her full attention, he said, "May I offer my condolences for your terrible sorrow." The woman's eyes filled with tears, and she motioned for him to take the empty chair across from her.

At this point in the story, Marshall catches his breath and sighs as it suddenly occurs to him where he has heard this story before: at a faculty cocktail party in Berkeley. A colleague in the French department. An anecdote about how André Breton had met his wife. The colleague, a svelte, worldly woman who had always rather intimidated Marshall, was wearing heavy, sweet perfume—gardenia, maybe, or nightblooming jasmine—and a low-cut black dress and was standing very close to him, almost whispering in his ear. He had definitely been aroused, although nothing came of it since he was there with Meredith, his lover, and a couple of days later he left for the Midwest. Telling the story, he seems to have conjured up the scent of jasmine. He sniffs the air, takes a sip of beer, disoriented.

"So what happened?" Hannah prompts him.

"We spent the night together." Marshall shrugs, as if to suggest the inevitability of it all. "She told me her husband and two children had drowned in an automobile accident, in Paris." He takes another slug of beer to give himself a moment—this is as far as the

French professor's anecdote went. He was on his own now, but he found he didn't need time; the story seemed to have a momentum of its own.

"She moved into my place," he continues. "We were in love, perfectly compatible, content. After a few months, we decided to get married—in June." He pauses again, for dramatic effect, but when he goes on, he is surprised to find his voice choked up.

Hannah reaches across the table and grasps his hand. "Take your time," she commands gently. "There's no hurry."

"She died." He looks away, across the lake. The sax player, as if in accompaniment to Marshall's performance, has switched from cool jazz to blues. "An aneurysm. She was at a Laundromat, the one on Euclid." Hannah nods. "Folding our sheets." Marshall is amazed at how these details just keep coming with no effort on his part. He remembers reading somewhere that the tiny unimportant details are what convince us something is true. Hannah and he are both silent for a moment, listening to the sax, the buzz of conversation at the neighboring tables that seems suddenly to increase in volume, the tinny yap of the sax player's dog—like one of those wind-up toys. Watching the dog, Marshall feels that some inner mechanism of his own, previously wound tight, has abruptly unwound.

"I'm sorry," Hannah says finally. "I had no idea."

Marshall busies himself with his beer, self-conscious now and feeling rather foolish, as if he has just emerged from an autohypnotic trance, but there is also a sadness, a deep ache, lingering inside his chest as if from an old wound. He remembers a Vietnamese student of his whose index finger was amputated at the knuckle. One day Marshall had finally asked him what had happened to the finger, and the student had said he didn't know. He had been an orphan, adopted at a young age by an American family. He had no memory of the finger and no one to ask. As he spoke, he'd stared at his maimed hand matter-of-factly, but Marshall had been haunted by the story, still often dreamed some gruesome version of it. Imagine, he'd said to Meredith in bed that night, having part of your body missing and not knowing why, how, when.

Looking at the sax player's dog, Hannah suddenly smiles and says, "Remember the day Stokely rolled in horseshit at Hilmar's farm and we took off all our clothes and took turns hosing him down?"

Marshall holds himself very still and just barely nods his head, not daring to look at her, not daring to breathe, hoping that she will continue.

"That was a nice afternoon," is all she says after a long silence.

He releases his breath in what sounds like an exaggerated sigh of disappointment or boredom, which causes Hannah to frown and fiddle with her wedding ring.

"I can't picture Charlie running around naked after a stinky dog," he says, attempting a good-natured laugh. To be honest, he can't exactly see himself doing such a thing these days. Even if Stokely were still alive.

Hannah shrugs and takes hold of his wrist, turns it to see the time. "I really do have to go. Tilden will be home from school soon." She slides her sunglasses on again and stands up. "Walk me to the bus stop?"

"I'll give you a ride." He stands up too, then says, "Wait a second. Be right back." He jogs down to the pier and tosses a five-dollar bill into the purple velvet case. As Marshall turns to go, the sax player makes a courtly bow in his direction and plays a flashy riff.

Hannah takes his hand companionably as they walk toward the Humanities Annex, where his car is parked. For the first time in the four months he's been here, he does not feel like prodding and shaking her. He is in a strange mood, hard to define—a moodless mood. He feels oddly displaced. As he makes small talk, he has the sensation that his lips and words are out of sync, but Hannah doesn't seem to notice. Every now and then she gives his hand a gentle maternal squeeze, as if to let him know she has not forgotten his terrible loss. Surprisingly, he feels no guilt, no regret, over his elaborate lie, no need to confess. Deep down he feels entitled to this consolation; he drinks it up like a thirsty brown-edged fern.

In the car, during the short drive to Hannah's house, they listen to a tape Marshall has just recently bought—Otis Redding's *Greatest Hits.* Hannah sprawls in her seat, one foot resting against the dash—an unladylike posture for a doctor's wife—and as they cruise down John Nolen Drive past the other lake, Monona or Mendota, it could be 1970, Marshall thinks. They could be in love. Or think they were. Marshall wonders if they ever were really. He hopes so, he really does. But as he pulls up in front of the white chalet with its cheerful geraniums, he has the sudden sad conviction that what Hannah and he had was just puppy stuff—wriggling, yapping, licking, biting—whereas Hannah and Charlie have the full-grown dog: he pictures two loyal and patient golden retrievers lying side by side on a stone hearth, year after year, their muzzles slowly turning white.

Hannah leans over and kisses him lightly on the cheek. "Call before you leave?"

He nods. "I'm taking Tilden to the movies Saturday. Thanks for lunch." He gives her a stiff hug. Over her shoulder he can see the lake, the one where Otis's plane crashed. The news has been full of Otis lately. Some organization raising money to erect a memorial on the shore of the lake, the twentieth anniversary of his death. "Is this Mendota or Monona?" Marshall asks as Hannah opens the car door.

"Monona," Hannah laughs.

"Monona," he repeats, determined to remember this time.

After Hannah disappears inside the house, he sits there in the car, looking at the lake and listening to the tape, tapping his fingers against the steering wheel in time to the music. Just sitting on the dock of the bay. He imagines Otis sitting in his plane at the bottom of the lake, perfectly preserved, like a ship in a bottle. Then he real-

The Rhythm of Disintegration

223

izes that, in fact, he is picturing the black saxophone player, and when he tries to picture Otis's face, there's nothing there—a blank. Suddenly he feels depressed, more depressed than he has ever felt in his life, grief-stricken. It is as if his story, his lie, has solidified into truth. He loves that woman with the drowned husband and children, loves the distracted way she sips her café latte, loves her sad dark-circled eyes, loves the way she folds their bed sheets—smoothing the wrinkles as if love depended on such small gestures. He wants her back more than anything he has ever lost, anything. He would do anything to get her back. He holds his index finger out straight against the steering wheel and thinks of his Vietnamese student and of his old friend TJ, who axed off his little toe to get out of the draft. He would do that, he thinks, for her, and not even feel it. He closes his eyes and pictures her and suddenly he recognizes her—or not so much recognizes her as knows who she is, why she looks so familiar. A little bit like Hannah around the mouth, like his high-school sweetheart around the eyes, even a bit like his mother—not as she is now but as he remembers her from his childhood, with a cloud of dark hair brushing his cheek, tickling him, as she bent over to kiss him good-night. The woman is the original loss, the mother of loss, the Ur-loss, the loss from which all subsequent losses flow, as if it is just one loss in different guises—all our lives—we lose the same thing over and over and over.

Hearing the crunch of tires on gravel, Marshall opens his eyes and quickly slides down on the seat as Charlie's silver Porsche sails into the driveway just beyond where Marshall is parked. In the late afternoon sunlight the silver car silhouetted against the deep blue lake shines like a shark. Slumped in his seat, Marshall watches as Charlie jaunts across the velvety green lawn, whistling like a man happy to be home after a hard day, a man with no regrets in the world. At the porch steps, he bends down and fiddles with something in the bushes. As he enters the house, shutting the front door behind him, a half-dozen sprinklers burst into action, whirling and sparkling away, cascading into the open window of Marshall's car, soaking his shirt and pants. He curses and rolls up the car window.

The sprinklers beat like heavy rain against the glass and he feels strangely disoriented, unreal, sitting there in the rain on a sunny day, like a movie actor on a sound stage. He remembers the tour Hannah and he took of Universal Studios the first summer they lived in California—simulated thunder, rain, lightning, even snow. He remembers that after the tour they drove out to the beach and had dinner with Hannah's old boyfriend and how upset he, Marshall, the current boyfriend, had been while Hannah and Rick had gossiped about old friends and laughed at in-jokes that had to be laboriously and unfunnily explained for Marshall's benefit. He wonders why it is that he and Hannah can't go to restaurants and laugh at in-jokes that they have to stop and explain to Charlie. He feels cheated, shortchanged, as if the past were a joint savings account that Hannah had unilaterally closed out. He wants to protest this unfairness, wishes he could haul her into small claims court and force her to give him what he wants. Which is what? What is it you want from me?—Hannah's question again. He knows exactly what it is he wants, but somehow he can't find the words to describe it. The words he tries and rejects all make it sound like both more and less than what it really is: an acknowledgment of loss. "If we lose the loss," he hears himself saying to her, "then what's left?" He thinks of simulated snow drifting prettily, like a sheet of blank paper.

It is hot and steamy in the car. He rolls down the window and lets the cool spray of the sprinklers wash over him. He rests his head against the back of the seat and shuts his eyes for a moment, tired. When he opens them again, Tilden is standing there staring at him. "Daddy," she frowns, exactly like her mother, "what are you doing? You're all wet."

"I'm waiting for the rain to let up," he says.

She considers this seriously for a moment and then smiles, as if she has just figured out the punch line to the world's most amusing joke, a little in-joke just between the two of them. Squinting into the bright haze of sunshine, she opens up an imaginary umbrella, then saunters around to the other side of the car and climbs in. "I'll wait with you," she says.

He flips over the cassette and snaps on the windshield wipers. Tilden giggles and waves to Hannah, who is watching them from an upstairs window, half-smiling. Marshall flashes her a peace sign. She laughs and flashes one back, then lets the curtain fall forward and disappears. There is a sudden loud clap of thunder, a flash of heat lightning. Tilden leaps onto his lap. He wraps his arms around her tight and sniffs her clean shiny hair, child's hair. It must be hereditary, he thinks, remembering Hannah's fear of thunderstorms, how she used to take her pillow and sleep in the hallway, away from all the windows. The thunder rumbles in the distance. Tilden shivers against his chest. He cranks up the volume on the tape deck. Otis is singing about tenderness, wailing, screaming his lungs out, like a dead man shouting to be heard.

Mr. Eggplant Goes Home
Alex Shishin

In the gray office at the private women's university sat three Japanese professors of English. They were all over sixty. Two were very white. Their hair was like dirty snow. Their skins were milky. The other had very brown skin, like desiccated leather. He drank heavily. One of the two very white English teachers also drank heavily, usually with the brown professor, while the other very white English teacher watched them in a superior sort of way. None of these professors of English knew English; they only pretended to. They hated any Japanese English teacher who did know English. They also hated foreigners. The university had hired a few foreigners as fulltimers and now one of them was up for a promotion. The three old professors had gathered in the chairman's office to discuss how to stop the foreigner from being promoted.

It was the office of the very white professor who drank. The first thing he had done as department chairman was to bully a few of the foreign teachers. The foreign teachers, unknown to him, had nicknamed him "Mr. Eggplant" because they said his face was shaped like an eggplant. Mr. Eggplant nodded his head as the brown teacher said, "The foreigner will have his own office, and he'll copulate with our students," and the other white teacher answered, "That'll scare the president; he's deathly afraid of foreigners offending the morals of our girls."

Mr. Eggplant stood up and walked out the door, not bothering to close it. The two others, used to his erratic behavior, said nothing. The brown professor went downstairs to tell maintenance to lock Mr. Eggplant's door. Mr. Eggplant took the elevator down to the first floor and went to the administration office.

"*Oi!*" he called to a female clerk. A terrified pimply young woman in a light blue uniform scurried over.

"My mother is ill. I am going away to my hometown for a few days. Get me a form or something to fill out."

"*Hai!*" the terrified young woman squealed. She went and returned. Mr. Eggplant filled out the form and put his seal on it, then went to the parking lot. He stood there for several minutes as his memory swam.

It was early November. The air was dry and laced with a faint hint of ice. In the mountains behind the university the trees were turning red and gold. In front of the university, which was situated on a bluff, was the city of Kobe, where Mr. Eggplant had lived with his wife for thirty years, where his daughter, now married to a Carlyle scholar, had been born. Mr. Eggplant fumbled the letter from his ninety-year-old mother out of his coat pocket and uncrumpled it. He read: "Come home immediately. Things are not well. I need you here."

When had he last been back to his boyhood home? How long had it been since his mother had written to him, or he to her?

A teacher who loved Nathaniel Hawthorne walked across the parking lot to her car. Since Hawthorne was his specialty, Mr. Eggplant hated her.

He caught a taxi for the Shin-Kobe Shinkansen station.

The automatic ticket machines confused him. He bellowed at the JR staff until he was able to buy a ticket for the Shinkansen to Okayama and transfer tickets to two local lines which would take him to his village.

He then went to a kiosk and bought himself three large cans of beer. His wife scolded him for drinking too much these days because the doctor had said it was bad for his gout, not to mention his liver and kidneys. A heavy drinker for most of his life, Mr. Eggplant suffered terrible mood swings and a constant dryness in his throat without alcohol. He envied the brown professor who had no wife to tell him to stop drinking. A bachelor, the brown professor spent almost all his income in bars. Mr. Eggplant enjoyed watching the normally shy brown professor flirt with the hostesses. It was painful to watch the brown professor drink by himself these days and not be able to join in. The white professor, who happened to be his wife's brother, was lately on orders from his wife to keep Mr. Eggplant from drinking. But now, traveling, he could drink all he wanted. He opened a can and drank. He felt his mind clear.

On the platform, it occurred to him to call his wife.

"I thought you would come home first," said his wife's worried voice. "I would have packed your clothes. You don't have a change of clothes."

"Send my clothes by mail," Mr. Eggplant said.

"I still don't see—are you all right? I mean are you feeling all right?"

"Yes, yes, fine. Except that *gaijin* is going to get a promotion. What kind of school is that, promoting *gaijin*. Hey, have you copied my paper yet? Use black ink. Last time you used blue. I want black."

"I'm working on it now. With black ink. Shall I send it to you in the village?"

"No, to the journal. Under my name. In nothing but black ink. Understand?"

In truth, it was his wife who wrote Mr. Eggplant's academic papers. She was fluent in English. He had never read Hawthorne in the original. Never could. This habit which they called "copying" had started from the beginning of their arranged marriage when he was a graduate student. He would scratch out a few notes, and she would write the paper. Quietly she had made his career for him.

"Are you sure you bought the right tickets?" his wife said. "Do you have enough money?"

"Yes, yes. My coins are running out."

"Do you remember how you used to take me out to dinner whenever you published?" his wife said suddenly, trying to sound cheerful.

"My coins are running out."

"All right then. Good-bye."

In her youth, Mr. Eggplant's wife, Natsuyo, had been a bright and beautiful woman who would have gone to study in America had her family been able to afford it. Being too poor to buy her a good education, her family had done the next best thing. They arranged a marriage for her with a scholar, the son of her father's colleague at the elementary school. She had tried to love Mr. Eggplant, who even as a young man was crotchety and irritable. Failing to love him, she was, however, devoted to him, living her ambitions through him. She had had but one affair during her marriage, from which, she was sure, their daughter had resulted. Mr. Eggplant never found out about the affair, which was with the mailman who still delivered mail in his neighborhood.

As the train arrived, his mind was still on this *gaijin* the university was going to promote. He was from Los Angeles or Texas or someplace like that. He also had a Ph.D. in Comparative Literature. Easy enough for foreigners to get Ph.D.s, he thought as the bullet train approached. Easy over there because foreigners always stick together.

On board, Mr. Eggplant sat down across from a thirtyish man in a business suit with a *Japan Times* on his lap. He took a beer out of the plastic bag he had gotten at the kiosk and opened it. He quickly drank the beer down and rolled the can under the seat. He opened the last can, took a sip from it and then put it on a tray by the window. The train started.

Mr. Eggplant looked out the window at Kobe and the Inland Sea. There was Sannomiya in the distance. He thought of the bars where the brown professor took him. Mr. Eggplant sighed, wishing he was in some small cozy bar now, talking to some mamma-san who, unlike his wife, did not nag . . . He took a cigarette out of the top pocket of his jacket and lit it.

"I'm sorry, I'm sorry—this is a nonsmoking car, *oji-sama!*" the young man across from him said. "I'm sorry. Perhaps you didn't see the sign." Mr. Eggplant looked up at the sign over the door. It had a picture of a cigarette with a line through it. He let the cigarette drop from his fingers on to the floor, then pressed his toe on it. Everyone was staring at him. He fumbled with the zipper of his briefcase, took out the latest edition of *Rising Generation,* opened it and read the table of contents. Rivals had published. He noticed with great alarm the *gaijin's* name—

"Excuse me, could I speak with you?" It was the young man across from him.

"Eh?" Mr. Eggplant said.

"Forgive me for mentioning the cigarette," the young man said smiling. "I really wouldn't have minded were I not allergic to tobacco."

"Too many nonsmoking cars these days," Mr. Eggplant said.

"Yes, I understand," the young man said. "I just happened to notice your journal. You wouldn't be an English teacher by any chance?"

When people were friendly they wanted something. "Are you looking for a position?" he asked.

"Oh no, no, no, not at all! I'm a businessman! I was just interested because I've recently returned from two years in New York. I'm quite fond of English, you see—"

"I was at Columbia University on my sabbatical," Mr. Eggplant said.

"That's wonderful!"

"Wonderful? I had to look at lots of Negroes all day. And my teenaged daughter turned feral."

"Feral?"

"Promiscuous! She got a scholarship to Barnard College, but I brought her back to Japan and put her into a proper girls' junior college. She would have become a prostitute if I hadn't."

"Oh. I'm sorry." The young man's face was red. He was about to return to his newspaper, but Mr. Eggplant kept talking.

"Too many *gaijin* in New York chasing after Japanese girls. As a young man I got a scholarship from Hyogo Prefecture to study at Harvard."

"That's wonderful! Gosh, I envy you!"

During that time Mr. Eggplant never saw the inside of a classroom nor met a single professor. After he had wearied of Widner Library—almost all of its books were in English—Mr. Eggplant cruised Cambridge and Boston until he found a bar run by a Japanese expatriate. That is where he spent most of his time during his year at Harvard.

"They have funny provincial accents at Harvard," Mr. Eggplant said. "You can barely understand them. Terrible English those people have."

"I really miss speaking English! I had a terrible time the first six months in New York because of culture shock, but then I got the hang of the language and had so much fun! Made so many friends. Mostly Americans. I was so sad when my company transferred me to Osaka. I sure do miss speaking English. I'm so lucky to run into you! I'll bet that as an English teacher your English must be great!" He spoke to Mr. Eggplant in the language.

Irritated by the sound of English, Mr. Eggplant waved a dismissive hand at the young man as he did when people at the university came to him to take up his precious time.

The young man hid behind his newspaper. Mr. Eggplant drank his beer. Before Okayama he was in the men's room, urinating painfully. He nearly missed getting off.

The local train was old, cramped, and littered with Styrofoam *bento* boxes and aluminum cans which rolled along the aisle whenever it turned a curve and shook. But at least here Mr. Eggplant could smoke without someone complaining. As it turned out, he became something of a celebrity in the front section of the carriage.

"Are you actually a professor? You actually read books in English?" an old man, a local farmer, asked.

"And you professors write books, don't you?" another old man said. When Mr. Eggplant nodded in the affirmative, they exclaimed, "Hehhhhh!"

"*Sensei*, I have a bottle of whiskey," a third old man said. "Would you like some? I'm afraid I only have paper cups."

There were six old men talking to Mr. Eggplant and smoking. The conductor entered the blue vales of cigarette smoke, glanced at the "No Smoking" sign over the heads of the old men, and announced, "Does anyone need to buy a ticket?" and walked on.

"So is your university private or public?" another farmer asked.

"Private," Mr. Eggplant said. "A girls' university."

"OOOOOOH!" his audience exclaimed together.

"So you can have many girlfriends, eh?" an old man said.

They cackled.

"Say, *sensei*, what about foreigners? Do you actually talk to them in English?"

"Yes, yes, of course," Mr. Eggplant replied. "I have to talk to them in English. They cannot learn Japanese. Because they do not have Japanese blood. When they try to speak Japanese it does not come out right and nobody understands them. So I have to talk to the *gaijin* in English. As department chairman, I am doing this all the time."

"What are they like, the *gaijin?*" another old man asked.

"All right when they know their place," Mr. Eggplant said. "But these days they don't know their place! Too many of them in Japan. Lots of them unqualified to teach, you know. Still they want promotions and all that. And they refuse to speak Japanese. Expect us to speak English to them."

"But it's not in their blood, you said," said one old man who was getting a bit weary of this professor.

"Say, what about foreign countries," another old man quickly cut in. "Have you been to foreign countries?"

"Yes, yes. I've studied at Harvard and Columbia. The *gaijin* don't think the way we do, you know. We have an emperor, we have customs, we have rules that everyone follows. We have polite forms of speech and all that. But the *gaijin* don't have anything like that, you see. Every one of them has his own way of doing things. You have to be careful with them. You never know what they are going to do, those *gaijin*. And you know something else? The *gaijin* know nothing about their own literature. How many of those *gaijin* at Harvard and Columbia know anything about Nathaniel Hawthorne? I had to teach them about Hawthorne, you see. Funny people, the *gaijin*."

A couple of listeners got up abruptly and without saying *sayonara* retreated to their seats. A few others, now quite drunk, stayed to listen to Mr. Eggplant talk about *gaijin*. They had to help him off at the end station where he had to transfer to a small local line that went up to his village in the mountains. Fortunately, one of the farmers was taking the same train and could look after him. At the tiny station, only a platform, he delivered the drunk Mr. Eggplant into the hands of his sister who was not pleased.

A short, strong woman of fifty-nine, Mr. Eggplant's sister had moved back to the family home after the death of her husband. She had spent the better part of her life working alongside her husband on their farm outside Okayama. She had sold the farm to developers.

"Here, put your arm around my neck. I'm putting you in the backseat. Didn't you bring a suitcase? That's right, Natsuyo-san telephoned to say she'd be sending it."

In the backseat, Mr. Eggplant groaned. His gout was acting up.

"We'll be home in a few minutes. You'll take a hot *o-furo* and you'll drink some ginseng tea. You'll feel a whole lot better in the morning." It was night now and very dark on the narrow mountain road that wound its way to Mr. Eggplant's village. As she negotiated the curves, his sister talked.

"We'll have the harvest *matsuri* next week. People are preparing. You can hear them beating drums. Fewer people left each year. Mostly old people. The young go to Okayama for jobs. Our young men cannot find brides."

Mr. Eggplant groaned.

"There is a big fight on now. I'm sure you read about it in the newspapers. There is a company that wants to turn this whole area into a resort. They'll be draining our favorite pond to build a hotel. You remember how we used to catch tadpoles there and bring them home in buckets?"

Mr. Eggplant had a brief recollection of himself and his sister and their late elder brother wading in a large pond down the mountainside a kilometer from their home. Their elder brother, conscripted into the Imperial Army, died in China—killed by *gaijin* soldiers, Mr. Eggplant reminded himself.

"We're starting a resistance to the company," his sister went on. "All the villages around are having meetings. We have a friend from Greenpeace who is helping us organize. He's an American named Mr. Mike. You'll be happy to meet him, I'm sure."

"Is that why you dragged me out here? To meet some *gaijin*. I refuse to translate for him, if that's what you want. I won't jeopardize my reputation—"

His sister was a patient woman. She let her annoyance with her brother contain itself before she spoke. "Mr. Mike has an interpreter already. Jiro-san, who will be working with us when Mr. Mike leaves. Mother wants to see you."

"What's wrong with Mother?" He had not thought of her during his journey.

"She is getting old. Still in good health. But she has an urgent need to talk to you about the property, as you are the oldest surviving son."

"Bother!" said Mr. Eggplant. "All this way to talk about that! Why couldn't she have waited until *o-shogatsu?*"

"She had a dream about death, elder brother."

"Nonsense! Ow!" Mr. Eggplant groaned as his sister rounded a sharp corner.

Inside his childhood house, an old wooden building through which the wind seeped, Mr. Eggplant felt both at home and uncomfortable.

His mother, a stout and robust woman who smoked American Camel cigarettes without filters, scolded her son for drinking too much on the train. "Now off with you to the *o-furo* and then sit with us at the *kotatsu.* I left your father's *kimono* by the *o-furo.* You will wear your father's clothes until your suitcase arrives."

After the hot bath, his gout felt better. Sitting at the *kotatsu* eating his mother's *nabe* and drinking his sister's ginger tea, Mr. Eggplant asked, "Just how long do you expect me to stay here with you two. I have work, much work at the university. Things are not well there—"

"Let us have you for a week, my son," his mother said quietly. "We have much to talk about. And your old playmates want to see you. They are very proud of you, you being such a great professor and translator and all."

"Somebody said you had a dream about dying," Mr. Eggplant said.

"Ah that! That!" his mother laughed. "That is only a dream. I was in the hospital in the valley last week. The doctor said I'll live to be a hundred if I stop smoking. Ha, I'm too old to quit my bad habits, I told him." She lit a Camel. "But that's no reason for you to start drinking against your doctor's orders."

"This is annoying," Mr. Eggplant said. "I'm a busy man!"

"You know something," cut in his sister. "Old age is when our essences come out. I mean we hide what we really are all our lives, but it is in old age that all our covers are finally taken off."

"It is late and I'm tired," Mr. Eggplant said. "Where is my bed?"

"In your old room. Come, let me help you up. There. You'll find it changed, I'm afraid. We had to put your things in storage in the loft. I've prepared your *futon* already. And there is an electric heater for you. Call if you need anything."

"I want to go back to Kobe," Mr. Eggplant grumbled.

The electric heater was on when he went to bed and off when he woke up the next morning. Mr. Eggplant saw his white breath and rose to turn the heater on.

"Ow!" The gout in his leg was terrible.

"Ah, you're up!" his sister said, sliding back the door. "It's 10:30 already! You were exhausted. Come have breakfast. Your old friends are going to make a special visit to you at noon for lunch. They are very anxious to see you."

"Ow!" Mr. Eggplant cried. "My leg! It's this horrid cold up here!"

"It's drinking too much," his sister laughed. "But it is unseasonably cold! We'll get snow this afternoon! Natsuyo-san telephoned after you were asleep. She said to tell you that the paper is copied and that she is sending it today. Here, easy does it, elder brother. Up you go!"

At breakfast, Mr. Eggplant ate his miso soup with rice and cold fish and looked out the window. The sky was the color of slate. Beneath it the harvested rice dried on bamboo racks in the odd-shaped rice paddies. Farmers, short-legged and bent gnomes, were covering the racks with black plastic sheets to protect their crop from the coming snowstorm. Mr. Eggplant noted the brightness of the various shades of brown—earth, grasses, rice sheaves, and bamboo poles—under the threatening sky. He noted too that some of the houses in the neighborhood still had thatched roofs, though most, on government recommendations, had switched to fireproof tin roofs.

"I must get back to Kobe," he said.

His mother, reading a newspaper and smoking a Camel, muttered something. His sister, who was in the kitchen preparing lunch for their guests, called out, "Did you say something, elder brother?"

"I said I must get back to Kobe!" he said a little louder.

"You will; just rest for now. Oh by the way, I telephoned your university at nine. There is no problem about you being with us."

"Things happen behind your back when you are gone," he grumbled.

"What did you say?" she called.

Mr. Eggplant did not answer.

He was not cordial to his old playmates when they came to call at noon. There were four of them, three women and one man. If they were offended by Mr. Eggplant's silent greeting to their cheery *"O-hisashiburi!"* they did not show it. They gathered around the *kotatsu* like disciples before a revered master. All were bent, gnarled, and tan. Their faces and arms were spotted with ocher freckles.

They had never known or even been this close to anyone more famous than Mr. Eggplant. Mr. Mike Offenberg from Greenpeace was not really famous, though his photograph had appeared in the local newspaper. Their old playmate, the professor of English sitting before them, a severe expression on his long whitish face, had lectured all over Japan and had gone to foreign countries and spoken to their people.

They offered him their simple gifts: homemade *sushi,* cakes, cut fresh bamboo shoots. His mother and sister got down on their knees and bowed deeply to the guests. The guests also got on their knees and bowed deeply. The great man smiled for the first time.

He loved adulation more than anything else in the world. And these gnarled people had been his disciples when they were all children.

Presently his mother brought two heavy folio-sized leather-bound scrapbooks. It had all of his achievements from when he had graduated from high school to the present. It was his life. There were parts he didn't wish to remember, like the fact that his graduate adviser did not like him and he had to take his first university post in Kagoshima. But the rest of his life had been a success. His wife had seen to that.

One of the gnarled old women suddenly began to sing, "A-B-C-D-E-F-G—" Everyone's face lit up.

"Do you remember teaching English songs to us, *sensei?*"

It had been just after the death of his brother. He must have been eleven. English had been outlawed as an enemy language and no one was allowed to teach it. Perhaps the grief and rage over his brother's death had made him take the textbook with children's songs and introduce it to a few select playmates. He had taken them into the forest outside the village and taught them the songs the enemy's children sang. The little book had Japanese *kana* translations and simple musical scores.

"Where did that book come from?" one of the old ladies asked.

"I heard an American airplane dropped it," another old lady replied. *"Sensei,* do you know?"

Mr. Eggplant shook his head. "I've forgotten about the whole thing," he said.

"Well I sure haven't," the old man said. "I still remember, 'Mary had a little lamb, little lamb, little lamb.' I never would've learned *romaji* if it wasn't for *sensei."*

"You never suspected your son was teaching us English, did you?" an old lady asked Mr. Eggplant's mother.

"No, never!" she laughed. "I would have been so frightened I don't know what I would have done. I only learned of it when he was teaching in Kagoshima. You are the few people of your generation in the village to have learned *romaji*. I still cannot read it! How many of you were there?"

"Seven," the old man said. "What amazes me is how *sensei* taught himself *romaji*. Oh, he was amazing, that's for sure."

"Oh, he was that," an old lady said. "And he was very strict. He beat us when we made mistakes, or if we were too loud. They were dangerous times you know. But no matter how badly he beat us, we always came with him when he called us with our secret password. And we never tattled no matter how severely he beat us. *Sensei* knew the dangers his family faced if we were found out. Oh, he was a brave boy."

"My brother, the subversive," Mr. Eggplant's sister chuckled.

Mr. Eggplant looked away. Yes, he had betrayed his country to the *gaijin*. "It has never bothered me," he had said to his wife long ago. "So what if I helped defeat the forces of the emperor? Yes, this is Japan. But in Japan you do what is best for yourself or you are left behind. Had it not been for that little book of children's songs, I might still be in that village, a simple farmer."

After the guests had gone away, bowing and wishing their childhood teacher good health, Mr. Eggplant's mother collected the scrapbooks and was starting to put them back in their shelf when she broke down and cried. His sister put her arms around her. "It'll be all right in the end, Mother. I'm sure it will," she said. "We'll care for him together."

Mr. Eggplant watched the four walk away along the dirt path leading up the mountain. There had been seven of them in the secret English cabal. Three had died. There had, it seemed, been others who had adulated him. Twenty years ago people filled the house when he came to the village. Now there were only these four . . .

"I must go back to Kobe!" he exclaimed.

"It is snowing," his sister said. "The train is surely canceled. And it'll get dark soon."

Mr. Eggplant looked out the window. The village roofs were topped with snow and the rice fields were white. He looked at his watch. It was 3 P.M. Time had shot by. How?

"You barely touched your lunch," his sister said. "You must be hungry."

"I want a drink!"

"Not with your gout."

"I am thirsty. Bring me whiskey!"

"No. I will bring you some ginseng tea."

The pain in his leg had subsided. Mr. Eggplant tried to stand. "Ow!"

His mother and sister helped him stand.

"It's still there, isn't it?" his sister said. "Best you lie down for a while. There, there. Let's go to your room and have you lie down."

It was night when he woke from his nap. There was a light on in the living room. He tried to stand and the pain in his leg stabbed him. He groaned. No one came. He rolled over on his stomach and got on all fours. Holding on to the wall, he raised himself. He needed a drink. There was a liquor cabinet in the living room. It had been there as long as he could remember. Mr. Eggplant hobbled out of his room. No one greeted him. He hobbled over to the liquor cabinet and opened it. It was full of liquor. Mr. Eggplant quickly opened a whiskey bottle and drank from it greedily. He drank until he felt warm and light. The liquor seemed to dull the pain in his leg. About to cap the bottle, he dropped it on the *tatami*. Its contents flowed. He tried bending down and felt dizzy.

"*Oi!*" he cried. "*Oi,* help me!"

His mother and sister were not there.

"*Oi!*" he called again. Reaching for the edge of the liquor cabinet, he upset a pile of papers, including a letter written in a familiar hand. The letters fell into the whiskey. The letter with the familiar handwriting was from the brown professor.

"Forgive me for writing to you instead of his wife. She is very devoted to him and would only scold me," it read. And: "You must find some excuse to keep him there for his own good." And: "At times he is very lucid, at other times he has prolonged outbursts of temper. He has wrecked the relations between our professors and with at least one foreign university. Our students are despondent. The curriculum for next year is uncertain. Our foreign teachers have given him an English nickname: 'Mr. Eggplant.' I am taking over as department chairman in his absence."

"Betrayer!" Mr. Eggplant cried. "Where is everyone? I must return to Kobe."

Mr. Eggplant virtually sprinted out the door despite his gout pain. He stood in the darkness. Light snow was falling and formed a thin powder on his house slippers. Except for the lighted windows, the village was black. Where were those four village idiots now that they were needed? Where in hell was his own family? Mr. Eggplant shuddered, and not because of the cold, but because he suddenly felt he was the last person in the world.

He saw car lights in the distance. A taxi was approaching. Inside was his sister. Their mother had had a mild heart seizure, and she had driven her to the prefectural branch hospital's emergency room in the town below. The doctor had put her under observation for a week. Frantic to return to her brother, she had tried to start her car in the hospital parking lot and found the engine frozen— nothing would start it. She had hurriedly explained to the guard that her sick brother was home alone, and she'd take care of the car later. She then caught the cab that Mr. Eggplant saw.

"*Oi!* Taxi!" Mr. Eggplant stood in the road and waved his arms. "*Oi!* Stop!"

Fireworks exploded in front of him as blood vessels ruptured. He fell in the snow-covered mud like a statue from a pedestal.

As freezing muck filled his nose and mouth, Mr. Eggplant had a vision of a summer afternoon long ago when he had led his seven English students deep into the bamboo forest to study the forbidden book. He heard them singing "A-B-C-D-" in earnest but hushed voices, a few octaves above the screaming cicadas. As the light diminished in his brain, he remembered how much he had cherished each of them. Dying, he admitted that the rest of his life had been a lie.

Q: Questing
Gordon Weaver

Quaid answers to his name, but likes to be called Q, which is how
he addresses himself in moments of what he considers profound introspection. *Q, thinks Q, for queries.* As in: *How'd you get where
you are, Q?* And: *And just exactly where is it you think you are, Q?*
And, more to the point: *Where, Q, do you think you're headed?*
These questions pose themselves most often when he's flying the
freeways. Such answers as have come to him so far are unsatisfac-
tory, but he persists. He thinks of his existence as something on the
order of a mission, a search, seeking.

    Q, thinks Q, for quest.

    Monday through Friday, he maintains a soothing illusion of
confidence. Monday through Friday, Q flies the freeways. To and
from the four classes he teaches, one each at four schools located in
the far four corners of this sprawling megalopolis. The four part-
time teaching gigs at four schools generate a near-poverty level income, a most spare living. Q doesn't, can't, won't call it a life, not
just yet.

    Monday through Friday, Q flies the freeways to and from the
four women he courts without, to date, success. Of these four
women, only one is alluring, one has apparent psychological problems, one makes him feel intellectually inadequate, one may be less
than wholly female in orientation. None has been willing to engage
in sex with him.

    But on the freeways, Monday through Friday, driving defensively against the relentless high-speed, seemingly suicidally reckless traffic, Q takes heart from the mere fact of motion, mobility, movement. Flying the freeways, to and from, Q is encouraged by the concept, however only theoretical, of direction, destination, of implied goal.

It is the weekend, Saturdays and Sundays, Q dreads, fears. Because weekends are stasis; Q is in stasis, going nowhere. Weekends are forty-eight hours of potentially devastating considerations. In stasis, Q might be compelled to truly, seriously think. Sometimes he cannot avoid it.

He thinks of his four part-time teaching gigs at four schools: City U., remedial composition; Martin Luther College, expository prose; Pere Marquette College, introductory rhetoric; St. Mary's College, Shakespeare's Major Plays. He thinks of the total of seventy-six students he neither likes nor respects, most of whom exhibit for Q only indifference and disdain.

He thinks of the four women he pursues in seeming vain: Marinelle, who is fat and mannish; Vonda, who is sexy, but ignorant; Patti, who is intelligent and professionally focused, but moderately androgynous in appearance; Belle, who is the most compliant, but so moody he suspects she's maybe chemically out of balance.

He contemplates the stacks of student essays he should read and grade. He thinks of reading he has assigned, but not yet read himself. He broods about lectures and exercises he should prepare.

And he worries for the condition of his vehicle, a 1980 Honda: knocking rod, balding tires, broken exhaust pipe, loose steering, screeching brakes, rusted panels, tentative ignition. His Honda worries him most of all, for if it should fail, he will be immobile, in stasis, unable to fly the freeways, going nowhere.

In an effort to escape such weekend musings, Q resorts to alcohol, marijuana, and televised sports. Q will even watch golf. When he succeeds by these devices, his weekends are a kind of only semi-static blur. Booze or weed or television, or the combination of any two, sometimes all three, make for such peace as Q can know over a weekend.

There is no comfort in his cramped apartment, no haven. Though the rent is low, the neighborhood is bad. There is no solace in flaked paint, cracking plaster, and gurgling plumbing, no ease in the faint, pervasive stench of the worn carpeting that suggests the previous tenant kept cats, only infrequent relief from his fellow-tenants' raucous lives, no refuge from the thick cooking odors hanging in the building's hallways.

The sole mercy mitigating Q's oppressive weekend is the simple certainty of its limited duration, in the promise of Monday coming, when he can rise to its new light to hit the freeways for another week. He has not prepared his classes, does not believe any breakthrough with any of his four women is imminent, but at least, provided his 1980 Honda cranks, he will be on the move again. And he sets forth, Honda roaring and belching, pinging and clattering, on the road to somewhere, flying the freeways.

Monday is City U., English 101-Remedial, twenty-one of the least qualified of the poorly qualified, since City is open enrollment. Q has not graded the batch of essays he promised to return today, so must, negotiating the morning freeway rush, come up with a ploy. Q has a quiver full of ploys to fall back on when he needs to cover his incompetence or neglect.

There is a family emergency ploy, but Q has already killed off a parent—both his are long deceased—put a nonexistent sibling in intensive care with life-threatening trauma, already conjured two bouts of serious flu out of thin air. Mentally sorting his stock, he discards the blatant no-show due to fictional car trouble; he's pulled that twice already this semester. He passes over the weak assertion that he has lost-then-only-this-morning-found his briefcase, and elects the story that he became so engrossed in close reading and extensive commentary that he simply could not finish the work, which he'll promise on his honor to return at Wednesday's meeting.

Q wonders how many, if any, of his remedial comp students will buy into that one.

And Monday is the freeway, his mental fancy footwork complicating and increasing the risks on all sides of his wheezing Honda. Q brakes to allow a Yuppie's Volvo to dart off the entry ramp in front of him, driver's ear glued to a cellphone. Q spots a gap, pulls out and floors the accelerator to pass an oblivious soccer mom in a van traveling a dozen miles below the speed limit. Q hunches at the wheel, eyes darting to his tilted rearview mirror, in terror of the growling semi tailgating him. Back in the slow lane, his Honda rocks in the wakes of a stream of commuters blowing by on his left. A crick forms and deepens between his shoulders, his knuckles ache from his death-grip, his calf cramps, his lumbar region throbs. But he's moving!

How'd you get where you are, Q? Oh, thinks Q, it's a chain of events acting upon a nature ripe from birth for aimless, mindless response to unseen, unexpected ur-forces! He doesn't like to get into this in any detail. He's diverted, in any case, by the fact of Monday, the freeways to City U., his remedial comp class, the reassurance of routine. *Q,* thinks Q, *for quotidian.*

With luck, he finds a parking space, sprints cross campus to the Humanities Building, a massive concrete bunker-like structure he thinks suitable to be adequate shelter against missile bombardment. Then up four flights of ringing metal stairs, into his classroom just in time; were he even a minute late, at least half those present would have walked. It had happened. He would not have minded.

Q faces his remedials.

They're a motley lot, their attitudes toward him expressed dramatically by their choices of seats to the back and sides of the room, as far from Q as possible. They sprawl, slump, slouch, the only eye-contact made by a trio of glowering African Americans. The dominant mode of attire is grunge and head-shop chic. One acne-scarred girl sports garish tattoos and a gold nose-ring. One thug, T-shirt and farmer's overalls, is barefoot. A bearded, pony-tailed man Q's age could pass for a reclusive survivalist, complete with camouflage battle dress, is probably a Viet vet. Q prays he never asks about *his* time in country; Q spent his tour in Nam at Long Binh, assigned to the stockade's laundry, a R.E.M.F. never once in harm's way, but lies about his service whenever he thinks he can get by with it. Q sighs. His remedials sigh a collective response.

He kills as much time as he can with a slow roll call, comments banally on the weather and freeway traffic, tells a bad political joke, then gives the spiel on the papers he has not finished grading, his utter absorption in the task, rattling off a number of encouraging elements emerging in their prose, all this from whole cloth. He promises to have them in hand come Wednesday, and as a salve for their disappointment, which is not evident, dismisses class very early. Nothing mitigates the choral sense of relief that rises toward him, after which, like water running swiftly downhill, his remedials exit the classroom in smug, appeased silence.

Except for Salvatore, Q's connection. Salvatore is the perfect type of an urban street-rat, wraith-thin, sallow skin, lank, greasy hair, black garb set off with chrome studs, bad teeth, chewed nails, broken shoes. Q has an arrangement with Sal.

"You looking to cop, Prof?" asks Sal.

"If and what I can," says Q, adding, "And you the man," in an effort to sound suitably hip. He scores a dime baggie, good stuff, though less potent than what Q learned to enjoy, along with binge boozing, in the Nam.

In exchange for Sal's weed at discount, Q will give him an A for the course, having excused this slime from all assignments in the bargain. Q knows that if there were an even mildly appealing woman in the class who would offer him sex for a grade, he'd agree to that in a mini-second. He lost his virginity to a prostitute while on R & R in Bangkok, and has for the most part been frustrated in that regard since. This accounts for his playing four women at the same time—anything to up the odds in his favor!

Q, thinks Q, *for quim!*

Sal takes his money, high-fives him, slithers out of the classroom. After a quick stop at the nearest men's to wash Sal's touch off his hand and stow the baggie in his briefcase, Q is off to the student union commons. Monday is also fat, mannish Marinelle.

And there she is, awaiting Q at their customary corner table, away from the smelly cafeteria line and the clots of jabbering, loitering students. Marinelle *does* look mannish!

Her hair is cut shorter than the fashion for most men, her head a squarish block atop her near-square torso. Marinelle wears slacks and a blazer and sturdy brogans. Her hands are large, sausage-fingers blunt. She wears no makeup, no jewelry, no scent Q can detect. When he scoped out the talent in the English department office, she was the best prospect, clearly too plain—even homely—to be enmeshed in any relationship. The gal at the desk facing Marinelle's was the one who took his eye, a certified stunner, all bleached coiffure, blood-red lipstick and nail polish, glittering earrings and rings and bracelets, short skirt, heels, creamy legs, one blouse button too many unbuttoned to display cleavage that halted Q's breath a full beat, her perfume a luscious redolence of lilacs in full bloom.

The stunner obviously out of his class by a mile or more, Q bypassed her to chat up Marinelle. He thinks he may have aimed too low in settling on Marinelle, but any port in a storm.

She greets him with, "You blew your class off again, didn't you, Q."

"I let them out early for a little treat. They deserve a break from the grind now and then."

"Bull-fucking-shit," she says.

"So are we on?" Q asks to get her off the topic.

"On for what?"

"We've talked about this before, Marinelle. My place? We could rent a video, drink a little wine, I'll roll us a couple doobies. Some good shit just came my way." He's not absolutely sure he'd like to finagle Marinelle into the sack, wonders if she has too much body hair, doesn't shave her legs or armpits, has better defined musculature than he.

"In a pig's ass, Q," says Marinelle. And she says, "You're about as subtle as a kick in the balls, you know that?"

Semi-relieved, Q says, "So, you suggest. I'm planning on working in the library all afternoon, we can take off as soon as you get off."

"Bowling?" says Marinelle. "I feel like maybe bowling a few lines. I've got a yen for some of those pickled eggs they got at Century Lanes." Q's stomach lurches.

"Doesn't much excite," he says. They have gone bowling several times; Marinelle has never lost a game or a beer frame. She crows when she wins.

"How about shoot some skeet? That gun club down by the lake lets you buy a daily membership. I haven't hoisted a shotgun since who laid the Chink."

Q says, "I had enough of guns to last me in Nam."

"Will you can that crap, Q? You sat on your butt and toked in Vietnam." At least she does not, as she has more than once, call him a rear echelon motherfucker. They compromise on going to the batting cage at Sports-O-Rama; Marinelle says she played very competitive fast-pitch softball in her youth. Q believes her. "You probably swing like a pussy," she says. When he denies this, she says, "Loser treats," and, "Ain't got a hair on you if you don't take the bet!" He accepts the challenge, immediately regretting it.

Time for her to return to her desk, they embrace goodbye there in the corner of the commons, the rattle of metal trays and tableware, the babble of student laughter and vulgar language, cigarette smoke and steamed food smells mingling in the air. Her bearhug tests Q's spine and ribs.

He kills the rest of the day chipping away at some of his remedials' essays. He reads some all the way to the end, reads portions of
some, ends up only tearing the corners off last pages; when his students question this, he'll tell them he wrote a summary comment
there, then thought better of it. This ploy has worked before.

He picks Marinelle up when she clocks out, they go to the
Sports-O-Rama's batting cage, where she embarrasses Q, hitting her
balls farther, at higher speeds, than he can. He pays the freight. One
of Marinelle's best features is her willingness to go dutch, no small
consideration on Q's income, so this debacle hurts doubly. And she
rubs it in, says, "How's come you're so wimpy at sports, Q?" He ali-
bis by telling her his parents were past forty when he was born,
wholly unexpected, that his father kept his distance while his
mother coddled him.

"It made me the kind of a kid kept to himself a lot," he says.

To which she replies, "It shows, Q."

When he drops her off at her apartment, they do kiss a little,
dryly, outside her door. When Q tries to cop a feel, she fends him
off easily; she's clearly the stronger, more fit. Marinelle is many
pounds overweight, but there's iron under that excess!

Depressed, disgruntled, and out the cost of the batting cage,
only the freeways home soothe his withered spirits. Sal's baggie will
get him through the late evening, and, Honda belching cloudy, oil-
laden exhaust, weaving in and out of traffic at great risk, he's in
motion!

Q, thinks Q, for quelled again.

Tuesday mornings in his apartment don't trouble Q. He sleeps
in a little, slumber abetted by Sal's pot last night. And rises eagerly
because Tuesday means Vonda, at St. Mary's. Shakespeare's Major
Plays is an early evening class, so he meets Vonda on the campus in
the afternoon, and this prospect is such that Q can even put in
sonic time on paper grading if he's in the mood, doesn't turn to his
TV for auto racing or co-ed body building competitions or Austra-
lian rules football.

When Q hits the freeways for St. Mary's—and Vonda—he is charged, exuberant, focused. Vonda stirs his libido like no other. She has a girlie-mag body, silky long hair, deliciously pale skin, a stripper's strut he dearly loves to observe from the rear.

Q, thinks Q, *for quarry!*

On the downside, Vonda is dumb as a post. She has betrayed to him her belief that London is a nation distinct from England, didn't know the date of Pearl Harbor, much less Hastings, and mispronounces myriad words. Because she is so much younger than Q, she knows only what he tells her of Vietnam, leaving him free to fabricate war stories that spellbind her. When she asked him what he did through the years since, he told her he was finding himself, and she was incurious enough not to request elaboration.

But there's an upside to this, because her classmates, demure Catholic girls all, are almost her peers with respect to ignorance, so Q's free to wing his lectures on the Bard.

And he's flying the freeways again, to St. Mary's, to Vonda! His Honda trembles like a wino with the shakes, but he passes with aplomb more than one junker older than his, flips the bone at an arrogant young man in a Porsche, maddeningly inscrutable behind reflecting shades, who blows his horn to clear Q from his path, tailgates a stretch limo without trepidation. Q's on the move!

Exiting the freeway, Q is thrust into a different world, one he wishes he had been born to.

St. Mary's campus is all landscaped, barbered greensward, dotted with copses, ponds, and elaborate, well-tended floral beds. When there's a breeze, the swish of freeway traffic is obscured, the air spiced with the trill and warble of songbirds. Founded by the Sisters of Golgotha well before the Great Depression, college buildings are mini-cathedrals of dark gray granite, the hours announced by crystalline chimes. One of the few last bastions of religious higher educational tradition, as much finishing school as college, St. Mary's caters to the overly privileged daughters of solidly affluent Catholic families who still keep the Faith, or at least its forms. In addition to the conventional, noncareer oriented liberal arts, St. Mary's offers European summer travel, horsemanship, and numerous retreats to maintain and enhance the young ladies' moral fiber.

Q feels deliciously subversive when he fantasizes about Vonda.

He finds the dark interiors, all subdued tile and polished wainscoting and stained glass windows, a tad oppressive, and the teaching sisters, who wear headgear putting him in mind of Arab terrorists, their modernized uniform frocks a pale prison-blue, detract a little from his delight. The beads at their waists clack as they walk the shadowy halls, and they seem—rightly, Q concedes—to regard him with suspicion. But he bucks up, hands out smiles and greetings all around as he picks up his junk mail and heads back outdoors to find Vonda.

And she waits for him under a massive shade tree, on a stone bench donated by the Class of 1928, legs crossed, foot bobbing in time to a fast tempo Q hopes is a sign of strong emotional desires and needs. "Hi, babe," says Q.

"Hi, Q." There is no kissing or embracing on the campus, public displays of affection discouraged, faculty-student relationships of a personal nature anathema.

"Did you think about it?" he asks. It always takes several seconds for Vonda to respond to anything, as if she must rehearse her words to arrange them in meaningful syntax before speaking.

"I did," she says at last, "but my mom always wants me home right after night class. She says it's not safe out alone at night."

"Your mother's very conservative," says Q. "You wouldn't be alone. You'd be with me." Another downside is Q's inability to maneuver Vonda into seeing him after sunset. He's contemplated the odds against her agreeing to find a custodian's closet in one of the buildings, sharing his Honda's back seat in the parking lot, crawling into a bower in one of the wooded areas; they're too great to risk any such suggestion. He frankly has no strategy, no tactic, yet, but Vonda's enough to keep him working on it.

"Can I tell you something once, Q?"

"Tell away."

"I'm not getting it. I just don't catch on to this Shakespeare stuff." He'd hoped for some intimate revelation, but, then, Vonda often converses in nonsequiturs.

"You're doing fine," Q lies. He lies to Vonda with abandon. He has lied about his military service, about his age—Vonda is almost a quarter-century his junior—about Shakespeare, about her progress in the course, about the sincerity and tenderness of his regard for her. An upside is Vonda seems to believe everything he says.

"I won't be able to do the term paper," she says.

"I'll help you with it," Q says, suddenly seeing the possibilities rife in tutoring sessions in his apartment. "Don't fret over it," he says, and says, "So what else's new in your life?" He's fishing for an endearment.

"Nothing," she says, disappointing, then says, "Oh yeah. I almost forgot. I was watching this educational channel you said I should?" Q likes to think he can sophisticate Vonda, if only a little.

"And?" He waits for her to arrange her words.

"And there was this one program. About these boy singers in Italy way back, they operated on so they could sing high notes?"

"*Castrati*," says Q, thinks this might lead to a discussion of matters he'd like to get candid about with her.

"Yeah. I was wondering. Q, did they, like, cut off their vocal chords of these little boys to make them sing like they had women's voices?"

Q says, "Something like that," and would have elaborated, informed, but it's time for their class, the bell tower's chimes calling. Walking across the greensward, Q allows himself to straggle, get an extended look at Vonda's so delectable posterior. It all but dizzies him!

Q, Q thinks, for queasy!

Q savors calling the roll here. The dozen females arrayed in a seminar-style half-circle make him think of a chaste harem. Each and every one embodies the rich fruit of entrenched, honorable prosperity. Their hair shines, faces bright, postures demure. Their bright eyes regard him with parentally ingrained respect. They answer cheerily to their names, flash smiles, pens poised over notebooks, at the ready to record anything he tells them is significant, might show up on an exam. Eager to follow anything he reads from the text, their books lay open to *Hamlet*. Q reads from the plays a lot, fancies they find his voice thrilling, his interpretations dramatic.

For St. Mary's, for Shakespeare's Major Plays, Q's major ploy strikes him as near-genius quality. The day he signed on for this gig, he dashed to the college's small library to check out every critical and historical study of Shakespeare. St. Mary's faculty are permitted to hold books for the semester's duration, which means his students can't get their hands on anything that would betray his lectures for the pure bunk they are. The books lie safely locked in the Honda's trunk, will be returned only after the final exam and the receipt of his last St. Mary's paycheck.

On the first day of class, already targeting Vonda, he discouraged them from reading any of the text's introductory material or appendices; these he mines for some substance to leaven his discourse, lest it sound like absolute doubletalk. Tonight, he reads the passages in *Hamlet* where the prince makes vulgar puns in dialogue with Ophelia and his mother. When he runs out of these, Q turns to the topic of theatrical production in Elizabethan times.

The highlight tonight is Vonda raising her hand—Q encourages discussion; nothing fills the time and makes students think they're learning like class discussions!

"Professor Quaid," she says—he has repeatedly cautioned her not to call him Q in the presence of others, is always happily surprised she remembers, given her short attention span. "Professor," she says, pronouncing it *perfesser,* "why did they call it The Globe I was wondering?"

"Because," says Q, pleased with his immediate riposte,

"Vonda," he says, "it was globe-shaped." At once, Vonda and her classmates write this in their notebooks. *Q*, thinks Q, *for quick-witted!*

He dismisses them, as always, at least ten minutes early. Five minutes, he thinks, doesn't count, and it's no high crime to steal five more. If ever asked, he'll say he doesn't want these girls walking the campus in the dark.

The others gone, all saying goodbye, some how much they enjoyed tonight's class, Q escorts Vonda to the parking lot. She drives a sporty convertible of foreign make he is too proud to ask the brand name of. He steers her to his Honda, which looks less shabby in the fading light. When he kisses her in this falling dark, she's all tongue and writhing and snorting breathing through her delicate nose. Looks, thinks Q, and money, and an obvious potential for passion! Who needs brains?

When, without warning, she extricates herself from his arms and mouth, says, "I better go, Q," he feels like weeping.

"We could sit in my car for a while. Talk," he pleads.

"My mom'll kill me if I'm late," she says.

"Okay, but don't forget about the term paper. I'll help you. Consider it a signed contract."

"A contract?" She pronounces it *contrack*. "Oh. Okay. I get it. Maybe. If my mom says." That—mom's permission—Q thinks, will surely put the kibosh on that fantasy!

Q, thinks Q, *for quashed.*

"I'll watch until you get in your car so you'll be safe," he says. There's just enough light left to afford Q a long last vision of her exquisite rump.

Were it not for the freeway home, he'd feel cheated by life, snake-bit, but his Honda, one headlight dead, roars and rattles one-eyed through the deepening night, and this motion, his mobility, restores his equilibrium.

So ends Tuesday, St. Mary's, Shakespeare's Major Plays, Vonda. All, thinks Q, is maybe well that just might possibly still end well, as the Bard could have said. *Q, thinks Q, for quotable!*

Rising from his narrow, lumpy bed isn't easy for Q on Wednesday. Wednesday is City's remedials again, and fat, mannish Marinelle, and, worse, the dour, doctrinaire Lutherans of Martin Luther College, expository prose. And Martin Luther is Belle, about whose mental health Q is dubious. When his alarm clangs, he's tempted to roll over, sleep in, call in sick, but remembers he's exhausted that ploy for this semester.

Q, thinks Q, for quota.

But there are some saving graces. He'll cop a nickel baggie from Sal; he's closest to carnal intimacy with Belle, even if she doesn't seem to enjoy the contact much. This could be the day! And the freeways beckon, so he does rise, does wash and shave and evacuate his bladder and bowels, loads his briefcase, is off in his stuttering Honda.

Where are you, Q? he asks as he dodges morning rush traffic, maneuvering between the seemingly oblivious and the road-enraged, tires thumping ominously on the concrete's joints.

He's on the margins of contemporary urban life, living paycheck to paycheck, he confesses. He's underpaid for the nonperformance of four shit-jobs. He's strung out between four women he doesn't really care all that much for. He's of course without a clue as to his future prospects, if any. But, he reminds himself, he's moving!

At City U., his remedials, sullen as usual, don't disappoint, don't openly protest the arbitrary grades he's slapped on their essays. He kills this fifty minutes at the blackboard, chalking selected student sentences to illustrate egregiously illiterate errors in grammar, diction, and mechanics. Dismissed, they leave the room like paroled felons.

But Sal does disappoint. "Can't help you today, Prof," he says, "my stash's way down. You know," he adds, "I'm thinking of getting out of drugs totally. I mean, you know how many narcs there are on this campus? Man, it's, like, too hairy for the bread you can glom."

"How about Friday? It's a long weekend coming, Sal, I need a little help from my friend!" Sal says maybe, he can't commit.

Q spends only a short interlude in the commons with Marinelle on her break. "I'm not on for tonight," he tells her, thinking of Belle.

"Suit yourself, Q," is all Marinelle has to say. When he says he's sorry not to be up for something this evening, she says, "I'll buy that, Q. You're about the sorriest specimen I know. You really can be a peckerhead sometimes! I think your mama must have toilet trained you too early and weaned you too late, Q." Marinelle, he suspects, is a lost cause, is happily surprised to realize he couldn't care less. He'd like to know if she's ever felt lesbian tendencies, but lacks the courage to ask.

The freeway to Martin Luther doesn't lift Q's spirits much. Marinelle's ready to dump him, and despite her fat, mannish appearance, her masculine vulgarity of expression, and her perhaps inverted sexual orientation, it's no fun being shown the door. And if Sal stops dealing, where'll he find a new connection? And Belle's black moods unnerve Q, as does the ambiance of Martin Luther and his stolidly orthodox students there. He nearly loses his chugging, huffing Honda to a rusty clunker operated by a pony-tailed thug who brakes without warning in front of him.

Martin Luther is a beautiful campus, the peer of St. Mary's, but once inside the admin building, the gloomy, dim-lit atmosphere oppresses him, and Belle, propped on her elbows at the information desk, intensifies this ubiquitous miasma. She looks up as he approaches, but doesn't lift her chin from her cupped hands. "Hi, love," says Q, forcing a smile.

"Hello" is her entire response, after which she returns her mouth to its perpetual disgruntled pout.

"How're we feeling this fine day?"

"I don't know," says Belle. And says, "Sometimes I don't see the point of anything."

"You need cheering up," he says.

"If you say so."

"I do. And I'm just the one to do it! Meet you here when you get off?"

"I guess," is the best Belle can muster. Q's libido, normally sparked by Belle's potential, wilts, but he sneaks a quick kiss of her unopened lips, and affects a jaunty stride as he hurries off to his class.

Q feels like a leper, complete with bell and sign around his neck, that he should shout *unclean, unclean!* in the halls of Martin Luther, where tinted windows emit only a dingy light, and nobody speaks to him in passing, students, staff, and full-time faculty alike seeming wrapped in some profound, pessimistic introspection. And Belle's possibly seriously disturbed, and the students of expository prose he faces are rigid in their seats, expressions tighter than a bull's ass in fly-time, as though contemplating the long odds against salvation within the theology of the Missouri Synod.

But expository prose at Martin Luther is a breeze, because, while these students have no interest in nor affinity for the subject, they love to argue, orally and on paper. Leaning hard on the former, Q easily fills the time allotted by proposing a controversial topic, then sitting back and letting them jaw until the bell tolls in the hall. He goes light on written assignments, thus cutting down on the pa-per grading grind. He does fear these brainwashed Lutherans would mount a collective fuss if he graded strictly, so Q always inflates by a full letter to stave that off.

Today, roll taken, he says, "If I were to state that every woman has a right, given to her by law, nature, and God, to abortion on de-mand, what'd be your response?" For seventy-five minutes, he nods, prods occasionally, and pretends to take seriously their shrill,

Scripture-laden, simplistic and simple-minded espousals of right-to-life over choice. This is all the ploy Q needs to finesse expository prose at Martin Luther College. By class's end, he's regained his emotional equilibrium, goes to meet Belle at her information counter with tangible anticipation.

Q can hardly believe it; it looks like a sure thing! When he invites her to join him in his Honda, parked in the most remote reaches of the faculty lot with just this in mind, she merely shrugs, enters the back seat when he opens the door for her in the falling evening light. After much kissy-face and tonsil hockey, after a spate of frenzied groping and clutching, his breath labored, when he asks if he can unhook her brassier, he takes her silence as tantamount to assent.

"Do you like it when I do that?" Q asks after releasing her non-erectile nipple from his teeth.

"It's okay," Belle says.

"Do you like this?" he asks, reaching inside her waistband.

"I don't care," she says. That's when Q stops.

He leans away from her to get a look at her face, her eyes; she looks asleep on her feet, tranced, wholly without appropriate affect. She's dead-weight in his arms. "Are you okay, Belle?" Q asks.

"I don't know. I don't know anything," she says, staring back at him as if under hypnosis.

"What are you thinking about? Seriously, tell me."

"Nothing. Stuff," she says.

"Not sex?"

"Some. I guess," Belle says.

Q ponders, realizes he's at a crucial juncture here. He can proceed, but it would be something like an act of necrophilia. He can stop, hook up her bra for her, rebutton her blouse, take her home, and suffer the freeway to his apartment with a likely case of aching stones. In the pondering, Q finds himself thoroughly detumid.

"I think I better take you home, Belle," he croaks. She sits, silent, statue-like, as he gets her rehooked, buttoned, zipped. She's so clearly stunned by whatever ails her he doesn't even ask her to move to the front seat with him. Stasis! he thinks. He drives her chauffeur-like to her efficiency, his Honda a battered ambulance. Q sees her to her door, says, "Belle, maybe you should, like, get some counseling or something?" before she closes her door in his face.

Flying the freeways home in full night, he wonders, torn, if he's committed an act of gallantry or just failed to grab the main chance.

Q, thinks Q, *for qualms.*

Thursday begins with Q's mega-hangover. No weed to be had last night, he hit the vodka bottle way too hard in an effort to forget both Marinelle and Belle. Good riddance, he told himself. Best, he reminded himself, not to sleep with anyone who's as screwed up as he is! He doses his splitting head with aspirins, slakes his parched throat with tapwater, regards his hands, fluttering like a dog trying to pass a peach pit, with horrified contrition.

Q, thinks Q, *for quaffer.*

By the time he's on the freeways toward Pere Marquette, toward Patti, his headache's subsided to a muted hammering, his tongue's no longer sandpaper, his hands occupied with the steering wheel. It beats stasis!

Pere Marquette College, the all-male counterpart to St. Mary's, isn't a cheery prospect. Were it not for Patti, even if she does look slightly androgynous, there'd be no joy, no hope at all in Pere Marquette. His students there, Introduction to Rhetorical Modes, a euphemism for freshman comp, are only a shade keener than City's remedials, though cut from cleaner cloth. They're mostly diligent, but lack the deference toward him he enjoys from St. Mary's girls. The faculty's about half Jesuit priests, sternly serious men in black, dog-collared, who always seem to be watching him for evidences of intellectual or moral heresy. Q avoids them for fear his guilt will be revealed in even innocuous small talk.

And he treads carefully in conversation with Patti, who's way out ahead of him, finishing her dissertation, groomed for a Pere Marquette tenure-track slot, and tangibly brighter than Q. She's also way too direct for his taste. The first time he invited her for coffee, she looked him straight in the eye and told him she wanted him to know in no uncertain terms, for starters, that she wasn't sexually available. He finessed that one by telling her they were a match, then, because he wasn't sexually competent, which broke the ice nicely.

Q, Q thought, *for quipster.*

Introduction to Rhetorical Modes meets but once a week, a hundred and fifty minutes; Q almost never keeps them the full period. Today he drones just over an hour, then, prompted by plain tedium and the residue of his hangover, looks up at the crucifix on the classroom wall for forgiveness—he finds none—takes a deep breath, says, "That's all for today."

Before he can get out ahead of them, he's accosted by Farhat, a Bangladeshi exchange student Q means to flunk because his written English sucks, and he doesn't like his oily looks or his brown-nosing demeanor either. Farhat says, "Please, sir, why are we not having always all the time in class meeting?"

Q comes up with a pretty good one, he thinks, given his hangover remainder, which now seems to have settled in his stomach. "I'm conducting an experiment here. I'm doing a study to determine the optimum number of minutes a class should run. I correlate the length of a given class period with student performance on exams and writing assignments. It's too complicated to explain, but you get the idea, right?" Farhat assures him he does, grins stupidly, half-bows, departs. Q prays the little turd doesn't mention it to anyone; the Jesuits would have his head instanter!

After a stop in the men's, where he debates inducing regurgitation to quiet his gut, thinks better of it, and resorts to gulping more cold tapwater instead, he heads for Patti's office on the second floor, utterly without confidence in anything.

Where are you, Q? he queries.

About, he concludes as he climbs the stairs, to go down the porcelain facility! Marinelle and Belle are total losses, strikeouts. If she needs her mom's permission, Vonda's an astronomical long shot. If Farhat repeats that last baloney, he'll be out on his ear here. Sal's a shaky source now. His Honda could give up the ghost at any moment. And Patti's too hip to fall for any line he's capable of stringing.

Q, Q thinks, for *quite—doomed,* that is.

But he's wrong! Patti, wholly contrary to all conceivable expectations, offers herself!

When he enters her tiny office, Patti gets up from her desk, closes the door, turns, puts her small hands on his shoulders, says, "You look terrible, Q? Are you feeling ill?"

"Not particularly," he allows.

"I've made life difficult for you, emotionally speaking, haven't I, Q."

"No. I mean, not really. I mean, you have your principles, I guess. I mean, I'm not sure what you mean, Patti."

"Q," she says, gives him a provocative peck on the nose, "do you think you're ready to take this relationship to the next level?"

"Um," is all Q can utter.

"I am if you are, Q," Patti says. And says, "I think I'm ready for intimacy. We're two consenting adults, Q. Are you ready for this, Q?"

For a second, he's not at all sure. Does she mean here and now, on the floor, atop her desk? "Am I going to get an answer, Q?"

Q, thinks Q, *for quizzed.*

"Yes. Of course. Most certainly!" he barks. She smiles, kisses his nose again, and they arrange for her to come to his apartment on Saturday, stay the night. Q's ecstatic; the looming weekend holds no terror now!

Q splurges, takes her to lunch off campus, the last of his hangover dissolving into blissful bewilderment at this absolutely serendipitous windfall. She's no Vonda for looks, has no discernible breasts, hips narrower than her shoulders, a boyish face under bobbed hair, but Q believes his world has changed, become wonderful, rich with possibilities. Sex is sex, he reasons, and where else might that lead? Maybe things are breaking his way at last?

When she turns the talk to his career status, he lies with enthusiasm. What Patti doesn't know won't hurt her. He blames his situation on his Vietnam experience, which unsuited him for conventional vocations, on too many years knocking about from job to job, on a bad attitude toward his schooling when he finally availed himself of the G.I. Bill, on a hostile major professor who derailed his dissertation. Truth told, Q failed his doctoral prelims twice, was put out of his graduate program on his ear. Now he knows he's too old to find a secure academic niche without the terminal degree, and even if he had it, he'd never rack up the publishing credentials a phenom like Patti already boasted. Truth told, Q knows he's going nowhere in the academic racket.

"What made you decide to study literature, Q?" she asks. He tells her he always liked a good read, likes interaction with students' minds, thinks education a noble enterprise. Patti suggests that's pretty vague, and not a little innocent. He doggedly disputes this until she lets it go.

Q, thinks Q, *for quibbler.*

Buoyant, he leaves her for the freeways, Shakespeare and St. Mary's and Vonda. But Vonda doesn't much matter now, he's got Patti on his dance card for this weekend. Oh, life is looking good!

Shakespeare is no sweat at St. Mary's. Q natters a good three-fourths of the scheduled period on the topic of humors, tossing in what he vaguely remembers about The Great Chain of Being, and, pleading exhaustion, dismisses them early.

Vonda is as easy on the eyes as always, but there's still too much light left in the evening to consider luring her into the Honda. Anyway, with Patti locked in for the weekend, he's not significantly disappointed by this. After a few deep kisses, she says, "I'm still thinking about it, Q."

"Thinking about what?" he asks, preoccupied with Patti.

"About coming to see you this weekend, helping me with my term paper, etcetera." She pronounces it *eckcetera*.

"Etcetera," he corrects her, imagining their coupling, adding, "We can always do this another time, it doesn't have to be this weekend." Q feels a cold rush at the remote possibility of two women converging on his apartment; he's relieved when she notes she still feels she needs her mother's okay. Given that, he's able to fully enjoy the vista of her voluptuous gait as she goes to her foreign-made sportscar. Is it in any way abnormal, he wonders, to so exult in this voyeurism?

Q, thinks Q, *for quirk.*

And he flies the freeways home, ecstatic with growing anticipation.

Friday's equally without problems. His Honda sputters and balks, but he's on time for his City U. remedials, and holds them nearly the full period with a spontaneous spiel about sentences combining as a means of achieving a distinctive individual style; this comes to him like a gift, no effort, no hesitation, no backing and filling or audible pauses marring this effortless gush of hokum. His remedials are glum as ever, but seem to pay at least a perfunctory attention to his words.

A Friday bonus is Sal coming up, after class, with a dime baggie. "I thought you were getting out of the lifestyle, Salvatore," Q says.

"I still might," says Sal. "I'm not for certain sure yet, Prof."

"You the man, Sal!" Q says as they make the exchange, and would, were Sal's hygiene not so revolting, have hugged him.

He meets Marinelle at their commons table, having decided on a ceremonial kiss-off to salvage his pride, which he thinks should be hurt. "Marinelle," he announces. "I've come to the irrevocable conclusion we're not well suited, you and me."

"You're breaking my heart, Q," she says, breaks out in a gruff cackle.

Q : Questing

"Okay," Q says, "you've made your point. I just thought it'd be the responsible thing to do to make it formal, sort of, okay?"

"Don't do me no damn favors, Q," she says, and, "Don't let the door hit you in the ass on your way out."

"No hard feelings?"

"For shit's sakes, Q," she near-shouts, "will you the fuck please just fuck off!" He does, deciding there's no loss of pride in losing fat, mannish, possibly-dyke Marinelle.

That done, the freeways to Martin Luther are a walk in the park, though he feels a bit skittish about seeing Belle again.

But there's another Friday bonus. Belle's not at the information desk, the woman in her place a snowy-haired granny who, when Q asks after Belle, says, "I understand she's not well."

Feeling freed of Belle—he hopes she isn't truly clinical—he fills the class period by provoking his dour Lutherans with a statement, qualified as hypothetical of course, denying the existence of God. So he sits it out as they wax eloquent, outraged, for seventy-five minutes, in response. This clears the decks for the weekend, for Patti.

Might it not come to pass, if he plays it cooly, he speculates, that after this weekend with Patti he could arrange it with Vonda for the following? He could, he projects, alternate them on succeeding weekends! Such thoughts take his mind off the hazards of freeway travel and the varied ominous sounds his Honda generates.

Q's euphoria endures until nearly midnight, enhanced by Sal's good grass and not a little vodka. Just before the witching hour, Q happy as a sultan with an inexhaustible seraglio from which to choose as whim dictated, Vonda telephones. Mother, it happens, has given her permission to receive some out-of-class tutoring on Q's turf. She wants to come over Saturday evening. She pronounces it *Satiday.*

He's too shocked to figure a way around this snafu, only fleetingly indulges a fantasy *a trois.* Q mumbles he'll get back to her in the morning, evades the implications of this impasse via an extra-large joint and another pint of vodka that leave him senseless.

Q, is Q's last coherent thought in the wee hours of Saturday morning, *for queered!*

Saturday, the weekend, finds Q hungover to the max again, spaced out in his cannabis aftermath, semi-paralyzed with pain and generalized angst. Unable to focus, he shifts mentally from foot to foot like a child in need of a toilet, his thoughts a jumble coalescing into one persistent whimper, psyche wracked by emotional whining.

Is there any possibility of getting Vonda in and out before Patti's at his door? What excuse might suffice to delay Patti until Sunday, run Vonda through this evening, an assembly line mode? Flummoxed, Q's caught his ass in a crack, between a rock and a hard spot, up the proverbial creek without a paddle.

Q, thinks Q, *for quandary!*

His genius for ploys deserting him, he sees that canceling the entire operation is the only viable solution.

After all, Patti's less than voluptuous, her androgyny a mild turnoff. And what delight would there be in yoking himself to a woman his emotional, intellectual, and professional better? He can imagine himself a house-husband, cooking and cleaning while Patti rose through the academic ranks. Q pictures himself playing perpetual second fiddle to Patti's maturity of character and record of accomplishment. Okay, scratch Patti!

Vonda? Vonda's a veritable feast of the flesh, but how long would that be good for when she comes off like an inarticulate juvenile? There was money, the ring of security, in Vonda's high-bourgeois lineage, to be sure. But what chance he'd be in any respect acceptable to her family? And the difference in their ages amounted to a generation gap. No, drop Vonda! Wipe the slate, start anew!

It surprises him how easy it proves, how minimal is his regret, as he dials first one, then the other.

Q, thinks Q, *for quitter.*

"I'm not ready," he tells Patti, "for the next level."

"You are such a child, Q!"

"We can still be friends, right?"

"Grow up, Q!" she says, hangs up on him.

"We're just not compatible spirits," he tells Vonda, who begins to cry.

"I bet you never even really liked me, Q!" she says. And says, "You just played with my afflictions!" He presumes she means *affections.* He promises to help her with her research paper—on-campus of course—promises he'll see her through the morass of Shakespeare, but doubts he's heard through her blubbering. He hangs up on her.

Only briefly does Q revel in a surge of relief. Only briefly does this respite obliterate the facts of where this leaves him. Too soon, these reemerge, descend on him there in his rat-trap of an apartment like a poisonous cloud.

He has stacks of student writing he can't bear to read. He has hosts of lectures and lesson plans to formulate he knows he won't attend to. He has no booze left, and only crumbs remain in Sal's baggie. He has four part-time teaching gigs without a scintilla of certainty they will be there next semester. He has no women, no woman, in his life.

Where are you going Q?

Well, no law of man or cosmos says something can't break his way! A distant relative—he doesn't know of any—could die somewhere, leave him closets of money in the will. He could buy a lottery ticket, win zillions! He could apply to the VA, claim posttraumatic stress syndrome, be awarded total disability for life! He could meet a new woman, one who was intelligent and well read, enjoyed inherited wealth, was deliciously feminine and psychologically healthy, sexually innovative and responsive! He could, he believes, by sheer act of will create a new and admirable character for himself, a vivacious personality, kick his dependence on alcohol and hemp!

He could, just now, get outdoors, crank his fragile Honda, just fly the freeways for a while?

And then it comes to Q that it's only late morning of this Saturday, that Sunday waits in line to swallow him like a black hole.

Q, thinks Q, *for quark!*

And then he's no longer thinking. He hears nothing, sees only the drab featureless and mundane particulars of his cell-like apartment, aware only of the irrefutable fact of this weekend in which he's stuck like a man mired chin-deep in a swamp.

Q, thinks Q, *for quiet*—the absolute quiet of interminable stasis.

Fundamentals of Communication
Thisbe Nissen

Communications is not my field. I teach Fundamentals of Acting I
and II. I used to do The Dramatic Monologue alternating semesters
with Advanced Improvisation, sometimes even staged a production
spring term, but there have been cutbacks, and a new dean who
seems to think that art is as dispensable as coffee from the basement vending machine. Dean Ford would actually be a decent
enough guy if not for his unbounded democratic enthusiasm for sys-
tems of check and balance. He's gone gung-ho about "putting the
community back in *community college*," so suddenly he's been here
six months and we're all serving on eighteen zillion different com-
mittees "for the advancement of dialogue among students, faculty,
staff, administration, and community." The Rhetoric/Comp. people
were all in a snit for a while about the grammatical correctness of
"dialogue among," but that's pretty much died down now. Pat Rei-
ser in Economics suggested we form a committee for the Grammatical Integrity of Memos from Personnel, or GIMP, but we're all over-
committed as it is. The one committee Ford has foisted on all of us
is PEAN—that's the Peer Evaluation and Advisory Network—and it's
PEAN duties that have me here at 8 A.M. on a Tuesday morning sitting in on Dan Zweibic's Fundamentals of Communication.

Dan's not a bad guy, just a bad teacher. But he's so goddamn earnest it's going to break my heart to do anything short of lying through my teeth on Ford's PEAN form and proclaiming poor, dull Dan to be "dynamic!," "engaging," "professional," "adept." I would too, only no one would believe me. Dan's a mouse, a sad little mouse who must have pursued a communications major in college as a goal-project in 12 Steps Beyond Shyness. So here's Dan a few years later, doing the Community College thing with the best and the rest of us. 8 A.M.: preaching to the sedated.

A few compassionate, front-row souls are swigging cans of Mountain Dew purchased at the basement vending machines in an attempt to caffeinate themselves into a modicum of functionality. And the Dew may well have twice the kick of Coke, but even that's not going to do it for Dan's students this morning. Fund. of Comm. is a required course, meets four times a week for an hour and a quarter. I have heard—through the student/faculty/staff grapevine (UNITED IN GOSSIP WE STAND!)—that four days a week Dan delivers a seventy-five minute lecture on communication. Now, as a witness, I can testify to the veracity of this oxymoron. A lecture on communication! Need my PEAN report say anything more?

The lecture hall—well, Jesus, what's the administration expect when they schedule a Comm. class in a lecture hall?—is a steeply sloped auditorium, with Dan stuck down there in front of us like a baby in a well. I've snuck in at the back, and I'm not sure he's aware I'm here. In front of me a kid in a dark trenchcoat is drawing with a full box of 64 Crayolas what appears to be a birthday card for a person called "Jeannine" whom, it would seem, he loves. A few seats down, a girl who looks like she's still in her pajamas is writing a letter, or rather the first five or six lines of a letter, over and over on sequential pages of her spiral notebook. Every few minutes she snaps up the sheet she's been working on, flips it with an angry crackle around back and begins again. "April 15. Dear Wallace, I'm in class, which sucks, which you probably figured since I'm sitting here writing you a letter." Another row down from Friend-of-Wallace, two women pass a looseleaf binder back and forth in written conversation. From the back, one of them looks a little like Emily, my delight-of-a-daughter, who's sworn that "if it's the last thing" she does, she's moving out of state as soon as she turns eighteen this spring and that she'd "sooner die" than take classes at the same dippy college where her mother "entertains the local bimbos." Her language is clichéd, but what about this situation isn't? I have no right, I'm told (guess who by?), to expect "a goddamn thing" from her. And, goddamn it, should I not have expected just that? Just precisely that.

The Emily-Girl reads her friend's latest message installment and dissolves into silent laughter, and that's more than enough to dispel her similarity to my daughter who would not giggle, I don't think, if her "life depended on it." In the aisle of these girls' row, a young couple have eschewed the convention of desks and are sprawled on the steps. The boy, with his bobbed dark hair and tortoise-framed glasses, leans against the wall. The girl—long, fine white-blond hair skimming past a jaw that might be called horsey, but is nonetheless striking—rests against her sweetie, her back propped between his open thighs, her own legs tucked beneath her. She's slipped off her shoes, a pair of tiny cork-soled clogs that sit on the carpeted step like two pet mice heeled beside their owner. The couple are among the few in the hall who are actually looking toward the front of the room, but I don't think they're listening any more than Wallace's friend or Jeannine's lover.

It's when I see Dan climbing up the aisle stairs that I realize I'm not listening either. He's describing a film of some sort, and it becomes clear that he's headed up to man the projector from the back of the hall. Dan seems to spot the stair-couple for the first time when he's about five steps below them, and there's a shudder of something like panic that crosses his eyes—this is an unanticipated obstacle!—and I can picture the adolescent that Dan really is inside seized with the adolescent fear of having to maneuver his way past a pretty girl. A pretty girl entwined with a pretty boy, the suggestion of everything that exists between them sprawled right there across the step. The girl leans toward the wall a bit to allow Dan passage, but she doesn't actually move over, just performs the gesture, the suggestion of movement. Dan seems to freeze, unable to move forward. He lifts his head, his eyes flit about, and it's then he notices me, my tell-tale PEAN clipboard out on the desk. Instantly, his hand rises in greeting, like a child's imitation of an American Indian—How. Dan's face cracks a goofy smile of utter relief, as though I were the familiar face in the crowd, the friend appeared suddenly to rescue him from his momentary logistical crisis. I smile back stiffly; a few heads turn to see who I am. I find myself nodding absurdly, as if I can coax Dan up the stairs, past the hurdle who is this girl, the way I once rooted Emily down the slide, up the monkey bars, onto the tire swing—I think I can, I think I can—The Little Professor Who Could. And we're all just poised there, waiting to see what will happen.

Suddenly, the boyfriend, in a moment of divine inspiration, scoops the girl's clogs from the step, one-handed, and holds them above his head. He is the drawbridge, the starter gun, the butler gesturing come in, come in, and somehow, miraculously, Dan is willing to accept this young man's offer to let him pass safely: the coast is clear, full speed ahead. Dan scuttles wordlessly past, flips a light switch at the back of the hall, and resumes control of his subject: show movie, project projector, provide narration, for transcripts see textbook, Dynamics of Human Interaction, p. 472.

On the steps, the boy has set the girl's clogs back on the floor beside them. The girl is wearing a sleeveless shirt, and in the dim film-light I can see the boy now place his hand on the warm skin of her back just between the shoulder blades. He's wearing sandals himself, and one of the girl's hands rests atop his exposed toes. They are still, eyes trained to the screen, but all the energy is there, in these touch-points. They sit, shifting occasionally, glancing at the glowing wall clock, waiting for 9:15. I can't see them as well now, in the shadows, but I catch an occasional movement in one of their hands, the caress of a finger, the press of a palm.

Contributors

Contributors

Thomas Beller has worked as a staff writer at the *New Yorker* and the *Cambodia Daily*, and now works as an errand boy at Mrbellersneighborhood.com. He is the author of *Seduction Theory*, stories, and *The Sleep-Over Artist*, a novel, and is editor of *Open City*.

Amy Knox Brown's stories have appeared in the *Missouri Review*, *Other Voices*, *Witness*, *American Literary Review*, and the anthology *High Infidelity*, among others. She is the recipient of a Henfield/*Transatlantic Review* Award and a Work Scholarship from the Bread Loaf Writers' Conference. She holds a Ph.D. from the University of Nebraska-Lincoln and a J.D. from Nebraska's College of Law. She lives in Washington, D.C.

Ron Carlson's fiction has appeared in the *New Yorker*, *Harper's*, *Gentlemen's Quarterly*, *Playboy*, *Ploughshares*, *Story*, and many other journals. He is the author of several books, including the short story collections *The Hotel Eden*, *Plan B for the Middle Class*, and *The News of the World*.

Dan Chaon grew up in rural Nebraska and attended Northwestern and Syracuse. He is the author of two collections of short stories: *Fitting Ends* (1996) and *Among the Missing* (2001). His novel will be published in 2002.

Art Grillo holds degrees from Drew University, Emerson College, and the University of Wisconsin–Milwaukee. His stories and essays have appeared in such magazines as the *Cream City Review*, *Passages North*, and *Washington Square*. A resident of the San Francisco Bay Area, he teaches at San Jose State University and City College of San Francisco. He is at work on a novel about the Marine Corps.

Gillian Kendall has been writing short stories and essays for fourteen years. Her work has appeared in a variety of magazines, from *Glamour* to *Girlfriends: The Magazine of Lesbian Enjoyment* to the *Sun*. She taught creative writing and journalism for three years at a small school in the South and now works as a technical writer in Silicon Valley.

Stephen King is a first-prize winner of an O. Henry Award for a story that appeared in the *New Yorker*. He is the author of many novels and short story collections, including *Hearts in Atlantis, Bag of Bones, Misery, The Stand, Night Shift, The Shining,* and *Carrie*. His latest nonfiction book, *On Writing: A Memoir of the Craft,* was published in 2000. He lives in Maine.

Rebecca Lee's stories have appeared in the *Atlantic Monthly, Zoetrope,* and the *Chicago Tribune,* and on National Public Radio. She is a graduate of the Iowa Writers' Workshop and was a fellow in the writing program at the University of Wisconsin–Madison. She teaches at the University of North Carolina at Wilmington.

John McNally won the John Simmons Short Fiction Award for his short story collection, *Troublemakers* (2000), and is the editor of *High Infidelity: 24 Great Short Stories about Adultery* (1997). His next book will be an anthology of humor by writers of color, which the University of Iowa Press will publish in 2002. He holds degrees in English from Southern Illinois University (B.A.), the University of Iowa (M.F.A.), and the University of Nebraska–Lincoln (Ph.D.). He has taught fiction writing at Southern Illinois University, Western State College–Colorado, University of Nebraska–Lincoln, University of Wisconsin–Madison, and the University of South Florida in Tampa.

Thisbe Nissen is the author of a story collection, *Out of the Girls' Room and Into the Night,* and a novel, *The Good People of New York*. A graduate of Oberlin College and the Iowa Writers' Workshop, she now makes her home in Iowa City.

Contributors

Sondra Spatt Olsen is the author of *Traps*, a collection of short stories. Her fiction has appeared in such places as the *New Yorker, Mademoiselle, and Redbook*. She lives in New York.

Lucia Perillo was awarded the prestigious MacArthur fellowship in 2000. She has published three volumes of poetry: *The Body Mutinies*, for which she won the PEN/Revson Foundation Poetry Fellowship; *Dangerous Life*, which received the Norma Farber Award from the Poetry Society of America; and *The Oldest Map with the Name America*, which appeared in 1999. Her work has appeared in the *Atlantic Monthly*, the *New Yorker, The Pushcart Prize* anthology, and *Best American Poetry*, among others.

Richard Russo's novel *Empire Falls* was published earlier this year. He is also the author of *Mohawk, The Risk Pool, Nobody's Fool* (which was made into a major motion picture starring Paul Newman), and *Straight Man*. His work as a screenwriter includes *Twilight* (co-written with Robert Benton and also starring Paul Newman) and *The Flamingo Rising* (an adaptation of Larry Baker's novel). His fiction has appeared in such places as the *New Yorker, Harper's, Granta*, and *Shenandoah*. He lives in Maine.

Joe Schraufnagel is a former writer for the satirical newspaper the *Onion*. Born in Elroy, Wisconsin, he has a B.A. in Communication Arts and an M.A. in English Linguistics, both from the University of Wisconsin–Madison. "Like Whiskey for Christmas" is his first published short story. He lives in Brooklyn, New York.

Alex Shishin teaches in a private college in Kobe, Japan. His fiction, nonfiction, and photography have appeared in numerous publications. A book of essays, *The Shy Voice in American Literature*, was published by Seiji Shobo in Tokyo. His short story "Shades" was anthologized in *Broken Bridge: Fiction from Literary Japan* and "Mr. Eggplant Goes Home," which first appeared in *Prairie Schooner*, received an Honorable Mention in *Prize Stories: The O. Henry Awards, 1997*. Shishin's Ph.D. is from the Union Institute.

Marly Swick is the author of two novels, *Evening News* and *Paper Wings*, and two collections of short stories, *Monogamy* (also titled *A Hole in the Language*) and *The Summer Before the Summer of Love*. Her fiction has appeared in the *Atlantic Monthly*, *Redbook*, *Playgirl*, *Gettysburg Review*, and elsewhere. She lives and teaches in Columbia, Missouri.

Gordon Weaver is the author of four novels and nine story collections, the most recent of which is *Long Odds: Stories* (2000), where "Q: Questing" also appeared. More than a hundred of his stories have appeared in literary magazines and have been reprinted in several anthologies, including *Best American Short Stories*, *Prize Stories: The O. Henry Awards*, and *The Pushcart Prize*. Recognition of his work includes two NEA fellowships, the O. Henry First Prize, the St. Lawrence Award for Fiction, the Sherwood Anderson Prize, and other citations. He is currently adjunct professor of English at the University of Wisconsin–Milwaukee, where he teaches fiction writing.

Tom Whalen has published stories, poems, essays, and translations in numerous publications, including *Ploughshares*, *Paris Review*, *Iowa Review*, *Michigan Quarterly Review*, *Georgia Review*, *North American Review*, and many others. He lives in New Orleans.